THE MAN BEFORE YOU

SHALANA BATTLES

CHAOS PUBLISHING & DESIGN LLC

THE MAN BEFORE YOU

For information:

https://shalanabattles.com

Editing by Laura LaTulipe

Cover design by Designed with Grace

ISBN print: 978-1-7356514-7-7

ISBN ebook: 978-1-7356514-5-3

First Edition: February 2021

❀ Created with Vellum

ALSO BY SHALANA BATTLES

SOUL JUMPER

The sun woke Eloise and she cursed herself for not shutting the dining room blinds. In the night, her blanket somehow ended up on the floor and her dog, Rossi, had claimed it as her own. Eloise saw Reagan in everything in this house, and when she stepped even a few feet from the safe recliner, she found herself struggling to breathe. Eloise wished she knew what Reagan was thinking. She wished she knew what he'd want her to do with his things, now that he was gone. Would he want her to get rid of them? Would that be the same as erasing him from her life completely? Would he want her to keep everything that reminded her of him so that she'd never forget? She couldn't even look at it, so she guessed it didn't matter much. Eloise pushed the footrest of the recliner down and stood to make coffee, then went up the stairs. She kept waiting to hear the door and his boots over the tile floor, as if he were just late, and not dead.

His shoes were still lined up on the floor of their closet. His shirts all hung, gray work shirts on the bottom rack, button-ups and T-shirts above them. She couldn't make herself move past their doorway. She could see into the walk-in closet to her left and that was as much as she could bear. More than ever before, Eloise was thankful that their L-shaped bedroom hid their bed from view. If she entered their room and actually saw their bed, or the razor on his side of the sink, sitting next to his mouthwash and deodorant, she'd lose it.

Eloise turned her back on the room that once brought her laughter and love and walked back downstairs to retrieve her coffee. She'd be sleeping in the recliner again tonight.

When Eloise met her husband, she wasn't looking to settle down. Meeting him, falling in love with him, was a whirlwind. He was never expected, and exactly what Eloise needed. She was twenty-three, in graduate school, and making big plans. She was a hot mess, just out of a relationship and in an apartment, by herself, for the first time in four years. Eloise had a variety of roommates over the years, but the last eight months her ex-boyfriend had been living with her. The run-down place was far from comforting with its ripped blue carpet and dated kitchen. At the time, Eloise had no idea how she'd be able to pay the rent without her ex, but as with most complicated things in her life, Eloise chose to ignore that fact until she had no other option.

The point of having no other choice came the night before rent was due, with Eloise sitting on the cold tile in her kitchen, balling over the fact that she'd have to do something drastic. The next morning, she gathered up some of her gold jewelry and for the first—and so far only—time in her life, took it to a pawn shop.

Eloise sat down in her recliner, almost the only place in her home that didn't make her skin crawl. She started thinking about Reagan, and before she could stop them, tears were streaming down her cheeks. Any resemblance of a smile was brought to her face by thoughts of her friends Nickie and Jack and the way they'd rallied around her at her lowest point, before the idea of the life she had now had even started to materialize.

"I *refuse* to sign up for a dating site!" Eloise had told Nickie as they cleaned her kitchen together. After her ex had moved out, Eloise wanted to deep clean, move things around, just make the place feel like it was her own again.

"I met Gage that way and I wouldn't trade him for anything," Nickie said as she opened a new spray bleach bottle.

"You met Gage on a site for sex." Eloise was beyond thankful that Nickie was here to help her. She actually wished she'd move in, but knew Nickie would stay living at home as long as that was free, and Eloise didn't blame her.

"And? Three years later we're engaged and happy. You deserve to be happy."

"I'll think about it." Eloise picked up her phone and sent a message to Jack. Now that her ex was gone, they could hang out again. Plus, he could help her move the furniture.

Eloise looked around at her living room now, the beautiful tile and freshly painted walls. Thinking about her and Nickie in college cleaning her sorry excuse for an apartment made her want to laugh, but she felt like she had to swallow it down in respect of Reagan. Jack did come that day, and he brought pizza. It was the most fun Eloise had had in months. They sang and danced in her kitchen, her broom and mop their mics.

Eloise switched on the television. She didn't remember the last time she ate or showered and had no desire to start functioning again. She pulled the blanket up around her neck as the doorbell rang. Rossi jumped up and started barking. Eloise placed her hand on top of Rossi's head. Whoever it was could leave their "I'm sorry" and their stupid-ass lasagna tray on the porch and leave. Eloise turned up the volume and ignored the knocking that followed the doorbell. Rossi stayed standing, but quiet.

"Eloise! Open the door, please. I know you're home." The voice was followed by more pounding and Eloise clicked the remote volume up three more notches.

Maybe one of the neighbors will call the police and complain, she thought.

"Eloise, it's Jack." The noise stopped and she felt as though the wind had been permanently knocked out of her. She froze, waiting to see if the silence would stay. It didn't.

"Eloise, open the damn door." The male voice roared through the entryway and Eloise's breath hitched. It couldn't be him. She hadn't heard that voice in ten years and yet the sound of it made her feel like she'd never gone without it.

Eloise stood and wrapped the blanket around herself tighter, hoping it would magically become a shield. She debated not opening the door, but if Jack was anything like he used to be, he wouldn't go away. Eloise would probably leave a month from now and find he'd been living on her porch. Rossi rose with Eloise and matched her stride. Eloise took a quick glance in the mirror hanging in her entryway, knowing full well she could pass for a person who'd been sleeping behind a dumpster, and then swung the door open.

Jack. A man Eloise hadn't seen or spoken to in ten years. He straightened from his leaning position over her window. He stood too tall, too straight. His feet spread apart too evenly. Rossi moved to place her body between Eloise and Jack, shifting her gaze from Eloise to Jack.

"Eloise." One word, then Jack snapped his mouth shut. Eloise closed her eyes and waited for him to look her over. She knew he would. "I wish there was something to say, but I know nothing will make this any easier." Jack's voice was this cross between being out of breath and a whisper, and Eloise wondered where the screaming madman he was a second ago went.

"Why are you even here?" Eloise noted Jack locking his fingers in front of his waist. He looked different and exactly the same.

"I wanted to check on you." When Jack spoke, he didn't

move. Rossi's body was still stiff, so Eloise rubbed behind her ear to let her know that they weren't in danger.

"Jack, it's been such a long time and then you show up here, six days after I bury my husband to check on me. You've got some nerve." Eloise turned and walked back in the direction of her recliner with Rossi on her heels, leaving the door open.

"I'll go. I just wanted to make sure you were all right. Long time or not, Eloise, we were always good at being friends." Eloise listened as Jack stepped inside and the door closed.

Eloise smiled, grateful her back was still to Jack. She didn't feel like she should be smiling at anything, not yet. He was right. They started out as friends after meeting at the movie theater they both worked at in college. They'd go through various relationships and stop talking out of respect, but they would eventually find their way back to each other. After every breakup or big life event, after any accomplishment, or heartbreak, they'd talk. It would be small talk—*how are you, congratulations on this or that, I'm sorry about whatever*—and then they'd go on with their lives. They never technically dated, but for five years, anytime they were both single, they were a couple who never labeled each other as such. That all changed when Eloise met her husband. She stopped talking to Jack entirely.

"You should go, Jack." Eloise forced herself to turn around and meet his eyes. "You don't even know me anymore. I don't know why you came."

"I came because I *do* know you and we both know it." Jack handed her a folded piece of paper. "My cell. I wrote the number for the hotel I'm staying at on there too. It's fine if you don't want to see me, but when you want to see someone, just know I'm here." He turned, opened the door, and took the three steps off the porch. Eloise held the paper in her hand and watched as he got into his truck, not daring to breathe even when the engine roared to life. She couldn't make herself say anything. She couldn't believe he came.

Eloise stood staring out her front door. Jack wouldn't come back, she knew that, not unless she called him, which was not happening. How dare he show up like that. Eloise quickly went from being shocked to being pissed. Ten years. It had been ten years. What the hell was he thinking?

Jack's truck floated down her street like a ghost ship. The lights of his breaks spoke volumes to Eloise, but instead of turning around the ship sailed into the night. Eloise wrapped her blanket in tighter and looked up at the sky.

"This could be bad, Reagan," she said to the stars, tears filling her eyes. Regan knew she had a friend named Jack, because he was frequently mentioned when she and Nickie told stories about their college days. But Eloise never had the guts to tell Reagan how deeply they were attached. She always thought if he knew, he wouldn't believe her love for him was real. She didn't want him to spend their life together questioning her feelings. She knew that was selfish, but she loved Reagan and didn't speak to Jack the entire time they were married, so she didn't see the real harm in it.

When she lost Reagan, the only way she could keep living was to focus on her sadness. Nickie thought she was crazy, but all she had was her pain to remind her that she was still alive. Jack would see right through her twisted plan to wallow in her self-pity, to, in Eloise fashion, ignore all things that made her uncomfortable, and that was the problem with him showing up. It took everything Eloise had to get up each morning and now Jack was here, and she knew in her heart that he would ruin what little comfort she had left, because the truth was, Jack did know her and she knew he'd force her out of her sorrow, something she never wanted to face.

When Eloise walked back into the house, she felt even more

out of place than she'd been feeling the last six days. Jack had stepped in her house. Her house with Reagan. He had a way of taking over anything he touched and now he'd been here. What in the hell was she supposed to do with that? She thought about the way he stood on her porch and had to fight a smile. This had to be Nickie's doing. She wasn't sure whether to hate her or thank her. Eloise went to her kitchen and threw open a cabinet, her anger ranging in her like a fire, consuming her thoughts of Nickie and Jack. Her guilt was seemingly always waiting for her to think a happy thought, to risk a smile, so it could put her back in her place. Before she could talk herself out of it, she pulled out a plate and threw it against the wall. Rossi was pacing, whining, and clearly confused. She let the tears fall as she smashed plate after plate. The house was so fucking quiet she knew she was going to go insane. With each broken plate, she cried harder.

"Why, Reagan?" she screamed as she threw another dish. "I'm here. I'm here alone and lost and then smug-ass Jack Brennan comes knocking on my door like it's no big deal." She grabbed another plate and held it in her hand. "I don't want him, Reagan. I chose you! And you're not here. How could you leave me like this? You said always. You said forever." Eloise threw the plate full force at the wall across from her. "How in the fuck am I supposed to do this, Reagan?" She slid down the wall, crying, folding herself in a ball. Dying wasn't Reagan's fault, but he sure felt like the one she should blame. She had to blame someone. No one expects to be widowed at thirty-three.

Eloise looked around at her glass-covered kitchen floor and forced herself to take a breath. She was so tortured in that moment, but she'd cried every last tear she had. The tears would come back, that she knew. They'd creep up on her, replenished, they always did. Eloise stood, careful to avoid the glass and walked to her recliner. She scooted as close as she could to the arm of the chair and patted the small space next to her. Rossi, a boxer who was obviously much bigger than a lap dog, jumped up. She'd deal with the rash decision to break every plate she owned in the morning. She thought about calling Jack. She knew he'd come over, and that he'd clean the glass. She knew what he'd say, and that he'd stay until she fell asleep and then sit there with her all night, but she couldn't. Even after ten years, she knew. She couldn't call him because the thought of him coming over, of wrapping her up in his arms, looking into his eyes and feeling safe, choked her. Jack had saved Eloise from herself many times in the five years they were close, but he couldn't save her tonight, because tonight it wasn't just her and him. It was her and him and enough guilt, pain, resentment, and lost time to eradicate them both.

The first thing Eloise saw when she opened her eyes was her cell phone. She pushed it off the arm of the chair, it was way too early to be thinking about Jack. She didn't want to stand up, because standing meant facing last night's tantrum and she wasn't ready to sweep the shards of glass. Rossi was snoring quietly, still in the chair. Eloise closed her eyes and tried to make herself fall back to sleep. She wished she could sleep forever. Sleep until her thoughts about Jack disappeared and her guilt over Reagan left with them.

It was hours later when Eloise picked up her phone and the thousand plate pieces off her floor. She opened her contacts and hit Nickie's name.

"Hey, El." Nickie answered before the phone rang a second time.

"What in the hell, Nickie?" Eloise breathed into the phone, not attempting to hide her anger.

"I take it Jack showed up?" Nickie coughed and Eloise knew she was trying to hide her laugh.

"Why would you tell him to come here?"

"I didn't. I told him about Regan and that you needed some

tough love right now."

"Tough love? God, Nickie. Say some shit like that, obviously he'd come."

"It's not like that, El. You two, well, you know how you were. I figured he could help you, help you in a way no one else can. This isn't about banging him, but, if you do that, too, great." Nickie didn't hide her laugh that time. "This is about leaning on someone who knows you at your core. This is about healing."

"I don't want to lean on him. I don't want to heal. I want everyone to leave me alone and stop trying to make me feel better about the fact that my husband is dead." Eloise cursed herself for starting to cry. *Damn tears always reappearing.*

"El," Nickie started calmly. "It's barely been a week. I can't imagine how you're feeling right now. This is still raw. But someday you're going to want to feel better, and I just figured an extra friend couldn't hurt."

"I wish you wouldn't have called him. It's been ten years. I don't even know him anymore. He sure as hell doesn't know me, even though he thinks he does. Jack is just one more thing to deal with when I can barely handle breathing right now."

"You don't have to deal with him, El. Call him or don't call him. Though I hope you do, because regardless of what you say, you two do know each other. It was deep, and it was soul-level, and that kind of knowing never goes away."

"Damn you, Nickie."

"I love you, too, El," Nickie said before hanging up.

J ack got into his truck smiling. Eloise, still feisty as ever, even in pain. When she refused to open the door, he'd debated kicking the bottom of it to make a louder noise but was happy now that he'd continued just pounding with his fist and ringing the doorbell. Nickie had told him Eloise would be this way, but screw her, he wasn't letting her off that easy, regardless of how bad she felt. "Tough love, Jack." That's what Nickie had told him, and that's exactly what he was there to deliver.

He couldn't get over how depressed she looked, and that took the smile right off his face. She had clearly been crying and definitely wasn't eating. When she first opened the door all he wanted was to pull her into him, but he forced himself to stay put. He'd perfected standing still in the Army, and if Eloise thought she could shake him with her swollen eyes and anger, she was about to be disappointed. No matter how tough he made himself appear, it hurt him to see her. He'd seen Eloise in rough shape before but nothing like this.

Jack rubbed his hands over the steering wheel, watching her on the porch. Eloise wouldn't stop him from going. She might call, once the anger wore off, and he could do nothing but hope she did.

Jack threw his hotel key by the television and plopped on the bed. He saw Eloise anytime he closed his eyes, and had for the last ten years. He knew he was pathetic. She didn't want him. She chose someone else, but he never stopped thinking about her. After seeing her face tonight, all he wanted was to comfort her, be her friend. No one was there for Jack when his brother died. There was no one to remind him that it would get better when his mother took her own life. It cut him wide open to think of Eloise grieving alone.

When Nickie called the day Reagan died, he knew something was wrong. She never called. Their friendship had been reduced to emails every few months after Eloise met Reagan.

Jack stood in the shower, more thinking than showering. He wasn't sure what he would do if she didn't call him, how long he should wait. The old Eloise would have called him the same day a relationship ended, but this wasn't a relationship. This was a marriage. A marriage that had lasted eight years with two years of dating before that. This wasn't a breakup either. This was something Eloise didn't want, and didn't ask for. She didn't just walk out of her marriage. Her husband had died. Jack knew how much Eloise hated feeling out of control, and he had no doubt that the lack of control over this was destroying her. Jack knew this was different, but still found himself hurt over the fact she hadn't called. Jack leaned his head back and let the water cover his face. *She didn't call because this is nothing like before*, he told himself. Sex with him wouldn't fix her hurting heart, not this time. He just wished she had called for the other reason she sometimes did: because she needed a friend.

Before Jack got into bed, he checked his phone. Nothing. Her number never changed, Nickie had told him that. He could call her, but he wouldn't. She had to decide to let him back in. Jack hated her a little for the way things ended, but his love for her never failed to overpower that hate. He hoped she'd call. He hoped that they could talk about the last ten years. He hoped they could help heal each other, because even though Eloise was broken now, Jack had been broken since the day his brother Drake died. He needed her too. For years he needed her friendship, but that wasn't an option after Reagan. Jack didn't want Eloise to be like him, full of open wounds, because she had no one to help her find the light. He closed his eyes and focused on the hope that they could make each other's wounds disappear, praying that keeping it close would make it a reality.

Jack woke himself up screaming. He had night terrors most nights, depending on what trauma decided to haunt him. When he reclaimed his grasp on reality, he slipped on some shorts and a T-shirt to get breakfast in the lobby. He figured if he was in Houston, he may as well enjoy it. Regardless of if Eloise called or not, he could check out the city before going back to Grand Junction for the remainder of his thirty-day leave.

After getting coffee, Jack pulled up Nickie's number and hit send.

"My, my, I'm popular today," Nickie said.

"Good morning to you too. I take it El called you already?"

"Does it surprise you?"

"Not in the slightest. What are you doing?" Jack heard a lot of noise on Nickie's end.

"I'm at work, sorry. She's mad, Jack. She's hiding it well, but I could hear it in her voice. It didn't take long before she was done talking about you."

"Yeah, she's probably going to be mad at us both for a while." Jack brought his mug to his lips and took a long drink.

"I don't care. Let her be mad. She'll get over it, and she'll thank us."

"I hope you're right, Nickie."

"You've always cared too much." Nickie paused and Jack imagined she was choosing her next words carefully. "She needs that now, even if she thinks she doesn't. I gotta go, but keep me posted and good luck."

"Thank you, Nickie. And you're wrong. I've never cared too much, at least not enough that it ever mattered to her."

Jack said the words, but in reality, he knew he'd always cared, probably too much like Nickie said, but now it wasn't about him, and for the first time with Eloise, he wouldn't let his feelings get in the way. She could push him away all she wanted and he wouldn't care, wouldn't give up on her, because he loved Eloise and so did Nickie, and one way or another, the two of them were going to keep her from decaying in her damn living room chair.

CHAPTER 2

Waking up in the recliner each morning continued to do a number on Eloise's back. It seemed no matter how much she stretched, popped it and her neck, she couldn't get the knots out. It had been three days since Jack came. He should feel special. Eloise couldn't count how many people banged on her door since Reagan's funeral, and Jack was the only one she opened it for. People kept texting her that it'd get better, that she'd be okay. They told her to take care of herself. Eloise thought about sending them a picture of her in clothes over a week old and see what they'd say to that. Nothing seemed to matter now.

"Why should I take care of myself when the one person I loved more than anything on this earth is gone?" She breathed into the empty room.

The recliner had become her home inside her home. It was where she slept. It held her Kindle and TV remotes. Her blanket shield was there and a water bottle that she hadn't had to refill yet because she couldn't make herself choke down more than a few sips.

Her cell phone was about to vibrate off the arm of the chair.

She hit ignore to make it stop, wishing people would just leave her alone. The phone started to wiggle again. As she reached over to pick up her cell, Eloise recognized part of Jack's phone number.

"What?" she snapped.

"I'm surprised you answered."

"Me too. What do you want?"

"I told you, I want to know you're okay, and don't say you are, because you aren't."

"My husband died nine days ago, so no, I'm not okay, but you can't fix me, Jack."

"I've never tried to, but like I said the other night, we've always been good at being friends. Let me be your friend." His voice fell quiet and Eloise listened to his breathing on the other end of line, steady and slow, every breath patient. She didn't want any friends, but what if someday she did and no one was left.

"Fine." It was all she could manage.

"Take a shower, Eloise. Put on clean clothes. Can you do that?"

"Yeah. I'm surprised it took you this long to call."

"There's that honesty I've so missed. I've talked myself out of calling you for the past three days, but I can't just sit in a hotel forever, I have a job."

"Guess I should be happy you didn't just up and leave."

"It crossed my mind. I'll see you in a couple hours. We can go eat and catch up."

"I can't eat."

"Eloise."

"I'll try." Eloise swore she heard his smile through the phone. She wanted to point out that he didn't ask her, he just expected that she'd go with him, but she didn't think she had the energy. If memory served her right, Jack wasn't one to bow out of an argument.

"See you soon," he said and hung up.

The phone felt heavy, break-her-wrist-from-the-weight heavy, so she set it back on the arm of the chair. If she left the house, maybe the calls and drop-ins would stop. Not likely. Now instead of coming to check on her, they'd gossip about her moving on with some mystery man and would drop by in hopes of finding out who he was. Screw them. Jack had always been respectful. Always. Of Eloise, of her relationships, and of the boundary that marked their friendship after whatever it was that they once had. One thing she didn't have to worry about was him thinking she'd move on to him, because he respected her enough not to try in the first place.

When Eloise stood up, her knees felt weak. She wished she could just stay how she was, but week-old pajamas were not the way to say she was doing fine. She fed Rossi and refilled her water dish. Eloise knew she wouldn't be able to walk through her room to the master bath, so she went up the stairs and into the spare bathroom. Her husband never used it and therefore, like the recliner, it was safe.

The water felt surprisingly incredible and Eloise couldn't figure out why she hadn't been showering this entire time. It helped lift her mood ever so slightly. She waited until the water ran cold to step out of the tub. She'd probably never use the walk-in shower in the master bathroom again. Eloise thought for a second about moving, about admitting that there was nothing left to keep her here.

Eloise chose a pair of army green cargo pants and a maroon shirt. An outfit that said she tried but was still comfortable. Seeing as how she refused to step into her closet, she didn't have a ton of choices, only the things still in the dryer from the day Reagan died. Eloise blow-dried and straightened her hair, taking her time, making sure that each red strand fell inward toward her face. She had cut her hair a few months before losing Reagan. It was long, down the middle of her back, and one day she had decided to cut it up to her chin. Eloise felt her smile appearing at the thought of Reagan hating it. He never said anything bad about it, one way or the other, it was just a feeling she had. Eloise applied her makeup with similar precision. Her lip liner took the longest, and when she looked in the mirror, she felt normal for the first time in ten days. Maybe Jack was onto something.

Eloise stood on the street and stared at Jack as he watched her. She knew he wouldn't come out. He'd wait and force her to make the decision to come in on her own. Jack was always that way, never pushy. When she was young, his go-with-the-flow attitude was appealing, but now for some reason, it annoyed her. She thought about Reagan. He was direct and strong, always had a plan and an idea. Eloise rarely had to make choices with him because most of the time they were already made. She'd found comfort in that over the years.

Eloise opened the door and stepped in. Jack grabbed her hand, and the only thing stopping Eloise from pulling away was the hostess smiling at them. They didn't say anything, just stood there until she was ready to show them to their table. The second they sat down Eloise's mouth flew open.

"Why are you always such an ass? Ten years later and that hasn't changed. Stand in here all smug and then take my hand without a single word like this isn't crazy weird." She took her napkin and placed it across her lap, a habit she'd had since she was a child, thanks to her dad.

"Have you ever considered that you're the ass and I'm just responding?" Jack filled each glass with water from the pitcher the hostess had left.

"Not once." Eloise didn't actually think he was an ass, but her anger always had a way of taking out anyone in her path, guilty or not, and Jack had experienced it enough to know that.

"Eloise you have always pushed my buttons, intentionally so, but why now? Why can't we just talk? I have never understood why you like watching me squirm," Jack said, making Eloise smile, because she knew that he did, almost always, actually think she *could* be an ass. She tried to piss him off, and it seemed she hadn't broken that little habit over the last ten years.

"I can't talk to you about him, Jack. I can't pour my heart out over him. Not to you, not to anyone." Eloise played with the napkin in her lap, her small smile morphing into sadness.

"You're not ready." It wasn't a question.

"I'll never be ready." Jack smiled as Eloise looked up.

"You can't just pretend your husband didn't exist." Jack looked at his hands, and Eloise waited, knowing he was considering his next words. "I know, from too much experience, that you have to mourn the loss of someone you love. If you don't confront it, it'll eat you alive."

"Why not? Seriously, who will stop me? I'm barely keeping it together here. You really think someone is going to question the very fragile Eloise?" No one had questioned her over the last few days, excluding Jack. They called, they tried to visit, but no one pushed her like he had, forcing her out of her cave, not even Nickie. Eloise ignored the fact that they had all tried, but Eloise wouldn't leave for any of them. She refused to acknowledge that Jack was the only one she'd let push her.

"Maybe not just anyone, but I will, and you've never been fragile. I still see the fire in your eyes. You think you're broken, but those pieces can be mended. You've always been honest with me. Let that work for you for once." Jack took a sip of his water.

He had her there. Jack was probably the only person Eloise had ever been completely honest with, including Reagan, but she'd take that to the grave. Jack had a rawness about him that was unmatchable. They were never filtered around each other, everything was always out on the table. She had never met anyone other than him who she could just speak to, no prior thinking needed. Eloise never worried about his feelings or pushing him away or whether he was being honest. She knew he was open, unafraid. She knew even her darkest thoughts wouldn't scare him. Jack always knew what to say, too, no matter what Eloise said first. He had a way of forcing happiness. Jack was sweet in a way that only he could be. Looking at him now, Eloise wondered if he still was that guy. In college, she could say some depressing things, some bizarre things, some awfully mean things, and Jack would always respond in a way that left her smiling. He never flinched, never wavered, never gave her that look that so many others did. The one that said she was too weird, too loud, too honest, too crazy.

"Where have you been?" Eloise changed the subject because she wasn't ready for the immensity that was Jack.

"Colorado mostly. I was stationed in Colorado Springs for a long time. I just recently got transferred to Grand Junction." Jack looked up as the waitress came back to take their order.

"Doing?" Eloise asked before also turning to the waitress. She knew Jack wouldn't answer until after the waitress left. The girl couldn't have been more than eighteen, but she looked at Jack like she'd marry him that instant. She barely spoke to Eloise, which was hilarious. Jack was handsome, she had to give him that, he always had been. The waitress touched his arm before she walked off and Eloise giggled at the uncomfortable look on his face.

"After I got back from Afghanistan the first time, they sent me to a ton of emergency medical training, so, that mostly, until they shipped me back out," Jack said, not mentioning anything about the waitress's infatuation with him.

"You joined the military?" Eloise was a bit shocked. When they were in college, he studied business. He was chaotic, partied way too much, but was also focused and driven. Leaving his dreams behind seemed odd.

"Yeah. I dropped out right after you moved, then enlisted in the Army."

"You didn't graduate?" Eloise couldn't believe it. "How'd you know I left?"

"I hit a rough patch. I needed out." Jack rubbed his hand down his beard, a new addition since the last time Eloise saw him. "Nickie told me."

"I'm not surprised. Do you want to talk about it?" Eloise reached out and touched his wrist, now wasn't the time to be insensitive.

"I thought you said this wasn't a heart-on-our-sleeves type dinner." His eyes burned into her hand.

"Not for me, but you can say whatever you want." She pulled her hand back and questioned touching him at all.

"Not a chance. I'm not opening my can of emotional worms when you refuse to." Jack pushed back from the table as the waitress approached with salads, again making Eloise smirk. She knew he was trying to give the waitress room to set down his bowl without touching him. So much about him was the same.

"This may be the first time we haven't just spit it out." Eloise couldn't help but laugh, both at their situation and at the all too eager waitress. They had always spoken their minds and now neither was willing to be that person.

"You show me yours." Jack winked at her, and Eloise watched as the waitress raised her eyebrows before leaving again.

"Look, Jack, if there ever comes a day where I can talk about Reagan, or think I can without completely losing it, you'll be the first to know." Eloise picked up her fork and started examining her salad.

"Looking for baby corn?" Jack asked as Eloise dug through her bowl.

"How in the world do you remember that?" Eloise loaded her fork, deeming the salad safe.

"You made your hatred very memorable." Jack picked up his fork now, not bothering to examine the contents of his bowl before taking a big bite. "I got depressed," he said after swallowing. "One day I was in school, I was the guy you knew, and then the next day, I was struggling to get out of bed. I knew I needed a change, so I enlisted and never looked back."

"What do you do in the Army?" His admission scared Eloise. She wasn't sure she was ready to think about or talk about Jack being depressed. It was an emotion she'd never seen concerning him. He was always smiling, always happy, when she knew him.

"My first couple of years I was infantry, but after my first tour, I trained to be a medic. I've been a Ranger combat medic for a while now." Jack looked around the restaurant.

"Wow. That seems so different from what you used to want." Eloise pushed the napkin holder closer to Jack, feeling a bit claustrophobic.

"Not so different. I always wanted to be the best of the best." Jack looked up, smiling.

Eloise was secretly happy to see some of his cocky attitude make an appearance. For a moment, she thought she was sitting next to a total stranger.

"But seriously, it's a team of men who proved their worth, not everyone can be in the Rangers."

"And what does that entail, being a Ranger?" Eloise felt her cheeks getting hot, she couldn't believe she was blushing.

"Whatever and wherever I'm told to go." Jack's tone was deeper now, and his smile was gone.

"Oh," Eloise said, unsure if she imagined the icy undertone to his voice. She wondered why he didn't want to talk about his job. It seemed a lot easier to her than talking about his depression.

"What about you? What have you been doing these last ten years?" Jack slowly shook his head, and Eloise wondered if he was trying to rid it of thoughts about the Army.

"I finished graduate school. I did a lot of random things at first, museums mostly, and I was a case manager for a while. I've spent the last five years teaching." Eloise thought about her students. She hadn't been back to her classroom since Reagan died.

"I can see you teaching. Do you like it?" Jack looked up just as the waitress set his plate in front of him, followed by Eloise's. Much to Eloise's surprise, she didn't stick around.

"I love it." Eloise glanced at her plate, his big eyes too much for her. There was a time when she loved his black eyes, a time when she'd seek out reasons to get lost in them.

"What do you teach?" Jack covered his entire plate of spaghetti in parmesan cheese.

"English. I run a mentor program too." Eloise picked up her fork and butter knife so she could cut her eggplant.

"Sounds very you, Eloise," Jack said before taking his first bite.

"How long can you stay?" Eloise wanted to shift the conversation away from teaching because she didn't want Jack to know she gave up something she loved because she felt she'd never be able to keep loving anything with Reagan gone. Teaching included.

"I'm off the next twenty-five days, I started with thirty." Jack took another bite and finished off his water.

"And then you go where?"

"Back to Fort Gunnison in Colorado until they send us out. It's a lot of training when we aren't on missions."

"How long will you be gone?" Eloise lifted the pitcher to Jack's glass.

"It depends. I never really know. Usually nothing over six months, though." Jack shoveled in a few bites before taking another drink.

"Wow." Eloise couldn't believe the length of time he'd leave, and she wondered if he'd ever been gone longer, but didn't ask.

"Nothing I haven't done before. Don't worry." Jack gave her a small smile.

"Wouldn't dream of it." Eloise's lips parted slightly.

"Do you want company for the next month or so?" Jack leaned forward.

"Absolutely not. Is that why you came here?" Eloise narrowed her eyes, and when Jack didn't back up, she shut them, their past flooding her memory. Jack was always the first person she called when she was single, and she had always been eager to be his first call too. The foundation to their unconventional relationship was sex. Eloise exhaled and opened her eyes, waiting for Jack to respond.

"I came here because I heard your husband died, yes from Nickie before you ask, and I wanted to check on you. I don't have to stay. I just thought you may like someone around. I can help do whatever you need." Jack's eyes never left Eloise and she wished he would stop looking at her like that. She felt stupid for thinking that he came here for the same reason she used to go to his apartment at all hours of the night years ago.

"I'll think about it." Eloise dropped her gaze.

"That's not a no."

"Shut up." Eloise couldn't hide her smile.

"Always so sassy." Jack stacked their plates, then grabbed the black folder that held the bill. He stuck his debit card inside and scooted his chair back as the waitress took the card and cleared the table. "I swear, El, I'd never cross that line. Not with you. I remember our past, too, but honest, I just came to check on you and to offer some help."

"I know that, Jack. I do." She reached out and touched his arm again, this time without thinking about it. "I don't know why my mind went there." Eloise waited for Jack to stand first after the waitress brought back his card. She knew he'd grab her hand again and walk her out. A lot about Jack had changed, she had a lot of questions, but some things that were at his core, she knew were still there.

Jack opened the restaurant door and escorted her out. "Eloise, if you change your mind, you have my number." He squeezed her hand. "I missed you. Thank you for having dinner with me." He lifted her hand to his lips, and she closed her eyes as he kissed it.

Jack kept Eloise's hand as he walked her across the street to her car. Eloise unlocked her door and slid into the driver's seat. Jack leaned down and kissed her cheek.

"Good night, Eloise."

"Good night, Jack." Eloise started her car, then Jack shut the door. As she drove off, she glanced in her rearview mirror and found Jack still standing on the side of the street.

J ack stayed standing on the street long after Eloise's car disappeared. The evening wasn't what he'd expected, but then again, he had no idea what to expect when he'd walked into the restaurant and told the hostess he'd need a table for two. He waited for Eloise by the door. She was never good with directions, and when he thought about the hostess pointing toward him and Eloise still struggling to find him, he had laughed then and it still made him laugh now. Seeing her through the glass window, stopped his heart. She looked amazing. He was thrilled to see that she had showered and changed her clothes. When his brother died, he felt like a shell until his first shower.

Jack stuck his hands in his jacket pockets and started walking down the street, not ready to go back to the empty hotel room. So much about Eloise was new to him, but a lot was the same ol' Eloise. She still couldn't stand the sight of baby corn. That had always been one of his favorite memories of her. The two of them ordering Pad Thai for the first time. She said no baby corn, got it anyway, and he spent the entire drive to her apartment throwing baby corn out the window, both of them in tears from laughing so hard, partly because Eloise refused to touch it and partly because of the lengths Jack would go to make her happy.

Where he'd been brutally honest with her before, he was filtered now, and he hated it. He didn't like not knowing how much of his life and his job he should disclose. He never had to consider her feelings before, not in the sense he had to now. Jack wanted to tell her about his team, the men he'd die for, the ones who had died, a few of them for him. It was a bond unlike any he'd had in his life—with two exceptions: his brother and Eloise. Jack had never thought of Eloise as fragile, not until the night he banged on her door and she opened it looking more breakable than he'd ever seen her.

CHAPTER 3

Eloise sat back in the recliner to sip her coffee in silence, twisting the white gold band on her ring finger. She hadn't had a bare finger in eight years. Looking down at her hand, Eloise thought she'd never be able to take it off. She finished her coffee slowly. Getting ready seemed pointless, but she remembered the way the shower gave her some motivation. If she was going to keep getting dressed at some point, she'd have to buy more clothes. She knew she'd never be able to walk in and retrieve the ones hanging in her closet.

After a shower, Eloise didn't think she could get as "dressed" as she had the night before, so instead, she chose leggings and a sweatshirt from her dryer. She needed to go grocery shopping, but she wasn't sure she'd make it through the store without breaking down. Passing the dining room table, she picked up her cell and found Jack's number.

Do you want to come over for dinner?

Eloise knew if it was just her who needed food, she'd never shop or eat again.

Suddenly you want to be friends?

Stop being a jackass. Yes or no?

Sure.

See you at 7.

She closed her messages and stuffed the phone into her purse. Maybe if she cooked and kept trying to eat, eventually it would work. If she kept pretending to be more than a shell, then maybe one day she would be. After Rossi was fed, Eloise grabbed her car keys, extremely thankful that she and her husband always kept separate vehicles. There was no way in hell she could drive his truck.

Going to the store drained Eloise. The mixture of pain, exhaustion, and anger she'd been experiencing since losing Reagan seemed to be growing within her. Eloise had to fight tears as she walked down each aisle at the store. Shopping was something she and Reagan did together, and passing the items he would have thrown in the basket made a lump grow thick in her throat.

Eloise wasn't sure how she should dress for dinner. It was just a dinner between friends and shouldn't be a big deal. Should it? She chose a pair of jeans from her dryer and a gray hoodie, going for the not-trying-hard-at-all look. She curled her hair and applied makeup, hoping he would be able to tell she did what she could. She thought back for a moment of who they were when they met. She was an eighteen-year-old kid fresh out of high school and starting college. Young, pretty, and confident. He was such a jock when they met and already in his sophomore year. He had played football in high school and still had super-ripped arms. He didn't take a damn thing serious, and always had a stupid grin on his face. He was at every party, smoked weed, and drank too much, but somehow still went to school and pulled good grades. He never had a steady girlfriend, because he was all about having a good time.

It was funny because when she met him at the movie theater, she was instantly attracted to him. She was smart enough to realize that no relationship whatsoever could come from it. He just wasn't that guy. He had that player vibe, and she knew it, but that didn't take away from her physical attraction to him.

She knew that she wanted him. Not in a boyfriend type way. She wanted to get to know him, definitely wanted to sleep with him, but before college, she'd only slept with one guy—her high school boyfriend—and just wasn't sure that she should be the girl who had meaningless flings. Jack had made that extremely easy, though. There was nothing awkward about it. She never felt self-conscious around him, it was impossible not to feel great with his huge grin and playful nature. There was no question of *was this going to be more*, because she never felt pressure to be his girlfriend. She had no expectations of him, or him of her, and honestly, the first time they slept together it was a lot more than sex. It was the start of an incredible friendship.

Her doorbell rang and unlike the first time he showed up, she didn't hesitate to open the door.

"Jack." Eloise unlocked the glass door. Rossi was pushing to get between Eloise and the door, a growl growing in her throat.

"Hey, Eloise." He wore jeans as well, but with a short-sleeved shirt that confirmed a decade hadn't caused his arms to get smaller. "Are you gonna introduce me to your friend this time?"

"Come in." She held the door open wide and he brushed against her as he passed. "This is Rossi." Eloise rubbed Rossi's neck. Jack kneeled to pet Rossi before he walked into her kitchen, Rossi keeping a close distance.

"Trying to get me drunk?" Eloise said as Jack set down the bottle of tequila he brought.

"If I remember correctly, it doesn't take much." Jack sat down at the breakfast bar like he owned the place. Rossi sniffed him and Jack held his hand out, palm down, so she could smell him. Rossi appeared satisfied with that and took her place next to Eloise.

"I made steak, fries, and salad. I hope that's okay." Eloise got the plates and started loading them with food, setting a plate in front of Jack. She snapped her fingers twice and pointed toward Rossi's dog bed. Rossi looked from her to Jack before lying down.

"More than okay. This looks amazing. I should cook for you sometime." Jack immediately started digging in.

"Oh right, I should've remembered that." Jack and his brother loved cooking. They had talked about opening their own restaurant while in college. It was the reason Jack had studied business. Eloise was suddenly worried that he was critiquing every bite.

"It's really just a hobby. I almost never have time to do any real cooking." Jack kept eating as he talked.

"You don't want to own a restaurant anymore?" Eloise grabbed two glasses. "You wanna start with tea or go straight for the tequila?"

"Cooking is what I do between missions. What I did between tours before becoming a Ranger. I still try and keep up with the changes and trends, learning as much as I can by reading and experimenting when I get the chance, but I don't get a lot of time stateside anymore, not enough to take a job. But someday I'll hang it up in the Army and open my own restaurant. Better start with tea." Jack smiled at her and took another bite.

"Jack has other goals?" Eloise filled their glasses with ice and tea.

"Shocks me too." Jack's fingers touched hers as he took his glass, and for a moment, Eloise saw the nineteen-year-old boy she used to know, happy-go-lucky, a goofball, and though she couldn't tell him, she had missed him too.

"Did you ever get married?" Eloise had a table, but they stayed standing to eat at the bar in her kitchen.

"No, El." Jack cut his steak, eyes on Eloise and not his knife.

"Kids?" Eloise took a bite and thought that standing to eat in her kitchen with Jack should feel uncomfortable, but it didn't.

"None that I'm aware of. Did you guys have kids?"

"Do you see kids?"

"Good point." Jack shook his head. "Did you want them?"

"Yes. I always wanted a big family." Eloise shifted her weight from one leg to the other.

"I remember, so why don't I see kids?"

"You blink and life kinda just flies by. Reagan and I talked about it, but we were both so focused on jobs, plus after I was done with graduate school, we moved a lot, traveled a lot, and it just never happened." Eloise swallowed. "Now it's too late."

"It's not too late. You could still have a family, El, kids even, if you wanted. Or just the kids on your own."

"I'm thirty-three years old, Jack."

"So? I'm thirty-four." He raised his eyebrows and Eloise chuckled, rolling her eyes. They finished eating, making light conversation. Jack tossed a couple pieces of meat to Rossi before he stood to pick up the dishes.

"I can clean, Jack."

"So can I, El." Jack tossed their paper plates in the garbage can. "Just relax."

"Thank you." Eloise watched as Jack placed the cups and silverware in the dishwasher and laughed as he walked back to the living room, tequila bottle and two glasses in tow.

"You aren't too old for a family, El." Jack handed her a glass before sitting down. "You'd be a good mom. A great one."

"Hah!" Eloise held out her glass for Jack. "I'm a mess. A kid wouldn't have a chance."

"Well, yes, you are a mess, but just right now. You aren't gonna stay a mess."

"You sound so sure." Eloise took a sip of the tequila and Jack followed.

"I am sure, El. I've seen you a mess before, not like this, I'll give you that, this is different. But you're also the strongest person I know. You *will* make it through this." Jack downed his glass and poured more.

"Thank you, Jack." Eloise finished her drink and held it out to him. Jack had definitely seen her as a mess, more times than she'd like to admit. Jack had seen it all. Various levels of drunk Eloise. Everything from slightly frustrated to see-red pissed, jealous, and mean—sometimes to him. He'd seen her confident, sassy, and sarcastic. He'd also seen her depressed, something Eloise would've hated if Jack hadn't been the one pulling her out of those dark holes. Eloise smiled at that thought, even though they were painful memories.

"What is it?" Jack stopped his glass just shy of his lips.

"You. Always pulling me out of my dark places. Did it before and now here you are."

"Happy to help." He extended his glass to hers, then they clinked together. "To finding the light."

"To finding the light," Eloise repeated.

Jack and Eloise got so drunk they couldn't see straight, and he had to sleep on her couch. It was only slightly awkward the next morning when he woke up and realized that she had slept in her recliner with Rossi.

"El, wake up." Jack shook her lightly on the arm.

"Jack, shut up." Eloise rolled over. Jack looked at her curled up, her back to her dog. Was this something she did now? Was getting drunk and sleeping in her living room a normal night for her? Jack didn't think she felt awkward about this. He did. He was at a loss for how to be around this version of Eloise.

"Coffee, beautiful?" The words were out of his mouth before he could stop them. It wasn't a compliment. Eloise was beautiful, but to him it was more of a nickname, something he called her frequently a long time ago. He hoped she remembered that and didn't take it as him crossing a line.

"If you want my ass out of this chair, yes, coffee, and try out those cooking skills on some eggs, handsome." Jack stopped moving when he heard the word "handsome."

"Move it, El." Jack set her plate where they ate at the night before, and laughed when he heard Eloise groan, *still not a morning person.*

"Bring it here."

"Move your ass, girl." Jack set her coffee next to her plate and then set his stuff across from hers. He knew she'd get up. Jack kept his eyes down as he listened to Eloise shut the recliner and stand. He could picture her without looking, twisting to pop her back, cracking her knuckles, and her neck. Eloise got up the same way anytime he was with her, and he was happy to see that not everything had changed.

"Jack, you said you'd help, did you mean that?" Eloise sat down in front of her plate and their eyes met for the first time that morning.

"Of course I did. What do you need?"

"A lot, but today...today I need to start deciding what of Reagan's to keep and what to get rid of, but I can't do that, Jack, I can't even look at his stuff."

"I can do it, El. I'll take care of it."

"How?"

"Well, seeing as you're not ready to face it, how about I box everything up? I'll pack it carefully and label it, and put it all in a storage unit, and when you're ready, it'll be there. And there's no rush, El, it doesn't have to be today, or even soon."

"I feel like I can't breathe in my own house. Everywhere I look, everything I see, it knocks the air out of me. The storage unit is a good idea, Jack. Thank you."

"I'll go get boxes after breakfast."

Jack came back after breakfast with a huge stack of boxes, packing paper, Bubble Wrap, and a receipt for a storage unit. As he moved, Eloise followed him, reminding him of how Rossi followed her. He knew she wasn't sure what to do. Jack didn't say anything, because he didn't know how to tell her that he understood her need to help. He didn't have the words to express his own understanding of the torture that comes after loss. Jack sneaked quick glances at Eloise as he worked. He was afraid that if he looked at her too long her somber eyes would suffocate him.

Jack turned Reagan's things in his hands, making up stories about how they made up Eloise's life with her husband. He packaged each item meticulously, carefully labeling every box with the items it contained and which room he took it from. After about an hour, Eloise finally gave up trying to pretend to help and sat down to read. When he saw her with her opened book, he let out a breath of relief that she finally seemed content in her decision to put this weight on him. Occasionally, Jack would walk into the living room and hold something up for Eloise's approval and then he'd go back to packing. He never brought something that was Reagan's. He would only bring things of hers that he found mixed with Reagan's stuff. He didn't want her to have to face his belongings that day. Jack may not be able to do a lot to ease her pain, but he could do this. He could give her a few hours of tranquility.

Jack felt weird about touching Reagan's things, but he didn't say anything to Eloise about that, because her trusting him to pack Reagan's stuff trumped any feelings of uneasiness. It hurt him when she said she couldn't even look at his stuff. Jack thought about Drake while he packed, because that was easier than thinking about Reagan. Jack's mother couldn't pack his brother's things, so Jack did, and then he packed hers too. Drake's stuff was hard to look at for a long time, but eventually Jack decided what to keep and what could be donated and thrown away. He understood about not being able to face the loss, because when his mother died, he felt himself break. He still had a few untouched boxes of hers, boxes that he may never be able to open.

When Jack's mom died, he felt abandoned. Drake didn't have a choice, so Jack never felt like he could be mad at him for leaving. But, his mother, she did, and she had another son, one who got left behind. Jack felt his eyes start to swell, and sat down on Eloise's bedroom floor. He was not about to cry in her house over his mother. He looked down at the photo in his hand. Eloise, Reagan, and Rossi. A family. Jack had always wanted a family. He and Drake both wanted that, which was why they never cared how many people crammed into their apartment each night. There was a time when he thought he and Eloise would be a family, but never had the guts to tell her that he had real feelings for her, ones that went way beyond sex. He'd spent every single day of the last decade wishing he'd done things differently, fought harder. He wished every morning that he would've told her that she was the only person in the world who had ever made him feel like he mattered, like he had something to offer. Jack thought of how close they were all those years ago, how they talked about everything, no boundaries, no comfort zones, just the real, raw, honest-to-God truth —the only exception being, how much they genuinely loved each other.

Once Eloise had given in, he went through the rest of the day barely seeing her. He was starting to get hungry, and decided he'd see if she was too.

"El, I'm fading fast. You can work me to the bone, but I still gotta eat." He came out of the master bedroom, watching as she shut her book, then reached down to scratch Rossi's ears.

"Do you want to go out to dinner?" Eloise stood, arching her back to stretch.

"Sure. That'd be great. I take it I'll still be starving for a while?"

"Yeah, I'm not going out like this." Jack eyed her pajamas, her unbrushed hair, and though he still found her breathtaking, he agreed that putting on clothes was probably best.

"Take your time. If I die, I die."

"So dramatic. I'll try and hurry," Eloise said, making Jack laugh. A decade had come and gone, but he knew that it'd be at least an hour before they left. Eloise had one speed when it came to getting ready, sloth. Eloise laughed too. "The things you remember surprise me."

"You spent a lot of time getting ready in my bathroom. See you in ten." Jack walked back into the master. He was one box away from being done in there and knew he could finish it before Eloise was actually ready to leave.

Forty-five minutes later, Jack and Eloise walked into the restaurant, which Eloise had found on her phone, as Jack drove toward town.

"Good evening," the host said. "Two?"

"Yes," Jack answered, still holding Eloise's hand. He never touched her when they were alone, but somehow recognized she needed the confidence to be out in the world without Reagan.

"How come you wanted to go out?" Jack asked after they were seated.

"I read all day, and just felt like I should get out."

"That's a good sign, wanting to be away from the house." Jack opened his menu and Eloise did the same.

They read through their menus, both setting them down after a few minutes. Jack watched the people in the restaurant and noticed everyone in pairs. Some leaning in close, some touching, and others who looked like strangers. He wondered what he and Eloise looked like to people.

"What can I get started for you?" the waiter asked as he approached. Jack looked to Eloise, waiting for her to order first. When she and Jack had their orders placed, the waiter told them it'd be right out, and moved to the next table.

"Shrimp enchiladas?" Jack eyed Eloise.

"What's wrong with that?"

"The grande burrito sounds better."

"To you." Eloise sipped her water.

Jack thought about how they fluctuated so dramatically from who they were, to the awkward versions they were throughout the day. Jack preferred the comfort of who they used to be. He understood their relationship then, was able to read her with accuracy. Now, everything Eloise did or said made him wonder what she was thinking.

"Thank you, Jack, for everything you did today."

"You don't have to thank me."

"I do. I couldn't have packed all those things," Eloise said. Jack thought of how different her thank you would have been ten years ago. They never would've made it out of his apartment. They definitely wouldn't have clothes on. Now, she could barely look at him and he knew she wouldn't touch him.

"Well, I came to help." Jack wanted to tell Eloise to draw a clear line. He knew she didn't want more than a friend, but did she want the friend he used to be, or some watered-down version of that?

When their food showed up, they ate in silence. Jack had a

million questions, but stayed quiet and waited. He figured he'd outlast Eloise, and he was right.

"What are you thinking?" Eloise looked up from her food, but didn't meet his eyes.

"The silence was killing you, wasn't it?" Jack pushed his plate back and then held out his hand for Eloise to hand him her plate. He stacked everything neatly for the waiter.

"Well?" Eloise stressed the word, drawing out the sound.

"I was thinking about lines." Jack flashed a wide grin and Eloise's cheek's flashed red.

"Lines?" Eloise bit her bottom lip and waited.

"That's all I have to say about that." Jack raised his eyebrows and pretended to look around the restaurant.

"You're such a punk." Eloise pushed her chair back, crossing her arms over her chest, glaring at him.

"Are you about to throw a tantrum." Jack's eyes bore into Eloise's as he, too, pushed his chair back.

"I hate you." Eloise looked away.

Jack watched her nostrils flare, and her chest rise and fall as she took deep breaths. Something he remembered she did to calm herself. Jack knew she was pissed, but he didn't care. Neither one of them had a clue how to act, he understood that. He didn't believe she did. Jack wanted to tell her that just because they never kept secrets before, just because he was always transparent then, didn't mean they could be that way now. They were different people. It had been ten years, but Jack knew Eloise wanted him to be the Jack she remembered. She said things, did things that were an undeniable tribute to their past, but she wasn't the Eloise she used to be. Their relationship had never been half-assed and that's what she wanted now. Jack couldn't do it. He couldn't be those people from ten years ago when she could handle it, and then just turn it off when she couldn't. The unfairness of that, the differences he noticed in her, even the small ones, that's what was pissing him off, and it seemed she wasn't too happy about it either.

"This *is* a tantrum." Jack stood. "It hasn't been long enough." Jack walked toward the front to pay the bill. Eloise huffed as he walked away, clicking her tongue. He pulled out his wallet and waited for someone to help him. He'd have to go back and get her. God, she could be such a pain in the ass. Eloise would sit there and let him drive off and leave her before she'd get up on her own, just to spite him. For a split second he considered walking out the front door, spite her instead, which made him laugh. Eloise won this game every single time, because he'd never actually leave her.

Jack paid the bill and walked back to the table, standing in front of Eloise's chair.

"Are we walking out of here hand in hand or we doing this the hard way?" Jack held out his hand. He had carried Eloise out of more public places than he could count because she was angry and stubborn, but he doubted she'd go that route now.

"You wouldn't dare, Jack. Not anymore." Eloise's arms were still crossed.

"We both know that I will, Eloise. Get up." Jack dropped his hand. "If I pick you up, your ass is getting carried all the way to the car, so don't scream at me to put you down."

Eloise stared at Jack, neither blinking. He honestly thought she'd stand. They weren't those people anymore, wasn't that what he'd decided? Eloise closed her eyes, a smirk spreading across her lips. It was that smirk that pushed him over the edge, and before he could stop himself, he grabbed her and threw her over his shoulder. Eloise didn't bother saying anything. Now that he'd picked her up, he'd keep his promise not to put her down even if she did scream. Jack walked straight to the front door, and didn't care that the entire place was staring.

"Have a good night," their waiter said as they passed.

"Thank you. You too," Jack said as he pushed through the door. He kept walking down the street to where he parked his truck. He didn't set Eloise down until he had the passenger-side door open.

"I cannot believe you actually did that." Eloise got in the truck and slammed the door.

"Yes you can," Jack said, then walked around to the driver's side.

"All you had to do is tell me what you were thinking," Eloise said once he got in.

"I did." Jack started the truck.

"You didn't explain what it meant."

"And that was grounds for a temper tantrum?"

"Considering you carried me out, I guess so." Eloise turned to look out the window. She'd overreacted, and they both knew it. He also presumed that she'd never tell him that, because that would mean admitting that she wanted old Jack and old Eloise. It meant she wanted him to carry her out of that restaurant just to be able to pretend for a moment that she was sassy and stubborn, instead of broken from the inside out. Jack believed that with his entire being, because though Eloise confused the hell out of him now, and in a way she never did before, he still had been intimate with her in a way no one else ever had, in a way no one else ever would.

CHAPTER 4

J ack had been packing boxes for days. Well, packing boxes and anything else Eloise could think of from cleaning to cooking to fixing things around the house. Eloise spent half the time barking orders at him, and half the time being annoyed by him. Neither of them had brought up the night at the restaurant again. He came over early that morning to help her clean out the gutters, and for the first time since he showed up, she felt like she owed him.

"Jack, I was thinking that maybe you should stay here until you have to leave," she yelled up to him from the bottom of her husband's ladder. It was easier to see Reagan's things when Jack used them. She could pretend that they were Jack's. He had gotten everything that he didn't need to work on the house packed and put in storage, and Eloise was finally able to take a breath, to walk into her closet, and she wanted him to know that it meant a lot to her, him staying and taking on all her requests. He never complained. He never even questioned her. He just did what she asked and would come back to her saying "What's next, El?" after he finished each task.

"Stay here, why?" He stopped and looked at her.

"Well, you're always here, anyway. The least I could do is make it so you don't have to keep paying for a hotel." Eloise used her hand to shield her eyes, because the sun made it hard to make out Jack's face.

"I don't mind, Eloise. I planned to spend my leave here checking on you and besides, I have nowhere else to be." Jack climbed down the ladder.

"Jack, this is a four-bedroom house and the only thing I even use is the recliner." Eloise could keep using the spare bathroom even if Jack stayed. She knew Jack well enough to know he wouldn't comment on it. Standing in the doorway of her closet was one thing. Using their shower, sleeping in their bed, that was a whole other matter that Jack couldn't fix.

"You're sure you don't mind?" Jack picked up the ladder and moved it down the house a few feet to reach the next section of gutter.

"If you keep doing stuff around here, I don't mind." Eloise took the steps to realign herself with Jack.

"Are you going to sell?" He climbed up the steps, not looking down.

"Yeah. I can't live here, too many memories." *Hell, I still can't even walk into my own bathroom.*

"Well, I can do whatever you need until my time's up, then hopefully, you can put the place on the market." Jack didn't turn to her, he just kept working.

"Thanks, Jack. I honestly think I'd still be in my recliner, wearing the same pajamas, if you hadn't shown up." Eloise went to walk back into the house. She hadn't meant to say that, but guessed he deserved to hear it.

"Eloise, wait." Jack jumped down off the ladder and as she turned, they were toe-to-toe. "Anytime. I know you would've done it for me." He took her hands.

"Can I ask you something?" Eloise glanced at their clasped

hands and then at his shirt as it moved with every lift and fall of his chest.

"Sure." Jack rotated her hands in his.

"What made you join the Army?" Eloise looked up. She wanted to see his eyes when he answered. Joining the Army was never something Jack wanted, and now he was here, a Ranger, and she had to know why, if he was staying.

"Do you remember my brother?" Jack stared down at his shoes.

"Of course I do. He was always nice to me. Even after you and I stopped talking, anytime he saw me, we talked." Eloise squeezed Jack's fingers. Whatever this was it was going to be hard for him to say.

"He died." His eyes didn't leave the ground. "College was never his thing. He was only there because he promised our mom he'd try. He always wanted to enlist, ever since we were kids. After he died, I just felt like I had to do it for him." He finally looked up at her, his black eyes never showing pain.

"I'm so sorry, Jack. Why didn't you call me?" Eloise wished her eyes could hide pain like his.

"It was after Reagan. I knew that once you married him our friendship was done. I knew I couldn't call you." Jack swallowed.

"I hate to say you're right." Eloise felt Jack's hands start to shake.

"Was he jealous?" Jack clenched his teeth.

"Never. He was always trusting. He was an amazing man. Way too good for me, in so many ways. I just couldn't talk to you because he was that good, you know? It wouldn't have been right. I had to be devoted to him." Eloise pulled her hands away and wrapped them around Jack, laying her head on his chest. His arms hugged her in tight. Her head still fit there as perfectly as the day she first laid it there over a decade ago.

"I get that." He rested his chin on her head.

"Are you going back to the hotel?" Eloise didn't move, everything in her told her to, but she felt safe for the first time in longer than she could remember.

"I'll need to get my stuff. Do you want to ride with me?" Jack dropped his arms and took a step back.

"Sure." She tried her best to look happy.

"Great. Let me finish up here and then we can go." Jack reached up to touch her face, but dropped his arm as his fingertips brushed her cheek.

Eloise walked away before she did something she'd regret. Back inside her house, she poured herself a glass of tea and stood at her kitchen counter. She could feel herself starting to sweat. How was it that he still had such an effect on her? She wouldn't let this happen. Jack wouldn't ever cross that line. He'd wait for her to do it and she couldn't. It wasn't fair to Reagan.

After about an hour, Jack came inside to get Eloise. He was soaked in sweat and grabbed a bottle of water from the fridge, drinking the entire thing before saying a word.

"You ready?" He put the lid back on the bottle and threw it in the trash.

"Yup." Eloise shook out her hands, somehow still not fully together.

When they got to the hotel, Eloise stayed in Jack's truck. It didn't take long for him to stuff his belongings into two duffel bags and throw them in the cargo bed.

"That's all you have?" Eloise asked as he climbed back into his truck and shut the door.

"Yeah. I only brought enough to last me my leave. The rest of my stuff is in storage in Grand Junction." Jack kept both hands on the wheel.

"Will you stay there after you go back?" Eloise looked out the window, the tension in this truck was ridiculous. She had no clue how they'd live together for almost two weeks. Eloise didn't want anything from Jack, not like that, not yet. She couldn't do that to Reagan. She knew that, but it didn't quiet the roaring feeling in the pit of her stomach.

"Yeah, that's the plan. I don't spend much time there. I'm either deployed or training on the base, but I found a house that I love and am working on buying it." Jack turned the radio on, but left it low.

"You don't want to have a place near family?"

"No. There's no one there anymore."

Eloise bit her bottom lip. They stayed quiet the rest of the ride home. When Jack pulled into the driveway, Eloise finally looked at him.

"I'll get the door for you." Jack got out quickly, grabbing his bags as he walked around the truck. He had one over each shoulder as he opened Eloise's door. At the front door, Eloise fumbled with her keys a bit, the proximity of Jack making her feel off-balance. They stepped inside and he dropped both bags.

"Make yourself at home. Take any room but the master," Eloise said, heading for the kitchen.

"Thank you, Eloise. This will save me a ton." Jack picked his bags back up and headed down the hall.

"Well, you've saved me more by getting this house ready to sell, so thank you," Eloise said to his back.

Eloise sat in her recliner and listened for Jack, but never heard him. She couldn't sleep knowing he was above her. The spare room he chose was almost never used, just a bed, two nightstands, and an empty closet. She took him some hangers when they first got back. Eloise wasn't sure if the next two weeks would be comforting or the reason she went sleep-deprived.

That night, Jack lay in a bed that wasn't his in a house he didn't own. Eloise never realized how much she affected people. She was this force that engulfed everything in her path. She was so caring, but honestly didn't see her power over others, over him.

He came here because he knew she'd be a wreck after losing Reagan, and she was, but he never planned to stay all this time, not that she'd ever know that. He'd call the airport in the morning and set up a flight out of Houston when it was time to return to the base.

The next morning, he tiptoed down the stairs. When Jack glanced at Eloise in her recliner, she appeared to be still asleep. He went into the kitchen and looked around, being careful not to open or shut the cabinets too loudly.

"Are you attempting to make coffee?" Eloise asked from her chair.

"Yeah, sorry." He sounded like she caught him doing something he wasn't supposed to.

"It's fine. The cups are in the bottom cabinet and everything to make the coffee is sitting by the pot." Eloise giggled, making Jack grunt in frustration. "You've made coffee here before," she explained.

"I wasn't fully coherent then, and yet somehow did a better job than now." Jack made the coffee, standing in the kitchen as the pot filled. He hoped his blue silk shorts and white tank top were okay with Eloise. He had no clue where the line was. The tile was cold under his bare feet. He poured two cups of coffee, putting creamer in hers, knowing that her coffee taste was another thing that hadn't changed, and walked into the living room.

"Here." When Eloise took the cup he offered, it made him think of his brother. Drake always made coffee and breakfast when Eloise stayed over at their apartment. It was a true bachelor pad back in college, four guys crammed into one place and never enough soap in the bathrooms. They'd wake up in the morning, walk out into the kitchen, and there would be Drake, making pancakes with a smile that people always said made him look like Jack. There were always people, and that was part of why Eloise loved staying there, something she told him often. Jack never pressured her for more and it was normal to have ten or more people eating Drake's breakfast each morning.

"Thank you, Jack." She smiled up at him. She let her other hand out of her blanket, but left it over her stomach and legs. Jack sat on the couch. "How'd you sleep?"

"Great. Thank you."

"Liar." Eloise ran one hand through her messy hair.

"Okay, so it was weird being here, but once I did fall asleep, it was great."

"I slept like shit." Eloise took another drink.

"Because of the recliner?" Jack looked the chair up and down.

"Because I knew you were above me."

"There's that honesty I've so missed." Jack's fingers tapped the side of his cup, a sheepish grin filling his face.

"Yeah, yeah. What are you doing today?"

"Whatever you tell me to."

"In that case, I'll make a list."

Jack started with painting, then moving and covering everything in every room except the living room. He told Eloise he'd do that room last because she slept in there, but he never asked her why. Jack remembered Eloise telling him once that he was good at being present without being overwhelming and he was desperately trying to be that for her now.

E loise was going through her kitchen cabinets, deciding what to keep, when her doorbell rang. She wondered if people would ever stop checking on her.

Out of habit, Eloise looked in the mirror by her door before swinging it open.

"El!"

"Nickie!" She embraced her best friend. "What are you doing here?"

"I had some time off and figured why not come back? You weren't in the best of spirits when I left last time."

"That was the day after I buried my husband." Eloise let Nickie go and took a step back so that she could come inside.

"El, are you okay?" Jack's voice came first and then his body.

"Jack, is that you?" Nickie gave Eloise a look that said *what the hell* loud and clear.

"Yes, it's Jack," Eloise supplied, shrugging at her friend. "It's nothing."

"Nickie?" Jack came all the way around the corner, grabbing Nickie and lifting her off the ground. "What are you doing here?"

"I could ask you the same thing."

"I came to check on Eloise and got stuck renovating her house." Jack laughed and gave Eloise a wink and a smile.

"She's got strong powers, Jack."

"I know. It's impossible to say no to her."

"I am right here," Eloise said, suddenly irritated at the two people who arguably understood her better than anyone else.

"We know," the two said together, laughing.

"Jack, will you take my bags upstairs?"

"Sure thing." Jack grabbed her two bags and headed up the stairs without looking back.

Nickie gripped Eloise's hand and pulled her into the kitchen. "What in the hell is he doing here?"

"Exactly what he said. Helping me."

"He stayed?"

"Yeah, is that weird? It's weird, isn't it?"

"Wow." Nickie shook her head. "I figured he'd stay a day, maybe two. I wouldn't have ever imagined he'd still be here."

"Well, at first he wasn't going to stay, but he ended up doing so much around here I felt bad that he was paying for a hotel."

"So you let him move in." Nickie placed a hand on her lips, before sliding down to her chin. "It's a bit weird. But, like a good weird. And have you guys…"

"God, no. My husband, well, are you insane?" Eloise was mad at herself for not being able to talk about Reagan and why she could never betray him that way, but Nickie was smiling.

"The heart wants what the heart wants, or in your case, the libido." Nickie laughed at her own joke and Eloise fought back a smile. Nickie was no stranger to the fact that Eloise had been attracted to Jack since the day she met him.

"It's not like that, okay. He's here as a friend and that's it. But enough about that. What are you doing here?"

"I told you. I have some time off."

"And you wanted to come spend it here?"

"Why not here? You're my best friend and you're hurting."

"Thank you, Nickie. I've missed you so much. How long can you stay?"

"Four days. Unless that's too long with your handyman around?"

"Stop. Stay as long as you want. Forever for all I care. He's just a friend."

"He was always 'just a friend,' wasn't he?" Nickie arched her eyebrows, emphasizing her point, while also trying, and failing, not to laugh.

"That's true." Both women turned at the sound of Jack's voice. "We're just friends. Same as always."

"Same as always. Like when you were just friends who slept together. Just friends who couldn't keep their hands off each other, like that?"

"No, Nickie. Not this time. This time we're just friends. Friends with no touching," Jack shot back.

"This time," Nickie said.

Eloise thought about her and Jack in college. Nickie had taken a back seat for a while after her and Jack met. Eloise was always at Jack's apartment, or at a party with him, or traveling somewhere with him. Nickie had told her later that at first, she felt abandoned, but then realized that she could join the fun. Some of the best memories Eloise had were after Nickie started to go to every party, and stayed over at Jack's, too, whose apartment was basically always full of people sleeping on couches and the floor. Nickie was like a sister to Eloise, her best friend, but even with Nickie, she never had the natural rawness that she shared with Jack, a trait most people would find difficult to obtain.

"What do you ladies say I make you some dinner." Jack headed for the kitchen.

"Can't wait." Nickie kept winking as Eloise rolled her eyes.

Jack set everything out on the back deck, and at first, Eloise wasn't sure she'd be okay eating there. Her husband built that deck.

Nickie was already seated, drink in hand, and as if he could read her mind, Jack grabbed Eloise's wrist as she looked out her sliding glass door window.

"Is it okay? I can move the stuff into the living room."

Eloise glanced at her wrist. It looked small in Jack's hand. "No, I'll be okay." She tried to smile, but had to take more than one deep breath before she stepped onto her deck.

CHAPTER 5

Having Nickie around made Eloise feel like the chunk of her heart that rotted away when she lost Reagan was starting to heal. She'd forgotten how funny Nickie and Jack could be together, her aching side frequently reminding her from laughing too hard. They sat on her porch, eating and drinking, probably having too much of both, and talking about a time when they were a lot younger and arguably not as wise.

"Do you remember when you dragged us to that neon party?" Nickie asked.

"Remember it?" Jack piped up. "That was the first time I kissed Eloise."

"Oh my gosh." Eloise knew she was blushing. "I'd forgotten that was the first time."

"I'm hurt." Jack mock pouted.

"Eloise couldn't shut up about that night," Nickie told Jack. "She probably forgot the kiss because she remembered the dancing."

"Nickie, I'm going to strangle you." Eloise lifted her hands toward Nickie's neck and Jack laughed so hard she thought he might fall out of his chair.

"No need to freak out, El," Jack said between his laughter. "I haven't forgotten the dancing."

"You two are impossible." Eloise stood and gathered their plates to take inside. Jack's face sobered almost immediately. Eloise smiled at him so he knew she wasn't actually upset before going back into the kitchen.

"I t's gotta be hard on her, the three of us like this again." Jack said to Nickie.

"I know it is, but I think it's also good for her. I can't imagine how she feels, but I know it wasn't helping for her to basically freeze herself in time, every time I called, she never had answers for how she was feeling or what she was doing. I talked a lot, and my guess is she didn't hear much of anything I said."

"Don't beat yourself up too much, Nickie. I think after Reagan, she was rooted in a place that no longer existed. Losing him petrified her and I think she would've rather turned to stone than move forward into unknown territory." Jack leaned back in his chair and saw that Eloise was rinsing off the dishes. He decided to give her a few minutes alone.

"So…" Nickie's voice made Jack turn back toward her. "Why did you stay, Jack?"

"Honestly, the same reason you came back. You know better than anyone that what we had was intense, sexually, and that everything grew from this deep friendship. I understood why we couldn't talk when she was married. But now, she needs a friend and I'd be lying if I said I haven't needed one for a while."

"You never said, Jack. You could have come to me. We only

email now and then, but you have me too. I know I'm no Eloise, but if you find yourself feeling like that again, you've got me."

"Thank you, Nickie. I just figured I best not put you in that situation with El. Us staying close while she couldn't hang out with us. It didn't feel right."

"I get that."

"How've you been, anyway?"

"Same. Working insane hours. I have no clue how I'll ever have a family if I continue to be a cop."

"I'm honestly surprised they let you in. Your record wasn't too long?" Jack couldn't help leaning back to check on Eloise again. He didn't try to hide his smile as she stood over the sink, swaying, as if singing.

"Hey now, everything I ever did was all in good fun and I never got caught."

"You sure did know how to have a good time." Jack looked back at Nickie. "I'm here for you too. I consider you a friend, and not just because of Eloise."

"Thanks, Jack. I'm glad you came. I think it'll do her good to remember what it means to feel happy."

They turned as the glass door slid open. Eloise was carrying a tray loaded with chocolate cake on three tiny plates. She set the tray down on the patio table, and Nickie and Jack both grabbed theirs without hesitation and a few giggles.

Eloise took her plate, then her seat in between them. Jack figured it had to be hard for her to be out on the deck, but he liked to think Reagan wouldn't mind, that he'd want her to be happy. Jack believed without a doubt that if Reagan were the one left behind, Eloise would want him to be happy.

"Well," Jack said as he finished off his cake. "What's on the agenda for tomorrow? How long are you staying, Nickie?"

"Just four days. I really wish it could be longer, but I have to go back to work. I had to beg just to get day four covered."

"We should do something fun tomorrow. I shouldn't be surprised that you two are the only people truly helping me during all this. Jack deserves a day off."

"Damn straight. She works me to death." Jack patted the top of her thigh twice and then stood, grabbing Nickie's plate first and then Eloise's. "I'll put this up and then I'm going to shower. See you ladies in the morning." Jack kissed the top of Eloise's head, and then Nickie's. Their laughter made him smile. He slid the door open and when he looked back at them, he felt a peace he hadn't felt in ages, probably since the last time they were all together. Eloise was, without a doubt, the best friend he'd ever had, and Nickie was easily a close second.

It didn't take long for Eloise and Nickie to follow Jack into the house. They waited until the sun finished setting and then both decided it was time for showers. When Eloise sat down in her recliner about two hours later, she laughed at herself. Nickie in one room and Jack in the other, and she was sleeping in a chair in her own home.

Eloise woke with a start, almost falling over the edge of the recliner. It had been a couple of nights since she had trouble sleeping. She tried to remember the nightmare that shook her awake, but struggled to recall anything other than Reagan and water. Reagan was always in her dreams. She thought he was drowning. She couldn't save him. She tried to figure out what else was in the dream, but it was too fuzzy. Sometimes she had such incredible dreams about him, him alive, that she woke up soaked in tears from feeling so happy in her sleep. Other times, like tonight, she had horrific nightmares, sometimes causing her to wake herself up from screaming. Eloise liked the nightmares better, because at least when she did wake up, she knew Reagan was gone. When she had a good dream about him, she had to remind herself that she'd never see him happy again.

Eloise heard Jack's nightmares too. He never talked about them and she often wondered if he was aware of the fact that he was having them. His screams would jolt her from sleep, and she'd stay awake for hours debating checking on him.

Like before, Jack woke Eloise while making coffee. Waking up to coffee each morning was growing on her, so she didn't mind. She heard Nickie walking above her and figured she'd be down soon. Eloise would ask her if she wanted to shop today, seeing as how she had worn and washed everything in her dryer much more than a few times.

"Good morning, Jack."

"Good morning, beautiful."

"I guess I should say *handsome* instead of Jack." Eloise smiled at the thought. Jack had always called her beautiful. The first time he said *hey beautiful* over text, she had replied *hey handsome* and it stuck. This was only the second time he'd used it since coming back into her life, but the first time it felt nice.

"Good morning to you both, nutjobs," Nickie said as she walked into the kitchen. "How's that for a nickname?"

"I think I like handsome better." Jack handed Nickie a coffee cup before walking over to take Eloise hers, creamer already in it.

"Thank you, Jack." Eloise loved the first drink of coffee in the morning and the way brewing it made the house smell.

"Nickie, will you shop with me today? And then I promise we can all do something fun tonight. I'm out of clothes."

"I'm always willing to shop. But, what do you mean out of clothes?"

"Don't ask," Jack said, giving her a look that clearly said *seriously, don't ask.*

"Never mind then. I don't need a reason for shopping." Nickie walked over to sit on the couch. They all had a second cup of coffee before getting up to get ready for the day.

Jack would finish some of the things on Eloise's list while she and Nickie were shopping. Then they'd go to dinner and to one of the bars that Eloise said she'd always wanted to go to, but never did. She and Reagan didn't drink much, but Eloise loved being around people and music. It was one of the few ways she and Reagan were different. Eloise loved the energy of people. She got a natural high just by being social, but Reagan liked to be alone and with Eloise. He had a few friends he was close with, but he didn't like spending time out like she did.

"I'll wait in your car," Nickie yelled as she walked out the front door after breakfast. Nickie was a bombshell. Eloise loved her naturally curly hair, which, when she didn't dye it, was a midnight black. She wore very little makeup, and needed none of it. Nickie loved dresses because they didn't squeeze her thighs and were easier to find in her size.

"Fabulous, beautiful, as always." Jack's voice came from the doorway. Eloise watched as he took deep breaths, as though he was trying to savor her.

"Thanks, handsome." Eloise ran her tongue across her bottom lip.

"Nickie is going to start honking soon."

"She's used to this."

"I remember." Jack took a small step back so that Eloise could pass. "Call me if you need anything, okay? Or if the shopping becomes too much. I'll come get you."

"I appreciate that, Jack, I do. Nickie should be able to handle me, but I'll tell her to call if she needs reinforcements."

"Have fun, beautiful." Jack reached for Eloise's hand, running his thumb over her knuckles. "Don't take this the wrong way, but I can't remember the last time I felt this good. You always seem to bring that out in me. I know you always thought I was confident and cocky and sure of myself, but the truth is…you make me confident. You make me feel like I'm always on top."

"I will, handsome. Don't work too hard." Eloise looked at her hand in Jack's and wanted to say more, wanted to tell him that she may make him confident, but he had always made her brave. She couldn't make herself say the words, so instead she looked in his eyes and willed him to read her mind. Jack waited a few seconds before lacing their fingers to walk her to the door.

When Jack opened the door, they both started laughing at the sight of Nickie singing and dancing in Eloise's front seat. The music was so loud that when Jack's and Eloise's eyes met, they both started yell-singing, too, and then it was Nickie who was laughing.

Nickie didn't bring up Jack until Eloise had picked out a few outfits, and Eloise secretly appreciated shopping without that pressure for a bit.

"So, what's the deal, El? He's been here a long time." Nickie held up a floral-printed shirt and Eloise shook her head no.

"I honestly don't know, Nickie. If I did, I swear I'd tell you, but I don't know. I don't know why he stayed, or why I let him stay at my house. I don't know why he makes my coffee every morning and works around the clock at my beck and call without ever complaining." Eloise took a deep breath to fight back her tears.

Nickie stepped closer to her and grabbed her hands. "We don't have to talk about this, Eloise. I just wasn't sure where your head was at."

"My head is drowning in guilt." A few slow tears trickled down Eloise's cheeks and she felt the squeeze of Nickie's hands. "Reagan was a good man, Nickie, a great man, you know that."

"Jack's a great man, too, El, and in your heart, you know that Reagan would want you to be happy."

"It's not even about that. I mean yeah, Jack is, well, you've seen him, but I feel guilty over everything. Over him packing Reagan's things, helping with the house, being my friend, being in the same damn room with him. It's like one day Reagan will come home and see everything changed, and he'll be hurt, betrayed." Eloise sat down on the floor, not caring that people were now staring as they passed. Her legs didn't feel like they could keep supporting her emotion and weight.

"What?" Nickie barked at a woman who stared a little too long and a bit too harsh, and then sat down next to Eloise. "El, Reagan isn't coming back. I know that man would move hell and earth to get back to you if he could, but he can't. He'd want you to have friends, a life, even love, and you'd want that if the roles were reversed. If Reagan somehow knows about Jack, I promise he's happy for you."

"I miss him so much, Nickie." Eloise's tears weren't slow anymore. Nickie didn't say anything, but instead, she hugged Eloise close, and that was enough.

After a good cry on the floor of a department store, Nickie and Eloise decided it was time for lunch. They looked at each other and smiled as they headed to Olive Garden. It was one of their things, and it held a lot of happy memories, and right now, Eloise could use all the happy memories she could get.

"I'm going to invite Jack," Eloise said as she pulled out her phone.

"El." Jack answered on the second ring.

"Jack." Eloise felt relieved. It was weird to her that his voice could do that. Nickie was amazing, but Jack was the only person who could say one syllable and make her feel at ease. "We're going to lunch. You want to meet us?"

"Olive Garden?" Jack laughed, and Eloise did too. Jack knew her so well, the parts that had always been her, he knew all of those. Eloise had changed, Jack had, too, but their foundation hadn't, their friendship hadn't seemed to, either, and Eloise smiled at that without feeling guilty for the first time.

"You know it, handsome." Eloise watched Nickie's smile grow.

"I would but I'm currently on your roof right in the middle of fixing a shingle."

"You sure? We'll wait."

"I'm sure. You guys have fun and we'll still go out tonight."

"You eat, too, Jack."

"I will, beautiful. You doin' okay?"

"There was a close call, but Nickie got it handled."

"Good. I'll see you in a bit."

"Bye, Jack. Be safe."

"I will. Bye, El."

Once Nickie and Eloise were seated and eating more bread-sticks than should be humanly possible, Eloise supposed it was her turn to question Nickie.

"How's Gage?"

"He's good." Nickie looked at her breadstick. "We fight more now than we ever have. It's been almost ten years, we've both knocked on thirty's door and walked in, he wants kids."

"You don't?"

"It's not that. I do. You just always think you'll have more time." Nickie's laugh caught in her throat. "I love my job. I love being a cop, and it took me a long time and a lot of work to get to where I am. I know that a child will change all that, and I'm not sure I'm ready to walk away."

"You guys got married so young. You've both had great careers, you don't think you can have both?"

"I want to say yes, but I also know that I'll take one look at our baby and want to give that child the world."

"I think it's supposed to be that way."

"I know. I just... I'm being selfish I guess."

"It's not selfish to be worried about losing yourself. Lots of women do, when they have children. Sacrifice everything, give up too much."

"But if I don't, I may lose him, and that really would be giving up too much. It'd be giving up everything."

"Not everything." Eloise smiled. "I get loving your husband, Nickie, you know I do, but you have to love yourself too. Gage loves you, you two will figure it out."

"Do you think I could do both?"

"I think you can do anything." Eloise reached out to hold Nickie's hand.

"Thank you, El." Nickie looked in Eloise's eyes. "For the first time I believe that. The idea of taking time off, taking years off, isn't so scary now. I have Gage. I can have a family and a career." Nickie took Eloise's hand. "Gage is solid. He'll help me. He has said as much many times, but somehow hearing you say that I can do it makes it true."

CHAPTER 6

E loise was happy that Jack wasn't still on her roof when she and Nickie pulled up the driveway. He was, however, sitting on the couch, showered, beard trimmed, and looking sexy as ever.

"Lookin' hot, Jack." Nickie threw a bag of breadsticks in his lap. "Midnight snack for you."

"Thank you, dear." Jack stood up and started to the kitchen, squeezing Eloise's hand as he passed.

It was an hour later before Nickie and Eloise came back down the stairs, both changed and with fresh makeup on. It was the most ready Eloise had gotten since Reagan died. She picked out one of her new dresses. She spent way too much money on clothes, but she knew Reagan wouldn't mind. He'd laugh and request a fashion show. That was one of the best things about Reagan. Eloise could buy clothes, makeup, purses, get her hair and nails and eyebrows done, spend hundreds of dollars, and Reagan would compliment her, that was it. He'd ask her if it was a new shirt she had on, tell her that her hair looked great, and beg her to scratch his back after getting her nails done. He didn't care about the money, and what Eloise didn't buy herself, Reagan bought for her, frequently as a surprise.

"There is a God," Jack said, flashing his contagious smile as Nickie and Eloise descended the stairs. Nickie did a little twirl at the bottom of the staircase, making Jack say, "Your turn, El," as Eloise mimicked Nickie. Jack's eyes got wide and he looked Eloise up and down in a way that made Eloise nervous. Jack held out an arm, Nickie taking one and Eloise the other.

The restaurant Nickie picked out, after reading endless online reviews, was packed. It was a sushi place and the second the three of them were seated, Nickie was ordering drinks.

"Pace yourself, Nickie." Eloise laughed as she looked at the menu. She was surprised at how nice it was to have a meal with Nickie and Jack. They always made everything so easy. By the time they were ready to leave, Eloise wasn't sure if they had stuffed themselves more of sushi rolls or of drinks.

Jack pulled up to the front door of the bar to let Eloise and Nickie out. Eloise noticed the doorman give him a nod. Jack told them their heals were too impressive to walk all the way across the large lot.

"Thank you, Jack," Nickie called as she shut the back door.

"Thank you, Jack." Eloise stepped out of the passenger side. "We'll wait by the door."

"For you two, anytime."

Nickie and Eloise were standing outside as Jack walked up, both of them chatting with the bouncer.

"Lucky man," the bouncer said to Jack as he again took them on each arm.

"That I am." Jack smiled, and Eloise knew that Nickie wasn't about to spoil his fun by saying she was very married.

Eloise wondered if she could say that anymore. That she was very married, happily married. Was she still married? She still wore her ring. She still felt married. Reagan, like Gage, wasn't jealous. Neither would have cared if Nickie and Eloise spent a night out without them, not even knowing they were with Jack, which Gage did.

The music was blaring and Eloise tried to remember the last time she went out. She couldn't. She and Reagan were best friends. They went fishing, and camping, and talked about owning a big place someday with lots of animals and kids. It was like Nickie had said: you think you have more time. Reagan liked staying in much more than going out, and over the years, Eloise began to think she did, too, until she watched Nickie and Jack walk straight to the dance floor, making most of the people around them step back and watch.

Nickie and Jack were incredible dancers. Eloise was awkward and was one of those people who had to *not* focus on what other people thought of her while she attempted to dance. But not Nickie and Jack. The way they moved was like watching art come to life. Nickie pointed a finger at Eloise, urging her to come dance with them, and Eloise felt her face get hot. She would watch Jack dance all the time in college. She'd stand with her back against the wall and watch him in awe. The neon party was the first time Jack got her to dance.

She was leaning up against the garage door, drunk people everywhere, all wearing white shirts that were covered in neon paint as part of the fun. Jack had walked up to her, standing right in front of her, too close, she could feel his breath. He had leaned in and pressed his lips to hers. Something she'd wanted since the second she first saw him. When he pulled back, he said, "Dance with me."

"You know I can't," Eloise told him, her hand on his neck.

"I promise you can. I know I can, anyway, and that'll be good enough. Trust me."

Before she could answer, Jack was pulling her away from the wall and close to his body. He didn't walk away from the door, didn't force Eloise to dance in front of people, he just held her close, turning her front and then back every few minutes, rubbing against her, kissing her, touching everything he could reach. After the fact, Eloise knew she had to have looked awkward and not anywhere near as good as Jack when he danced, but in that moment, she didn't care. The way he held her, the way their bodies moved together, he made her feel like she looked fabulous. Jack had always made her feel glorious.

With that confidence fresh in her brain, Eloise started toward Nickie, thankful when Nickie held out her hand. Eloise always felt better about dancing when she was holding on to someone else and Nickie was aware of that. She felt like mimicking the action was easier somehow. Jack smiled as the two of them danced, switching hands when Nickie needed to keep moving around Eloise.

Jack found himself following Nickie's rotation and thought about the very last time the three had been this way. It was right before Nickie got engaged, before Eloise met Reagan. They were at a Halloween party. Jack couldn't remember what he was that year, maybe Eloise would know, but she was a fairy, hot as hell even with plastic wings on. It was a house party and so many people were crammed into the living room that it was barely possible to dance, but they'd managed. They were sandwiched together, Jack in the middle. Tonight looked a lot like that night, but Jack hoped it wouldn't be the last time.

"Let's drink," Nickie yelled over the music, and they headed for the bar. Nickie held up three fingers and mouthed, "Surprise me," to the bartender.

Great, Jack thought, *we're all getting hammered.*

"Nickie, we drove here." Clearly, Eloise was thinking the same thing.

"And we can take an Uber home." Nickie didn't miss a beat. The bartender set the shot glasses down and no one asked what was in them before picking them up. The three friends eyed one another and then threw their drinks back at the same time, Eloise being the only one who had to swallow down a cough. It had been years, minus the tequila night with Jack, since she'd gotten trashed. Nickie motioned to the bartender and Jack leaned into Eloise.

"You don't have to do this. I'll take you home," he whispered against her neck and she didn't pull back. She turned her face into his, their lips way too close.

"I want to," Eloise mouthed before placing her lips to his ear. "I don't want to care. I just want to dance and laugh and drink so much that I'll hate myself the next day." She could, too, because Jack would never get drunk enough that she and Nickie would be at risk. He'd get them home safe, and he'd do it without even bringing it up.

"Then have a blast, beautiful." Jack handed her a drink, then Nickie hers, before picking his up. "That's it for me, boss," Jack told the bartender as Nickie was already motioning for shot number three.

"Come on, Jack, you can't be the only sober one."

"Trust me, Nickie, I won't be sober, but someone has to be not as drunk as you two, or we'll all end up sleeping on the pavement." Jack distributed shots again, this time leaving himself out.

"True, always the protector, big man. I'm going to call Gage before I can't see the numbers." Nickie walked off, likely to find some quiet.

Jack felt Eloise's gaze on him as he kept an eye on Nickie. He turned and raised his eyebrows as he caught her smiling at him.

"Always the protector," El explained.

Nickie was everywhere, playing darts one minute, dancing the next, and drinking after that. Jack sat at the bar and watched Eloise follow her around. Eloise always looked so uncomfortable dancing, but Jack loved watching her try all the same. Jack felt his phone buzz in his pocket, but didn't recognize the number.

> *Hey Jack. It's Gage. Nickie gave me your number.*
> *She doing okay?*

Jack lifted his phone and took a picture of Nickie dancing, a blurry snapshot of her smiling, sent it to Gage, and then saved his number. It didn't feel like it had been over two hours since Nickie had called Gage, but the clock on his screen confirmed it had been.

> *Thank you. Looks like she's doing great.*

Jack looked over at Nickie twirling like the ballerina in a music box and was beyond happy for her, because she had someone who loved her. She had someone who wanted her to have fun, but also be safe. As Jack watched Eloise and Nickie dance, he wondered if Reagan was that for Eloise. He knew that Reagan loved her, Eloise had made that clear, and that she loved him. What he wasn't sure of was whether Reagan threw fuel on her fire or if he was the type to try and extinguish her flame. He hoped he hyped her up, he prayed he told her every day how incredible she was, and he wished with his whole heart that she never felt like she had to change for him.

After about fifteen more minutes of tracking Nickie dancing and Eloise's attempt to dance, Jack watched as they crossed the dance floor to where he was sitting. Eloise took the seat next to him. Nickie stayed standing, ordered two more shots, but included two glasses of water. Nickie started scrolling through her phone and Jack prepared for them going to do something else as Nickie's face lit up like a Christmas tree before she handed her phone to him.

"Time to go," Nickie told him.

"Karaoke," Jack said to Eloise.

"Nickie, I can't sing."

"You can do all the things you say you can't." Nickie finished her water. "Let's go." Nickie grabbed Eloise's hand, pulled her off the chair, and started for the door.

"Hold on. I don't want you two out of sight," Jack said. "Sit here. I'll pay the tab and then, Nickie, I will take you to sing."

"Deal." Nickie scooted up on the barstool, still holding Eloise's hand, who was now forced to stand next to her.

Jack motioned for the bartender and asked for their check when she approached. When she handed his card back, he noticed her number on his receipt. She was still looking at him, so he pointed at Eloise and mouthed the word *taken*. The woman shrugged and turned away. Jack didn't want her waiting for a call that wouldn't come.

"All right, karaoke." He helped Nickie off the chair before grabbing Eloise's free hand. Less people looked at three people walking out holding hands than you would think. Jack was thrilled that the new location was within walking distance and that both Eloise and Nickie were still able to walk. The place was packed, but a lot less chaotic than the bar they'd come from. Most people were sipping on drinks and listening to the music. Almost no one was dancing, which Jack was sure Nickie would change.

"You're singing too," Nickie told Jack as she pulled them to where they signed up.

Jack quickly discovered that he'd be singing twice: once with Nickie and once with Eloise. Nickie signed up three times, once on her own, which made Eloise say she was envious of Nickie's confidence. Nickie picked all the songs, so Jack and Eloise had no idea what they were getting into. They found seats at the end of a long wooden table, which was mostly full. Nickie was in her seat less than four seconds before she was off to get another round of drinks, making sure to bring back one for Jack.

"You've gotta be mostly sober by now, so here." She set the drink down in front of him and instead of arguing, he threw it back, figuring he'd need it to sing in front of all these people, twice.

Jack grinned as he heard Eloise holler way above the crowd after their names were called, and when "Love Is a Battlefield" by Pat Benatar started, his grin evolved into a chuckle as Eloise jumped to her feet. Jack waited for Nickie to start, but by the chorus, he was scream-singing every line with her. Nickie circled him, playing off the sexual-tension vibe immaculately. Though he took his role as Nickie's boy toy seriously, Jack glanced at Eloise every few words to make sure joy was still plastered on her face. As the song ended, Nickie jumped off the stage and Jack motioned for Eloise to join him.

Jack saw the song on the screen before the music started. "When You Were Young" by The Killers. *Freaking Nickie.* Even drunk, she was trying to make a point. Clearly, she wasn't drunk enough.

"You're starting this," Eloise told Jack as she got on stage.

"You got it, beautiful." Jack's adrenaline was still rushing from singing with Nickie, and he had no problem continuing to ride that wave.

It only took three lines for Eloise to join in, and by the end of it, they were having a full-fledged concert, jumping around and all, most of the place up on their feet. Eloise and Jack both hit their knees for the guitar solo, and then Eloise dropped her pretend guitar to crawl toward Jack to finish off the song. Unlike Nickie, Jack used the stairs.

Eloise stayed on stage and waited for Nickie. Jack knew what they were singing by the shit-eating grin on Nickie's face and had no doubt that Eloise knew too. "I Touch Myself" by Divinyls. A song that had been theirs for years for no other reason than it always made them laugh. Jack watched as Eloise took a deep breath as the music started, knowing that she and Nickie were about to get real into this performance. Jack stood in front of the stage, singing right along with them as the two women pranced in circles looking more like they were modeling than dancing.

Nickie finished off their set with "Rolling in the Deep" by Adele, completely crushing it, and then chugged two glasses of water.

"Thank you, Nickie," Eloise said, leaning over to kiss Nickie's cheek. "You always know exactly what I need."

Nickie pushed her second glass of water away, replacing it with two shots, one of which she handed to Eloise.

"Let's order food and then go home. Jack will love us more if we can walk ourselves to the car." Nickie held up her shot and Jack watched as Eloise did the same. Nickie counted to three and both shots were gone.

Eloise leaned into Jack, then whispered, "Food, handsome." He didn't say anything, just nodded. He could hear both women laughing as he walked away to order. He didn't mind carrying them to the car if they enjoyed themselves. It was tough to say no to Eloise, but Jack was beginning to believe that saying no to Nickie would have even more severe consequences.

Once they ate, Nickie loudly announced that she was ready to go to bed. Jack didn't have to carry them to the car, but he did have to walk behind Nickie all the way up Eloise's stairs and help her into bed. Jack pulled off Nickie's shoes and covered her with a blanket before going back downstairs to check on Eloise. She was rocking in her recliner and her face told him she was excited to see him reappear.

"Why aren't you asleep?" Jack asked as he sat on her couch.

"Why aren't you?" Eloise countered.

"I wanted to check on you first. Nickie is out cold." Rossi jumped up next to Jack and he started to scratch her head.

"Sleep down here." Eloise's energy seemed to have disappeared and Jack wondered what had her so serious all of a sudden.

"What?"

"I just want you close. Up there." Eloise's eyes looked up at her ceiling. "It's too far."

She tried to stand and Jack jumped up to keep her from toppling over.

"I'll stay." Jack gently settled Eloise back in her chair. "Try and sleep and I promise I'll stay." He grabbed the blanket she kept folded nearby and covered her. Jack sat back down on the couch with Rossi and watched as Eloise closed her eyes and slowed her breathing. She wanted him close. He wasn't sure what to do with that.

The next morning, Eloise swore someone hit her in the forehead with a hammer. She didn't think she could lift her head off the back of the recliner if she wanted to. She cracked one eye open to see Jack in the kitchen, starting to get stuff for coffee and breakfast, then glanced at Nickie passed out on her couch. *Guess she didn't make it up the stairs.*

"You can't cook, Jack. I can't smell it. I swear to God I'll puke on you."

"Got it. No food for now. How you feel about smelling coffee?"

"I think I can handle coffee. No creamer today." Eloise pulled the blanket over her face. Jack's laughter echoed through the kitchen.

"Jack, I will throw something at you if you don't shut up." Nickie's voice sounded like she was speaking from six feet under fresh dirt.

"Good morning to you, too, Nickie." Jack shut a cabinet, but Eloise knew he was trying to be quiet. "Coffee now or later, El?"

"Now, please," Eloise answered from under her blanket.

"Nickie?"

"Try me again in about twenty."

"Gotcha," Jack said, then tapped Eloise on her shoulder.

She struggled to sit up, and when she was situated, he gave her the cup of black coffee. Eloise took a sip and watched as Jack went to go get his own. When he came back, Nickie's legs were already lifted, like she sensed him. Jack sat down and laughed quietly as Nickie set her legs down over his lap, never opening her eyes.

"Did she sleep down here?" Eloise whispered.

"She didn't start down here." Jack chuckled. "I was asleep on the couch and felt her at around four this morning. No idea why she got out of bed." Jack was struggling to contain his laughter. "So, I went upstairs and left her asleep."

"Shut up." Nickie begged.

Jack looked at Eloise. She wanted to talk to him, but not bad enough that she was willing to risk Nickie kicking his coffee cup out of his hand. Jack seemed to understand, putting his finger to his mouth saying, "Shh," as quietly as he could manage. They sat in silence, making faces at each other. Eloise had to hold her breath more than once not to laugh. It was a full twenty minutes before Nickie started to act alive.

"Okay, Jack, I think I can sit up now."

"You got it." Jack set his cup on the coffee table while Nickie lifted her legs so he could stand. They repeated the process in reverse when he came back with Nickie's coffee.

"You're a god," Nickie said, before taking a huge drink.

"I haven't seen you this smashed in a while, Nickie." Eloise said this while holding her fingertips to her temples, knowing full well that Nickie could say the same thing to her. The last time the two of them got drunk together was the night Nickie got promoted and that was over five years ago. The morning after that looked a lot like this one, but Reagan had been the one making coffee and it had been Gage under Nickie's feet.

"I think the last time all three of us were this messed up was that night at Jack's with the jungle juice and Bacardi. You remember that?"

"Remember it? I had to get Jack to kick his own bathroom door in to check on your passed-out ass." Eloise could laugh about it now, but at the time, seeing Nickie passed out on the bathroom floor terrified her. They had a yellow pitcher that night that they had stuck two straws in and would race to see how fast they could finish it before filling it up again. They both probably should have died of alcohol poisoning that night.

"Oh, to be young again." Jack squeezed Nickie's leg. "Drake was pissed. He was positive that we'd never get our security deposit back."

"But little ol' Nickie came in clutch and had Gage fix it before anyone was the wiser," Nickie said, then laughed. Eloise would miss Nickie more than she was ready to deal with when it was time for her to leave.

"Came in clutch?" Jack yelled. "It was your fault in the first place." He also laughed.

"If I remember correctly, there were a few times it was us babysitting *you*." Eloise winked at Jack.

"Exactly," Nickie followed. "Like that time we had to put new sheets on your bed because you barfed all over them. Eloise was pissed, having to walk out of your room naked to put those barf bags in the washer."

"Naked? Why were you naked?" Jack asked. Nickie and

Eloise were laughing so hard that Eloise had to take four deep breaths before she could answer.

"You threw up all over me," Eloise said between laughter. "You don't remember that? It was Drake's birthday."

"I remember us going to bed. I remember waking up with you. I remember nothing else."

"Ha! See, and you want to give me crap," Nickie said.

"What happened?" Jack asked.

"When I say you threw up all over, I mean all over, Jack. I was literally dripping and Drake would have killed me for walking that all through the apartment. I didn't have anything else."

"That's why when I woke up, we were both naked?" Jack asked her.

"Exactly," Eloise said, trying not to think about being naked with Jack, she couldn't. Thinking about those nights and mornings with Jack all those years ago was enough to make her feel more than guilty.

Eloise liked talking about Drake, because it made her guilt subside, and allowed her a moment of happiness.

The day was wasted, and no one got dressed or ready. Eloise and Nickie barely moved, but Jack made a lot of snacks throughout the day and they watched more movies than Eloise could name. They had a recovery day and it was amazing. Nickie waited until almost midnight to pack so she could leave the next morning, and Eloise tried not to cry right then.

"I'm going to miss you so much," Eloise told Nickie as she folded the last of her clothes.

"I'll miss you too. Maybe next time I visit I can call you auntie."

"Are you going to have a baby?"

"I'm going to talk to Gage about it. I think I can have a career and still be a mom."

"So do I." Eloise reached out and squeezed Nickie's hand. "I really do."

"Gage will be a great dad. I love him. He deserves to get what he wants. It wasn't ever about me not wanting kids. It was about me not wanting to lose myself, my identity."

"I'd never let that happen, Nickie. I'll remind you all the time that you were you before you became the mom version of yourself."

"Promise?"

"Of course." Eloise wrapped Nickie up in a hug. "You'll be a wonderful mom, and remain a kick-ass cop. You got this."

Jack stood with Eloise in the doorway the next morning as they watched Nickie drive away. Nickie wasn't even all the way out of the driveway when Eloise started crying. Jack placed a hand on her shoulder and squeezed lightly.

"She'll be back, El."

"I know. I just already miss her so much."

"It's going to be okay." Jack kissed the top of Eloise's head.

"I hope so," Eloise said, even though it wasn't going to be okay. Jack would leave, too, and she'd be left alone in the dark again, and she wasn't sure she could make it back out a second time without them.

CHAPTER 7

O nce Nickie had left, Eloise and Jack fell back into a routine much quicker than expected. It felt so natural to have him around and as much as she hated to admit it, she'd be miserable once he left. It started out being about helping her with the house, then helping her with herself, but now it was about the way he made the coffee each morning and how she had someone to go places with again. It was about not sitting alone hour after hour in her recliner.

When Jack was around, Eloise felt like herself again. She felt like the girl who ran through sprinklers and danced in the rain. She felt like the person who did an impromptu photo shoot on a stranger's motorcycle in a store parking lot. The girl who sneaked into pools and played truth or dare. She loved Reagan, but with Reagan, Eloise was a wife. She was career driven. She was serious. Jack reminded her that she was fun once too.

"What do you need done today?" Jack said as he walked into the living room. Eloise hadn't moved from the recliner since he handed her coffee to her over two hours ago.

"I have a bunch of stuff I want to donate. Can you help me

take it somewhere?" Eloise stopped thinking about being young, about life before worries, and stood to fold her blanket.

"Sure. I can finish trimming the trees out front while you get ready. Is there stuff you want me to take? I can start loading it." Jack stepped into the kitchen as Eloise placed her pillow and blanket on the recliner.

"Yeah, there's an end table thing, I'm not sure what it's called, in the dining room. That can go." Eloise walked into the kitchen, leaning over the counter toward Jack. "You may as well disassemble my bed." Eloise swallowed. "I...just. I can't. I'll never use the bed."

"We can wait on doing that if you aren't ready, El."

"No, it can go. I just don't want to look at it, and I can't go in there."

"I'll make sure you aren't around when I take it out to the truck. Anything else?"

"Yes." Eloise shook her head slowly, hoping to rid it of thoughts of her bedroom. "Everything in the garage can go."

"Everything?" Jack's voice hitched, as if in surprise.

"Yes. I don't know what half of it is, so I won't miss it. If there's stuff you want, just take it."

"Okay, if you're sure. Let's start there and then you can keep adding to the list."

"Your list is never-ending." Eloise reached over, laid her hand on Jack's arm, and squeezed. "Thank you."

"That's why I'm here." Jack leaned in, their faces only inches from each other and held her eyes before leaning back. Eloise shouldn't want him that close, but sadness took over as he broke their contact.

"I'll go get ready." Eloise turned and left Jack alone in the kitchen. She knew he'd probably have her bed taken apart before she was out of the shower and that was fine by her. She could go her whole life and never look at that bed again. She wondered if it was too much when she had Jack pack up the things she shared with Reagan in that room, intimate things, if that was crossing some line. Eloise knew Jack wouldn't say no, even if he wanted to. She just wasn't sure if she should have put him in that position. She wasn't sure if Reagan would mind. She had no idea what the correct way to pack up her husband's life was.

As Eloise assumed, Jack found her as soon as she was out of the shower and dressed. He told her to stay in the spare bathroom while he loaded the now disassembled bed.

"I figured you meant the bedding, too, so I bagged that up." Jack stood in the doorway.

Eloise hadn't thought about her bedding, but that seemed like the right thing to do. If she couldn't sleep in the bed, the linens should go too.

"Thanks, Jack." Eloise kept applying her makeup.

"I'm going to run this stuff to one of the churches or shelters, then I'll be back to go through the garage."

"Okay. I'll start thinking about what else can go." Eloise picked up her eyeshadow pallet and watched Jack's eyes follow her brush through the mirror, until he turned to leave.

When the front door closed the second time, Eloise knew Jack and her bed were gone, one of them never coming back. Eloise tried to picture the things in her house and which ones she could live without. When she did end up moving, would she want all new things? Her living room furniture had worked for her after Reagan's death, so that was all still safe. The spare bathroom and kitchen were also okay, but Jack should donate the things in the master bathroom, he was already going through the garage, and if she could talk herself into having him pack up her closet, she supposed all of that could go too. Eloise had broken every plate she owned, so she could either find those same plates, have mismatched dishes, or buy a whole new set. When Jack started cooking dinner on a regular basis, he made sure there were paper plates in the house. They'd used bowls before that, regardless of what they were eating, and he never asked about her glass plates.

What did a person keep when their spouse died? She felt like getting rid of all his things would be cruel and she'd regret it, but what would she do with his clothes and shoes, his razor, and green toiletry bag that he used for travel? She would keep the important things, photos, his wedding band, the watch his grandpa gave him, his sketchbooks. Things that were Reagan. Things she'd never be able to replace. Things she'd miss, or things she already missed about Reagan. Losing someone, Eloise was discovering, wasn't all at once. It didn't happen in a linear fashion. Loss crept up on her like a nightmare during sleep. She'd be okay, breathing, managing, and then in an instant, her air was gone.

Eloise hated the fact that she could feel like she was normal, and then see Reagan's artwork, or open a drawer and spot some-thing trivial like his sunglasses or truck keys, and her heart would stop as though she were drowning, suffocating, choking. As though she'd never breathe again.

Eloise heard Jack later that afternoon in the garage. He was making enough noise to let her know he was home and clearing it out. She wasn't sure what to do and didn't want to hover over him, so she decided she'd go through her own things. She had boxes of her own schoolwork, research, and endless books. Surely, she didn't need to keep everything.

"You ready for dinner?" Jack walked into Eloise's office to find her sitting on the floor and surrounded by loose paper. She definitely didn't look like she was making progress.

"Is it that time already?" Eloise held out her arms and Jack pulled her to her feet. "I guess I got caught up in here. I have so much read-ing, articles, and essays. Things I probably have no real use for."

"But somehow they're still hard to throw out?" Jack eyed the hurricane of papers.

"Exactly." Eloise cleared her throat. "Dinner, whatever you want to do." Eloise took a step back. Jack had been cooking them dinner almost every night. Eloise knew he loved cooking and frankly, she liked not having to worry about it. Without Jack, she'd probably still be skipping most meals. He cooked, but also made sure she ate. Eloise always said thank you, but what she meant was thank you for putting her back together.

"Well, you probably have about forty-five minutes until whatever I make is done." Jack leaned back and Eloise found herself smiling at his control, his certainty.

"Thank you, Jack. I'll try and get this stuff at least piled up." Eloise playfully nudged Jack out of the room and went back to trying to organize her chaos.

O ver the next few days Jack had the garage almost cleared out. Eloise couldn't get over how empty and different it looked. She didn't ask him if he kept anything, she didn't want to know. Besides, most of it was tools and paint, things Eloise wouldn't recognize as Reagan's if she saw Jack with them.

The night before Jack was set to leave, they decided to go out to dinner. Eloise dressed fancy, and she was meticulous with her makeup, apologizing to Reagan the entire time. *He's just a friend*, she kept telling herself over and over. Jack was a friend, arguably the best friend she'd ever had, and Reagan wouldn't mind her having a friend.

"El, our reservations are going to expire," Jack yelled from the bottom of the stairs.

"That's not a thing, Jack." Eloise continued to apply her eyeliner.

"It most certainly is. We're already going to be over fifteen minutes late. Move your ass."

"Call them!" Eloise poked her head out of the doorway to yell.

"No. I'm sure you look drop-dead gorgeous, now move it."

"You are such an ass." Eloise giggled to herself and continued to apply her eye makeup.

"Eloise, now."

"I hate you."

"Okay, what are you now, twelve?" Jack bellowed from where Eloise assumed was the bottom of the stairs.

Eloise dropped her eyeliner tube and her laughter vibrated the items on the sink. She composed herself and then took one last look before heading out of the bathroom.

"I knew it. Drop-dead," Jack said in a near whisper as Eloise stopped at the top of the stairs.

Jack wore a navy suit and Eloise thought he looked pretty drop-dead himself.

"Thank you, handsome." Eloise smiled and grabbed the staircase. Falling down the stairs would not be good for the hot vibe she had going. Eloise frowned a little at that thought, hot vibe, hot vibe, and no Reagan. Jack's eyebrows creased just enough that Eloise knew he caught her frown and likely the reason behind it. "I'm sorry, Jack." Eloise grabbed his extended hand.

"You never have to say sorry to me for missing him, El, never." Jack pulled her into his chest. "You loved him, he was good to you, those things make me happy. Don't ever feel bad because you had someone great."

"I just feel so guilty. Always."

"I'll never push that, El. I'll never try to make this more than what it is right now."

"I know." Eloise lifted her head off his chest so that she could see his eyes. "I know that, and that makes it even harder.

You're great, too, Jack. Always have been. But being your friend, it hurts, you know? It's been amazing having you here. Better than that. I wouldn't have ever made it through without you being here. But that will always mean he's not here." Eloise wiped the tear off her cheek, thankful she'd chosen waterproof mascara.

"I know, beautiful, I know." Jack placed a hand on her head. "It's okay to feel, El. To miss him, to love him, and I'm sorry it hurts having me here, and I'm sorry it'll hurt when I'm gone, but you...you never have to be sorry, not for anything, okay?"

"Thank you, Jack." Eloise wished she could say more. She wished she could tell him how much he meant to her. How much he had healed her. Maybe he knew, she hoped he did. It ripped her open to think about him leaving, and it ripped her open to think about moving on from Reagan. Everything felt wrong, but she'd think about that later, when Jack was gone and the darkness was still there waiting.

"You ready?" Jack said after a few minutes. Eloise needed some time to bring her thoughts to a happier place.

"Yes." Eloise took a step back, but Jack kept her hand and held it until he helped her into his truck.

The restaurant was packed and Eloise watched Jack roll his eyes as he parked, knowing full well he was thinking about how long it took her to get ready. She hoped they still had their table, but admittedly would laugh a bit if they didn't. She knew Jack wouldn't laugh at all.

"I got you." Eloise waited for Jack to come and open her door.

Eloise had never been to this place and she was excited to see what was on the menu. The hostess was a young, supercute blonde and the way she looked at Jack, Eloise knew they'd have a table.

"You realize that girl is about to drool?"

"She's probably looking at you," Jack whispered.

Eloise had to cup her hand over her mouth to keep from laughing. "I doubt that."

"Reservations for two." Jack flashed his smile and Eloise had to struggle not to roll her eyes, he was turning on the charm and being quite obvious about it.

"Yes, it looks like we did call you a few times before moving down the list, but I will put you right on the top and the next table is yours."

"Thank you." Jack blessed her with his smile again.

"Anything else I can do for you?" She fluttered her eyes at him.

Eloise felt Jack pinch her side, a warning for her not to laugh. Eloise wasn't sure it was going to work.

"No, thank you. I really do appreciate it. My sister takes forever to get ready." Jack winked at the hostess. *Winked* at her. Eloise knew right then he'd be getting that girl's number and wanted to make a gagging noise, but he was still digging into her side.

"Sister?" The hostess was obviously staring at Eloise's skin tone and likely wondering which one of them was adopted.

"Yup." Jack's eyes glanced quickly to Eloise and then back to the hostess.

Eloise decided to let him deal with his own mess and stepped away to sit and wait for their table. She smiled as Jack and the hostess flirted. She knew he was just having fun, mostly securing their table, and that he'd never call that girl. It wouldn't matter if he did, it wasn't like Eloise had any claim to him, but the thing about Jack was, he'd never pursue anyone when Eloise was an option. Eloise shook her head at herself. She wasn't an option. She had made herself not an option. That, too, was something of their past. It was always Eloise who would date, always Jack who would back off while she did, and then he'd date to pass time, but the second Eloise was single, somehow Jack was as well. The only time he dated someone first during their years of whatever it was they were, he asked Eloise first. Asked her permission. Something she never did. Eloise smiled at the memory.

"You say no, and I won't do it."

"Jack, I date frequently."

"I know, but I only date because you aren't available to me. This girl is cool. I really like her, but she's still not you."

"It's not my choice, Jack."

"I'm making it your choice," Jack had said that night.

"Pursue it. If something happens, call me," Eloise had answered then.

Now at the restaurant, watching him flirt, she'd say the same thing again.

Jack didn't talk to her for six months that time. It was horrible. She finally experienced how he felt when she ghosted him. It had to be that way, though, it had to be. It was different now, they were older, they could keep boundaries in place. Back then, as young and hormonal as they were, Eloise would cheat on anyone she was with if she tried to keep up a friendship with Jack. Jack knew that, too, back then, so they didn't, because it wasn't fair to the other people involved. When Jack had finally called, all he said was, "Wanna have sex?" Eloise didn't hesitate before saying, "I'll be there in ten minutes," and she was, and they did.

"Table's ready, El." Jack glanced over his shoulder, and when Eloise stood, Jack grabbed her hand, then made sure to pull out her chair when they reached their table.

"Thank you," Eloise said as he took his own seat.

"I was just playin'. You know that, right."

"Yes, brother, I do." Eloise giggled.

"Seriously, El, I'll never call her."

"I know that, but you can if you want."

"I know that, and I don't want to," Jack told her.

Eloise smiled as they looked over the menus. Then watched as the hostess was clearly telling her coworkers all about Jack.

"You should tell her, Jack. She's too excited to leave like that and never call."

"Eloise, *my* Eloise, cares about what happens to the likes of her?"

"I'm older now." Eloise snickered. She knew Jack was referring to the fact that if they were banging, it was because some girl was crying over him, but she never cared then. To be fair, Jack never asked about her exes' well-being either. When they were single, they were all in, and when they weren't, it was as if they didn't know each other. Yet, they could fall back together without missing a beat, weeks, months, apparently years, later, and there was something beautifully magical in that.

"I'll let her down easy before we leave," Jack said.

Eloise smiled, then frowned, feeling a little bad about breaking the girl's excited heart. Eloise really couldn't blame her. Jack was as good looking as they came. Add his looks to his personality, his heart, and anyone could see how it was easy to love him.

CHAPTER 8

Eloise couldn't believe Jack's leave was over. It felt like he'd just showed up and now he was packing to go. Eloise's hand found its way to her chest and she started rubbing it, trying to force the ache away. Losing Reagan was unbearable, but Jack breathed some life back into her. She wasn't sure she'd survive him leaving her too.

She stood in the doorway of his room and watched him fold his clothes and repack the two duffel bags he came with. He wore headphones and she loved watching him pack, smile at her, and sometimes sing whatever he was listening to. He turned his Bluetooth off so Eloise could hear the music too. He reached for her and she didn't hesitate. He pulled her into him and they danced, his arms feeling as safe as they had all those years ago.

"Jack, I…" Eloise looked down at her feet.

"This doesn't have to mean anything, Eloise."

"I'm just not ready." Everything in her was screaming at her to stop, but she kept moving.

"I know." He spun her slowly. "That doesn't mean we can't dance."

"I'm going to miss you, Jack." After she spun a second time, she moved closer to him, unwilling to fight the magnetic pull any longer.

"I'll miss you too." Jack kissed the top of her head, and finally Eloise's feet stopped.

"Can I take you to the airport?"

"I'd like that." Jack switched the song. "Something a little more upbeat for you." His smile made her face flame. "I used to jam out to this all the time. It's my tribute to you."

"I'm going to hate this, aren't I?" Eloise laughed. The song started and Jack pushed back from Eloise and moved frantically, clearly not trying to look good. "What is this called?" Eloise yelled. Jack had the music up way too loud and was still dancing around his room like a madman.

"Heartbeat," Jack screamed, still dancing. "Scouting for Girls. Dance with me." Jack threw a pretend rope to reel her in. Eloise played along and found herself shaking her head so hard her hair whacked her in the face. Their laughter was somehow in sync with the song. They danced around, twirling in circles, and ended the song by jumping on Jack's bed. When the song finished, they were both struggling to breathe.

"I think I needed that." Eloise fell back on Jack's bed.

"Dancing can be very therapeutic." Jack settled next to her. "One more time?" He turned toward her and her smile spread.

"One more time." Eloise jumped up and grabbed Jack's hand to pull him up, and as he hit play, they sang as they spun around. When the song stopped the second time, they knew they had to leave to make Jack's plane. The happiness and laughter that filled his room now seemed to be disappearing, replaced with all the sadness they had just danced away.

They sat in Jack's truck, silence enveloping them. Eloise turned to face him. He drove here, but she'd drive his truck back to her house and keep it there for him.

"I can't thank you enough for coming, Jack. I know I wasn't

the nicest at first, but having you here really did make things better."

"I'm glad I came. Thank you for letting me stay."

"Be safe seems like a silly thing to say, but I hope you're safe and careful. I'll think about you while you're away. Visit when you come back, okay?"

"Of course." He squeezed her hand. "You have my truck. You be safe too. Stay in the light."

"I'll try." Eloise reached out to touch his face. She wanted to feel him, because it would be months before she got another chance.

Watching Jack, a duffel bag over each arm, walk into the airport caused a heavy weight in her chest that she refused to identify. The weight her chest was bearing subsided as he turned once he got through the door and smiled at her. She waved and blew him a kiss before she realized what she'd done.

She had to scoot the driver's seat way forward to reach the pedals. She was happy that she could drive Jack's truck, be a part of him in a way she couldn't with her husband. She heard her phone ding and picked it up, thankful that she was still parked.

Miss me yet?

His name across her screen made her breath catch.

Maybe.

She hit send and waited. She'd have to move soon or people would start honking at her.

I figured we could at least talk while I travel and on base, but after that, I'm not sure if I'll be able to.

A few more days of Jack. I like that.

She hit send and hoped it wasn't too flirty. Pulling out of the line was easy, but finding her way in the airport traffic was another story. She tossed her phone onto the passenger seat and concentrated on getting to the right exit. Eloise thought of Jack the entire drive. She wondered if these few texts would be the last she'd hear from him for six months or longer. That thought scared her in a way that she wasn't sure how to process.

Eloise pulled into her driveway, then reached for her phone.

I like a few more days of you too.

Did you make it home?

Eloise read his messages twice and then responded.

Just got home. I'm sure you're on the plane, but let me know when you land.

She hit send, shut his truck off, then went inside. Her house was too quiet, so she turned her TV on before starting dinner. She moved around her house as if it wasn't hers. In a lot of ways, it wasn't anymore. When Jack was here, she could pretend that everything was fine. Now that he was gone, the emptiness was quick to remind her that nothing was okay.

He had only been gone hours and Eloise already realized just how much Jack actually did. It wasn't just his long chore list, it was things like this, coming home to an empty house, walking in and not seeing Jack scramble around her kitchen fixing dinner with a dishrag resting over his shoulder. It would be the next morning when she had to make her own coffee. It'd be the next few days when she had to go shopping alone, check her own mail, and answer her own door. He picked up her pieces by taking over the mundane parts of her life so that she could focus on breathing.

Eloise ate in her recliner, knowing she'd sleep there. She was looking for a movie to put on when her phone rang, Jack's name flashing across her screen.

"Hello." Eloise swallowed. Jack coming back into her life was never something she would have asked for, but now that he was here, she secretly wished he'd dive all in. The problem? Eloise wasn't sure she'd be able to do anything other than let him drown.

"Eloise, hi."

"Hi, Jack. You made it to Grand Junction?" Eloise had to focus on her breathing to keep herself from crying. All she did while Jack was around was tell him she wasn't ready, and though that was true, she was left feeling afraid. She was terrified that they weren't together, and not because he was in a dangerous place. She wanted to tell him she'd wait, to tell him to wait for her, to ask him if his heart was still with her. All of these questions would never leave her lips, because somehow, she'd always held his heart, it never left her and that was the scariest thing of all.

"Yeah, I just got to my house."

"I'm glad you called. I was thinking about you." Eloise spoke without thinking, but was happy she did. Lying to herself was getting exhausting.

"I'm always thinking about you. Sorry."

"Sorry?"

"If saying that was too much."

"It's fine. I don't mind, actually." That was the truth. She left out that she loved it when he flirted with her. She refused to tell him she had to fight herself daily in order to maintain her distance. She wanted to tell him "say more, remind me that I'm loveable, that I'm desired."

"I feel like I don't really know how to tell you goodbye."

"Then don't." Suddenly Eloise was panicked. Was that what this was? A goodbye. She couldn't lose him, not again, not when she just got him back. She also couldn't ask him to stay, because no matter how much she wanted to believe that Reagan wanted her to be happy, she still felt like she was betraying him.

"I have to. I'll be gone for months."

"So that's it then?" If Eloise wasn't so distraught, she'd think this moment was ironic. For years, it was her leaving him.

"I'll always think about you, Eloise, always have."

"Just be careful, Jack. Just come back." *Come back to me*, she added in her head.

"I plan to. Have a good night, beautiful."

"Good night, handsome." She hit the end button and threw her phone on to the couch to her right. She could feel herself starting to cry. Eloise pawed through her hair, trying to fight back her tears. She looked around her empty living room, without registering anything she saw, and the tears fell.

After Eloise ran out of tears, she forced herself to get up and take a shower. She didn't want to, but she had to try to keep moving forward. The worst part was not knowing when she'd see Jack again. He said he'd come back and she believed him, but not having a time frame was going to destroy her. Jack told her he had to go for training. That he may, or may not get deployed, but until then, he'd be training for mountain warfare. He could get deployed for a few days or it could be months. She hated all of that, hated the not knowing. Before Jack came back into her life, it was easy to picture him, to see the man she knew before, because she didn't know any different. She knew now, and that was both wonderful and painful.

Eloise sat in her recliner, her hair still wet, and wished that Jack was in the room above her. Her body was exhausted, but her mind felt wide awake. Eloise thought about the day Reagan died, even though she hated thinking about it. That morning, she had no clue what was happening to him, but there's no way Reagan didn't know that he was about to die.

Reagan had flown hundreds of times since he got his pilot's license, maybe thousands. That Friday morning he kissed her on his way out the door and she yelled, "I love you," to his back. The last thing she ever heard him say was, "I love you more," and then he shut their front door and never walked back through it.

The police told her it was engine failure. The coroner told her he died on impact and wouldn't have been in any pain. No one could tell her what Reagan was thinking the moment he realized his engine was failing. Not a single person could tell her if he was scared, if he thought about her, if he tried to be brave, or if he cried. Reagan was a smart man and a great pilot. Eloise knew he would've done everything in his power to safely land the plane. The crash meant he had exhausted every option. Eloise had flown with him more times than she could remember, but that morning she had a committee meeting at work she couldn't miss.

Eloise wiped the tears off her cheeks. She should've missed the meeting. The meeting her teaching assistant interrupted when the hospital called the school's office, trying to find her. The long list of missed calls on her cell made her guilt grow. Her phone was always on silent at work, and usually in her desk drawer. She should've been on that plane too. She'd be dead, but at least she would've died with more answers than questions. She would've been there to hold his hand, to tell him that she loved him the most. She would've witnessed his final moments and would have the closure she desperately needed now. Instead, she was in a meeting that really didn't matter in the grand scheme of things. Eloise barely remembered leaving work that day. She couldn't remember any of the drive to the hospital and was still shocked she didn't die on the way there. When they told her the news, she sat in the hospital room for hours, holding Reagan's hand. She remembered a nurse telling her to take all the time she needed, but she didn't need time. She needed her husband. She sat there but she didn't remember what she said, if she spoke at all. She just kept holding his hand, afraid to leave, because it would be the last time she ever touched him.

J ack looked at the phone in his hand, wishing he could call back, wishing he'd asked if she ate dinner. The worry in his head would drive him nuts. He would have to put her out of his mind, not because he wanted to, but because he had to focus on the task in front of him. His life, and other people's lives, were depending on that focus. Eloise couldn't consume him, even though it'd be easy to let her.

Jack hoped that training would take up his thoughts and energy until they sent them out. The base in Grand Junction was brand new and his unit would be one of the first to train on it. The Army built it for extreme weather conditions training, and Jack knew he'd be spending more time in high elevations with low temperatures. His days would be much more structured here and he'd need that to keep thoughts of Eloise at bay. He lay back and tried to fall asleep, knowing his alarm would be going off in what would feel like the blink of an eye. Jack clasped his hands and twirled his thumbs around each other, something his grandfather used to do. He moved them closer and closer, until they were almost touching, focusing on the motion, until he fell asleep.

Jack woke four minutes before his alarm and cursed the universe for taking those extra seconds of sleep. It was only four thirty his time, but he wanted to call Eloise. If he didn't call her now, it would be hours later, after a full day of training, before he would be able to talk to her. He could text her, but that meant he wouldn't hear her voice. Something in his gut told him to call, so he clicked her name on his phone.

"Hello?" Eloise sounded like she wasn't fully awake.

"Good morning, beautiful," Jack said. "I'm sorry for waking you up, but I wanted to talk to you before training starts."

"You can wake me up anytime. What time is your training? It is way, way too early for physical activity."

"We start in thirty minutes. How'd you sleep?"

"Okay, once I fell asleep. I thought a lot about Reagan last night, about his plane crash. I hate that he was alone."

"He wouldn't have wanted you there, Eloise. You have to know that. He loved you. He'd want you safe."

"I know, but I still hate it. I wish he didn't have to face that alone. He knew, Jack, he had to have known what was going to happen. I know he probably tried to prevent it, but there was a moment when he knew he wouldn't be able to. He realized he was going to die, and he was alone." Eloise was sobbing and Jack wished he could hold her.

"I miss you, El," Jack said, trying to think of something to make her feel better. "You can't beat yourself up over not being there. I can promise you that Reagan was thanking God that you weren't."

"Thank you, Jack. I just go in this vicious cycle of blaming myself and feeling guilty, and whenever I catch myself almost feeling happy, I go right back to feeling guilty. I hate that I even want to feel better. When Nickie was here I was so happy. I wasn't faking it. You guys made it easy to forget for a while that I'm beyond repair. Does that make sense?"

"It makes sense, El, and I promise it will pass. When I lost Drake I couldn't imagine ever feeling like myself again. It just takes time. Drake was sudden too. It's not the same as losing a husband, but I get it in the sense that I could never have prepared for it." Jack held the phone between his ear and shoulder and stood to get dressed.

"What happened to him?"

"Motorcycle accident. He rode all the time. He even rode when you knew him." Jack pictured his brother on his motorcycle. He'd spent more time on that bike than he ever did in class. Drake only made it one semester before dropping out. His crash happened three days after he enlisted. Drake was so happy the day he joined the Army, the happiest Jack had ever seen him. Drake had done what he could to make their mother happy, but that day he did something because he wanted to, and Jack would never understand why God would take a man before he lived out his dream.

"I remember."

"He went out and some guy ran a red light. I was in class when it happened. My mom called, hysterical. I never went back to school." Jack moved the phone to his other ear and then pulled his socks on.

"The guy?"

"He lived, and for the first time in my life, I hated someone I never even met."

"Drake deserved such a full life. He'd be so proud of you, Jack. Of everything you've done to honor him."

"Thank you, Eloise. Reagan would be proud of you too."

"Maybe not right now. But, one day, I hope he is."

"It just takes time. I gotta go, beautiful. I can't be late. I'll try and call you tonight."

"Be safe, handsome. Good luck."

"Thanks, El. Bye." Jack hung up the phone before he overthought it.

J ack's training and days were always the same, but he and Eloise fell into a routine that he loved. Every morning for the past three months he'd call her. She reassured him each time that she didn't care that it was five thirty in the morning her time, because she was thrilled he called. Every night, the same thing, he'd call and they'd talk until he had to go to avoid sleeping through his alarm. It felt like time was flying. He wondered if Eloise felt the same, or if time was moving slower for her.

The morning after Jack's unit was finished with their training, they got called to the debriefing area and Jack was dreading what they would say. He'd done this enough to know they'd be deploying.

"Where do you think they're sending us?" Chase, a man Jack had known for the last ten years, asked as the unit stood to get their orders.

"No clue." Jack honestly didn't care where it was, he just hoped it was a quick mission. When they got sent out, talking to Eloise would get a lot harder and he hated thinking about giving that up.

"Gentlemen, I've received orders today that we're being deployed. I don't have specifics yet, but once I do, we'll have a detailed briefing," First Sergeant Beckett told the men. "We've got four more days here, same training schedule. Make sure your stuff is ready to go."

"Yes, sir," the unit replied in unison.

"Dismissed." Beckett turned to walk toward the office buildings and the men started to talk among themselves once he was out of sight.

"There's no way we've been doing all this mountain, cold-ass, snow-ass training for them to send us somewhere hot," Chase said to Jack. "I fuckin' hate the cold."

"Same," Jack said. "But two-hundred-degree weather ain't my favorite either."

"I need to call Allie. She's gonna flip. Crazy how easy it is to pretend we work a regular nine-to-five when months pass without us leaving. Back to reality." Chase took off, almost jogging, and

Jack wondered if he should tell Eloise about his new orders. He didn't want to scare her, but he didn't think he should leave her in the dark either. They were just friends, or at least he kept telling himself that. He didn't really have to tell her, but then she'd wonder why he wasn't calling each morning. He couldn't put her through that, just disappear and leave her wondering where her wake-up call went.

Jack called every day, twice a day, and he'd bet those calls were the reason she was getting up, getting ready, and moving forward. Eloise still seemed so broken, and as selfish as it was, Jack wanted to be her reason to keep going. The more mature part of him hoped that one day she'd be strong enough to live for herself, to find her confidence and independence again, but he didn't feel like she could yet.

Jack picked up his phone. His call would scare her. He never called in the middle of the day.

"Jack," Eloise answered. "Are you okay?"

"I'm fine, El, but I have some bad news." Jack took a deep breath. "I'm being deployed."

"What?" Eloise whispered. "You can't go. I'm finally starting to feel normal, Jack. I have a routine that makes sense to me. I know that's a lot to put on you, but the thought of losing my bearings now…"

"You're not putting anything on me, El. I'm aware of all that, but I can't change this. I swear to you, if I had any control over it, I'd already be standing in front of you." Jack wanted to tell her that he never stopped wanting her. That it had always been her and no amount of time or distance or life-altering pain would change that. But he didn't, because he wasn't a hundred percent sure she wanted to hear those things, and he couldn't risk pushing her away. "In the next few days. I won't be able to call anymore. I can't give you an exact date, that usually changes. I didn't want you to worry when I stopped calling at the crack of dawn."

"You can't call at all?"

"I don't know, El. It'll depend where I'm at, what I'm doing. I'll try." Jack wasn't sure if that was the best idea. Would it hurt worse to have him call a few times, maybe send messages, or would it be better to just wait until he could tell her he was safe and back on base. She could be waiting months for that call.

"I don't know how to do this, Jack," Eloise spoke quietly, and Jack could tell she was crying.

"Well, good thing is, I do."

"Ass."

"Sometimes." Jack smiled, happy he decided to tell her. "But, also serious. I do know what I'm doing. Everything is going to be okay. The second I get back on this base, I'll call you."

"You'll call me tonight?"

"And every morning and night until I deploy." Jack bit the inside of his cheek so he wouldn't tell Eloise how much he loved her, missed her, ached for her.

"Be safe Jack. I'll talk to you tonight then," Eloise said.

Jack didn't want to hang up, but if they kept talking, he'd end up spilling his guts and professing his love and that wasn't going to help anything. Not yet, anyway.

"Have a good afternoon, beautiful. I'll talk to you soon."

"Talk to you soon, handsome." Jack waited for her to hang up first, watching as her name flashed twice on his screen, and then disappeared.

CHAPTER 9

J ack was sitting on a huge boulder, his butt felt like a block of ice. He longed for the days where he was soaked in sweat and the sun seemed like it would never move out of its high spot in the sky.

"Brennan, why you sitting out in this shit?" Chase asked as he walked up, pulling a beanie over his ears.

"Thinkin' I guess," Jack answered. Prior to being with Eloise for weeks, everyone he knew called him by his last name. It seemed weird now when Chase said it. Chase's was one of the rare ones who always got called by his first name.

"Can't you think inside where there's heat?" Chase sat down next to Jack, but didn't look happy about it.

"I suppose. I kinda just sat down."

"Women or money?" Chase's breath floated in the space between them.

"What?"

"Brennan, I've known you a long time. And I've only ever seen you think so intently when you were worried about a chick or worried about money."

"She's not a chick."

"So it is a girl." Chase didn't try to hide his smile.

"*The* girl," Jack said. Chase knew all about Eloise. Jack had known Chase since he enlisted almost a decade ago. After losing Drake and enlisting, Chase helped Jack and now they were brothers, just as close as he and Drake had been.

"You saw her?" Chase's eyes went wide. Jack was embarrassed. He'd told Chase all about Eloise, but in a pining and pathetic way. He didn't want Chase to judge him for his choice to visit Eloise.

"Her husband died," Jack said flatly.

"Shit."

"Exactly."

"And how did her husband dying lead to you sitting here allowing yourself to turn into an icicle?" Chase rubbed his gloved hands together.

"I stayed my entire leave." Jack was looking at his hands in his lap. "I just went to check on her, you know, make sure she was okay. She wasn't. Far from it, actually. That may have been the worst I've ever seen her look." Jack thought about the times back in college, nights when Eloise wasn't herself, the nights she felt lost, the nights she cried. Ninety-nine percent of the time that woman was solid and the brightest light, but when the days creeped in where she felt hollow, Jack remembered it getting too dark sometimes. When they were kids, he was just thankful that those days were few and far between, but now he was old enough to understand that their impact could have caused her fire to be lost forever.

"Did she ask you to stay?" Chase asked.

"Not at first, but then she needed help so she could list her house. So, I started helping, and her list kept growing until I was staying in her spare room so that I didn't have to lose my ass in a hotel."

"You stayed with her for your full thirty days?" Chase's eyes had disbelief written in them, and Jack wanted out of this conversation.

"In Texas, yeah, but it wasn't like that. I did the stuff she needed, made sure she ate, shit like that. There wasn't anything else happening."

"And then you left, which I take as the reason for you freezing your ass off?"

"Yeah, I just don't know what to do now. We talked every day during training. I just don't know if I should wait to contact her until we're back. I don't want her worrying about what we're doing here."

"Brennan, she's going to worry either way, probably more if you ghost her while we're here. If you want to keep in touch with her, send a damn message. Don't sit out here freezing. Worst case, she doesn't answer. Best case, she does. You said you were always friends first, so why not now?" Chase stood and jogged a few paces in place.

"I just don't know if it's what she wants."

"Well, you ain't gonna find that out sitting here. Message her, man." Chase extended his hand to Jack, helping him off the rock.

"Thanks, man." Jack pulled his phone out of his pocket, walked until he found a Wi-Fi signal, pulled up Eloise's Facebook, and clicked on the message button. He did want to talk to Eloise, that was a given. Not talking to her for the past week had about killed him. He should be back stateside soon, as long as the mission went as planned. He hoped that would bring her some comfort.

Three days after Jack mentioned leaving, Eloise woke up at five thirty, her body used to the early hour after months of doing it, but there was no phone call. Her phone's clock flashed six in the morning, proving Jack was gone, fighting somewhere she'd probably never see, probably didn't even know existed, and now she could do nothing but wait for him to return.

Eloise tried to stay positive, but for the last week her tears were uncontrollable, spewing from her body nearly every minute of the day. The only time she wasn't crying was when she was blessed with sleep, and that wasn't often. Nickie called and texted almost daily after Eloise told her Jack had deployed, and when Eloise answered she always told her she was doing fine. Eloise hadn't been fine since the day Jack left. Somewhere in her, she believed Nickie understood that, but was trying to give her space while still checking on her.

Eloise sat in her recliner, thinking about whether she could manage to skip another meal. She didn't feel hungry, but at some point she would have to choke something down. She heard her phone ding, but couldn't make herself reach for it. When she was forced to get up to pee, she grabbed her phone on her way to the bathroom and her jaw dropped as the bubble with Jack's face sat on her home screen.

> *El- I realized once I got here that the reason I didn't know how to tell you goodbye was because I never wanted to. I figured it would make you smile to get a message from so far away. I can't say exactly where we are, but I can tell you it's cold, way too cold for me. I never want to be this cold again. I can't thank you enough for letting me stay with you, and*

> *for talking to me the last three months. They*
> *were some of the best times I can remember.*
> *Not that college was bad. I wanted to email*
> *you because I miss you and figured you may be*
> *feeling pretty lonely in that house, all by*
> *yourself and want a pen pal. If I'm wrong,*
> *well, don't write back.*
>
> *-Jack*

Eloise couldn't believe it. She thought her time with Jack was on hold and here his words were scrawled across her screen. She read the words again and again, touching them lightly with her fingers. If he saw her now, he'd force her to get up, to shower, to act like she was still alive no matter how dead she felt on the inside. He was good at that, at bringing out the pieces of her that she felt were buried with her husband. She wasn't sure what to say, but started typing anyway.

> *Jack- I swear you can read my mind. I was just*
> *sitting here thinking about you. I'm glad you're*
> *okay. I know you weren't sure about talking*
> *while you were deployed, but I'm glad you*
> *messaged me. If you have an address and*
> *there's anything you want sent, just let me*
> *know. The house is definitely quiet without you*
> *and the coffee definitely worse. You don't have*
> *to thank me, my house is market-ready because*
> *of you. And, as for the last three months, they*
> *kept me going. Your calls were why I got up,*
> *Jack. I'll never be able to thank you enough for*
> *that.*
>
> *Be safe,*
> *Eloise*

Eloise kept looking at their chat, hoping to see a new message pop up. After twenty minutes, she gave up and decided to make some dinner. He was probably busy. She suddenly missed being busy. Maybe she should go back to work. Four months ago she couldn't even think about her job, and now she considered returning. For her to go back to work, she'd have to start getting dressed again. It amazed Eloise how quickly one message from Jack could shock her back to life.

Eloise ate while she read, and Rossi waited patiently for her scraps. Once the dishes were done and Rossi was fed both leftovers and her dog food, Eloise curled back up with her book. Falling asleep in her recliner no longer felt odd to her. She was comfortable and comforted there. Eloise sat up in her chair the second she heard her phone ding.

> *I'm sorry that I didn't write back sooner. Honestly, sometimes you may be waiting days. I feel bad about that. I had to leave on a mission. We're back now. I'm going to get some grub and probably end up crashing hard. I hope you had a great day. I'll be thinking about you, El.*

She read the message a couple of times, debating on whether to write back now or wait until morning. His message was short, and he probably wanted to sleep, but she missed him and was up now anyway.

> *I'm glad you're back safe. I worried about you all day. I'm still not really used to you being gone. The house is so quiet. I had a good day, I guess. I sent my boss an email about going back to work. When Reagan died, I couldn't even think about work. I couldn't think about*

*leaving my recliner for God's sake. But you
know that. Now I feel like I could do it. You
forced me to keep living. Thank you for that.
Please keep talking to me, Jack. If you stop,
I'm afraid I will fall back into the deep, dark
hole that I climbed out of while you were here.*
Be safe.

A fter closing and opening their chat for the fifteenth
time, Jack finally had his message. He was shocked she
was awake, especially with the time difference. He
read her words and heard her voice in his head. He missed seeing
her every morning, drinking coffee with her, talking about their
day, and reminding her to do the mundane things that she stopped
doing once her husband was gone. She was afraid she'd fall back
into week-old pajamas and not eat. He couldn't let that happen.

*I will write to you as much as I can, but there will
be days I can't. That doesn't mean I'm not
thinking about you. It just means I'm busy with
work. Don't give up on me when I don't
respond. I think you going back to work is a
great thing. I bet the kids miss you. When
would you start? Tell me about the house. Is it
on the market yet? Do you know where you'll
move?*

Jack stared at the screen. He wasn't sure what else to say. Like
usual, he had no clue where the line was. It was easier to see
when they were together, because he could use her facial expres-
sions and body language as a guide, but now, he could say

anything he wanted and she could decide what to do with it. Should he tell her that he missed seeing her sleepy face, missed drinking coffee with her? Should he tell her he thought about her piercing green eyes and about kissing her pouty lips? Should he ask her if she thought about when they were kids as much as he did? Just kids, eighteen and nineteen years old when they met. So naive. He reread his message before adding to it.

> *You're all I've thought about since I got here, and I*
> *want you to know that. I know you're hurting*
> *right now and if I could take that pain from*
> *you, I would. Always.*

Eloise fell back to sleep holding her phone and didn't see Jack's message until nine in the morning. She reread the last two lines until she memorized every word. It would be dark where he was, and he was probably exhausted. That's what she told herself anyway. She could respond to the rest of his words easily, but had no clue how to address those last two lines. She set the phone on her end table the message still opened and went to take a shower.

Eloise reached the school by eleven. She was meeting with her boss to discuss transitioning back to work. She wanted to start part time to see if she could handle it.

"Eloise, it's so nice to see you." Mr. Maddux offered her his hand, and she shook it with intensity.

"You, too, Mr. Maddux. How have things been here?"

"Good for the most part. The kids have missed you, we all have." He gestured inside his office and she sat down in one of the chairs in front of his desk. He took his seat and, for a moment, the two just stared at each other.

"I've missed being here and I hope I can come back," Eloise started.

"Your job is yours whenever you want it. If you want to start part time, I'm sure we can work that out with your long-term sub." Mr. Maddux hit a button on his keyboard and his computer lit up.

"Great. I also may be moving. So can we play next year by ear?"

"Of course. You've been here five years, Eloise. We love having you. You're an amazing teacher and we will do what we can to accommodate you. Just tell me what you need." Mr. Maddux positioned his screen so Eloise could see the schedule.

After two hours of hammering out the details, Eloise was back in her car. She took her phone out of her purse. It would be late where Jack was, but she pulled up his message anyway. He didn't deserve her being a coward.

Eloise hit send and stuck her phone back in her purse. She wanted to sit there until he responded, but who knew how long that would be. She drove home listening to one of her favorite songs and sang the whole way. She felt guilty about it. She felt guilty about anything that made her smile. She didn't feel like she had the right to smile. Smiling should have died with her husband, but for that to happen, she'd have to stop listening to music and stop writing to Jack.

Jack's unit rolled in at just after ten that night and he was beat. His uniform was covered in dust and dried blood, some his, most not. The day had been one of the worst he'd ever had and now three men were returning home under the flag. Nights like this, he always blamed himself, all the men still breathing did. The difference was Jack had his hands on those men, and their deaths would always feel like his fault. Jack headed straight for the shower trailer without going to his bunk first. He needed to get today off him. The three men he lost were all married and two were fathers. He hated to think of their wives. Right now they were home, not expecting that their lives were about to never be the same. It always hurt, tore him apart, losing people, but now it was worse because he saw what losing her husband had done to Eloise, experienced firsthand what it would do to those men's wives.

Jack made quick work of the shower, and was thankful when Chase handed him a towel.

"Saw you beeline for the showers and figured you could use a towel," Chase said as he turned his own water on.

"You thought right. Thanks, man," Jack said, drying his ears and wrapping the towel around his waist. "I'll get you another one."

"No worries. No one here wants you walkin' back to quarters naked."

Jack fought back his smile. "Can't argue with that."

"Will you cook tonight?" Chase looked hopeful.

"Don't I always?" Jack said without looking at Chase.

Jack always cooked when men got injured, or worse. The men would sit around and talk about their fallen brothers, because even though no one said it, none of them would sleep that night.

Jack put on fresh clothes and opened up his Facebook. He hoped there'd be a message from her. He could really use it after today. He sat in his desk chair and waited for what felt like an eternity for his phone to load.

I'm thrilled to hear that we can keep talking.
Thank you for agreeing to continue to save me.
I can wait for your messages to come in, don't
worry about me giving up on you. I just met

*with my boss. I start Monday. I'm going to
work half days for a while and see how I feel,
and my long-term sub will keep covering the
rest of the time. I told my boss I may be
moving, and he is willing to just let me do
whatever. I'm sure he pities me, but it makes
me feel bad that he is so understanding. The
house should be on the market in two weeks.
My real estate agent is going to take pictures of
it Tuesday and thanks to you, it looks a lot
better. Once the house sells, I think I will go to
Colorado. I have my job here, but I can get
another one. Don't think I'm crazy, I've only
been there once, but I think I need a place
where everything is new and there's nothing
that reminds me of Reagan. I feel like we're
always talking about me. How are you? Truth
be told, I haven't stopped thinking about you
since you left, and you've taken away more
pain than you realize.
Be safe.*

Jack kept reading the message and getting hung up on *how are you* each time. How was he? He was terrible. Should he tell her? He couldn't *not* tell her. Eloise told him he saved her. Maybe she could save him too.

*I'm not doing so great. I hope you're up. It's seven
a.m. there, so maybe I'll get lucky.*

I'm up. What's wrong? Are you hurt?

Her response was immediate. Jack didn't know what to say. He was hurt, but not in the way Eloise thought.

> *We lost three men tonight. I'm not hurt, not really,*
> *some scrapes, no big deal. I just blame myself*
> *for losing them. They have families. Families*
> *who will never be the same. Losing men is*
> *always hard, it's losing a brother all over*
> *again. I've never had anyone to talk to about*
> *this before. I know you can't fix it, but I felt like*
> *I had to say it. Three soldiers died tonight and*
> *someone out there, away from all this hell,*
> *should know that. Someone good.*

Jack licked his lips as he fought his tears. He wasn't sure what he expected from her. It wasn't right to put those deaths on her, because he knew she'd feel responsible for taking his pain away, but there weren't words in existence that could take that type of pain away. Jack didn't know how to need someone. He sure as hell didn't want to need anyone. Drake and Eloise. Those were the only people he'd ever depended on and he lost them both. He had Eloise back now, in a way, but that didn't mean he always would. He couldn't let himself need her. He couldn't let himself need anyone. His phone buzzed, disrupting his thoughts.

> *I won't say I'm sorry for your loss. I hated when*
> *people told me that they were sorry for my loss.*
> *How could they be sorry for my loss? How could*
> *they even begin to comprehend my loss? You*
> *don't want sorry when someone you love dies,*
> *you understand that. You never once told me you*
> *were sorry. I wish I could absorb all that pain for*

*you. Don't let it consume you, Jack. Not there. I
know you've suffered a lot of loss, and you know
all of this already, but I had to say it, because it's
too easy to let the darkness swallow you.*

Jack stared at his screen. Eloise's words were exactly what he needed, and he was beyond grateful that she answered so quickly. He hated to admit that he wanted to throw all reason out the window and jump feetfirst into needing her in his life, into making sure he never lost her again. He couldn't have that argument with himself now, though. He couldn't lose himself here. He had men depending on him, people who needed him to keep them safe. He failed tonight, but he couldn't let that failure take over. Like he told Eloise, as much as it hurt, he had to keep moving forward.

*I needed your words so badly, and I can't tell you
how thankful I am for you. I will keep moving
forward if you do. Maybe together we can
reach the light.*

CHAPTER 10

Together we can reach the light. Eloise had to sit down after reading that. She felt as if she couldn't breathe, but also like the only chance she had of breathing again was through Jack. It was confusing and painful. He was her light, and the guilt she felt over that was the darkness pushing forward, threatening to consume her. Eloise knew she was going down a questionable road with Jack, she just wasn't sure why it was questionable. She thought maybe it was because she still felt married most days, or maybe it was the fact that they'd been down this road before and it was a dead end.

Eloise knew Nickie would argue that it never went anywhere because Eloise didn't want it to. Everyone always blamed Eloise for it not working out, and she'd always taken the brunt of the responsibility. Eloise was fun, but she was never *Jack fun* back in college. One of her biggest flaws at eighteen was thinking too much about where she wanted to be at twenty-eight, at thirty-five, at fifty. She made too many decisions based on her desired future instead of enjoying her actual present.

She never felt as though she pushed Jack away, but she didn't exactly pull him in close either. It was a weird thing, their relationship, because she was closer to him than anyone else, ever, but when it came to labeling their relationship, she couldn't do it. She told everyone Jack wasn't boyfriend material, but maybe *she* wasn't really girlfriend material. No. She would've been a great girlfriend to Jack. Eloise knew that it was fear that stopped her. She was afraid of losing something that wasn't hers to lose. If she had labeled it, made the immensity of it real, then the loss would come at a greater price.

It was ridiculous, because now she saw she may not have lost anything. They could've worked out. It made no sense to push someone away because your feelings were so intense they terrified you. Why didn't she dive into them headfirst?

Eloise was thinking through this as she planned for the next morning. She was starting work and felt more nervous and anxious about going back than she did on her first day five years ago. She felt like someone else now, like the girl who started teaching five years ago disappeared, ran away, or died with her husband. Eloise felt that way most days. The line marking her identity as Eloise and as Reagan's wife only got blurrier as more days passed since losing her husband. She grabbed her phone and dialed Nickie's number.

"Hey, El." Nickie always picked up, and Eloise loved her more each time.

"I have a question." Eloise put Nickie on speaker phone so that she could wash her face as they talked.

"Let's hear it."

"Do you ever feel like the person you are is dependent on your husband?"

"Sometimes. Why?" Nickie responded without hesitation.

"I don't know who I am anymore. I was one person when I was young, the person Jack knew, and then I became Reagan's wife, and now I don't know who the hell I am. So much of who I am was Reagan, and now, I'm scared I'm letting Jack shape me into someone too." Eloise dried her face and grabbed her moisturizer.

"Eloise, I love you, so take this with love, but Jack has never tried to shape you into anything. He's always let you be wild, be free, be any person you wanted, and you know that. As for Reagan, that happens, honey, after you're married for a long time. Pieces of you rub off on each other."

"I'm afraid it's more than that. What if I lost myself? I made so many decisions based on our plans, our life, our future. My career, my hobbies, the freaking house I live in. None of it is just mine." Eloise pulled her toothbrush out of its holder and added toothpaste.

"Take a breath," Nickie said, then paused as Eloise took a few deep breaths. "You made sacrifices, babe, and compromises, but that would have happened with anyone."

"I don't feel like you lost yourself."

"In some ways I have, but I always find my way back somehow, and you will too. Your entire world was turned upside down. It's understandable that you'd question your identity. It's not a bad thing that who you were, who you still are, is tied to your husband."

"I'm going back to work and I'm not even sure I want to. I miss the kids, but I don't think I miss the job. I had so many things I wanted to do, and I feel like I've done none of them." Eloise squeezed foundation on her forehead and cheeks.

"El, you have a freakin' master's degree. You love teaching, or you did, and if you don't anymore, you will find something else. You get to choose what you do now."

"That's what terrifies me, Nickie. The freedom. What if I choose wrong? Reagan always had a plan. He made most choices for me. I loved him for that. He took all the hard parts of life on himself and now, I have to face all those things. You were right.

Jack has never tried to shape me, but is that good? He just stands back as I go insane?"

"He'd never let you go insane. But, he likes you how you are. When you're silly and serious. When you sing as you do the dishes or act weird. I can't explain it, El. He likes your core, he loves your core, but he'd also do anything to protect you."

"I know." Eloise said after spitting and rinsing her mouth out. She didn't feel better. She wanted to, but nothing seemed right. When she was Reagan's wife, she knew who she was, and now she felt as if she were watching herself on a movie screen, going through the motions. She felt normal when Jack was with her, the weeks he stayed, she felt extremely normal. But he was gone now too. Maybe that was what scared Eloise, the thought that she didn't have any identity at all unless she was tied to someone else. "Maybe it's good I'm alone for now. I miss Jack. God, I miss him. And I miss Reagan, every single minute, I miss him. But, being alone forces me to find myself separate from anyone else."

"It's okay to love other people, El. A person who tries to make the people she loves happy. I've known you a long time, and you never seemed lost to me. Sure, you changed goals, but that happens. Who you are is still in there."

"Thanks, Nickie." Eloise wanted to believe her. When she was in college, she wanted to study veterinary medicine and open an animal sanctuary. After she met Reagan, her dreams evolved into becoming a teacher because she'd be finished faster and have a good schedule when they decided to have children. She never regretted it, but that was when he was here. That was when she did it for their future. Now she just felt like she gave up what she wanted for no reason because her husband was dead. Reagan dying wasn't his fault, but she blamed him for abandoning her. The empty hole his dying caused demanded that she question her future and her identity and she loathed him because of it.

"Anytime, El. I love you."

"I love you too. Talk to you soon." Eloise hit end and applied ChapStick before making her way back to her recliner to sleep.

Going back to work wasn't as easy as Eloise had hoped. She woke up late, and that usually ruined her whole day. She hated feeling rushed. Eloise liked waking up in the morning and enjoying her coffee, taking her time, and being able to drive the speed limit. Today she would be going at least ten over to make it by the bell. Not the best way to start back.

Her door was covered in "welcome back" signs and notes from her students and she had to choke down tears as she read them. The bell rang two minutes after she got there and students quickly started filing in, hugging her as they passed.

When the tardy bell rang, her class was completely full with many more students than desks.

"What are you all doing here?" Eloise asked.

"We had to see you and you won't be here after lunch, Mrs. Masten," Jasmine, a girl in one of her afternoon classes, supplied.

"So you're all just ditching first period?"

"Of course not," Paige, a student actually in her first period, said. "We told Mr. Maddux."

"If it's too much, they can go." Mr. Maddux stood at the doorway, surprising her.

"No, Mr. Maddux. For today, it's fine. I'm happy to have them back." Eloise was thrilled that all her students showed up that first day. Not a lot of teaching took place, but the students told her about the last few months and their substitute, and Eloise tried not to cry as they talked about missing her.

At lunch, Eloise decided not to eat at work. She wasn't sure she was up for talking about her husband with other teachers and they'd ask. She was sure they all meant well, most of them came to the funeral, but after a full morning of interacting with over a hundred freshmen, she just didn't have it in her.

J ack tried to talk himself out of video calling Eloise, but had no real reasons besides seeing her face might be too much for him. Messaging was easy because it was all words on a page. If he saw her, it would be all he'd think about until he saw her again. He guessed that was similar to how he lived now, her face at the airport, blowing him a kiss, burned into his brain.

He thought about writing her a handwritten letter to distract him from calling, but decided he should just email it so she got it quickly. The freezing temperatures today must be making him delusional. Maybe he should ask Eloise where her line was. He could call her beautiful, but could he flirt with her? Could he tell her how incredible she looked, better than when they were together before? Would she care that he'd noticed all the things that had changed and remembered every detail that had stayed the same? He probably shouldn't tell her that her hips were slightly wider, but sexier, or that her skin still looked as soft. He didn't think he should admit how he'd do anything she asked just to see her smile. When he thought about her green eyes, he knew that all she had to do was look at him and he'd give her the world—or die trying. That had to cross the line.

When Eloise quit talking to him there was never any closure. She just quit, like she had done before. The difference this time was that she never started talking again. Before Reagan, she'd quit and then things with a guy would end and she'd come back to him. He waited, always, and that never changed. He'd spent the last decade waiting, but he never wanted things to end up this way. He wanted Eloise to be happy, and Reagan made her happy. Jack had loved Eloise since the day she first texted him *wanna have sex* and nothing else. No explanation. They had been working together for over a month and the way she just asked for what she wanted made his heart stop. She was fearless and he loved it.

When he had texted back, he wondered if she'd actually go through with it. Those thoughts disappeared when she showed up an hour later. That first night was still one of the best nights of his life, because he knew in that moment that he was born to love Eloise and he'd never felt happier. She looked excited when he met her in the parking lot, excited and nervous. He didn't say anything, just grabbed her hand and led her straight to his room. She was there for a reason, and he was all too willing to accommodate. They didn't say a word until after, and that made it even more wonderful. She had gotten up to leave, but Jack didn't want her to go. It was just sex for her that night, but it was already so much more for him.

"Stay with me," he had said from his bed as she searched for her pants.

"You don't have to do that, Jack."

"I know, but I want to." Jack waited, and then started laughing as she pulled her shirt back over her head and lay down next to him.

"Thank you for tonight. I needed it."

"Anytime." Jack remembered kissing the top of her head. He never asked her why. Why she needed it. Why she texted him. Why she picked him. He never asked what happened that day that led her to his bed, and it was years later before he started wishing he had asked. After that night, *wanna have sex* became one of their things and they said it countless times over the years. That was the first night of many that she spent the night, and when Drake knocked at seven the next morning to see if she was staying for breakfast, he loved her even more when she answered him.

"I'd love to," Eloise had said from Jack's bed, and Jack will never forget how big his brother smiled.

With Eloise's smile on his mind, he hit the call button. He stared at the phone in his hand and counted the seconds until Eloise's face filled the screen.

"Eloise, can you hear me?" Jack knew his face had to look dry, and he hoped that wouldn't worry her.

"Yes, Jack, hi." Eloise paused and Jack felt her eying him carefully. "I'm going to mail you some ChapStick. Are you okay?"

"I had a few minutes and thought I'd try to catch you. How was your first day?" Jack licked his lips. For some reason Eloise mentioning the ChapStick made him self-conscious.

"You remembered. I just got done. I'm about to drive home. It was good. Every one of my kids was there this morning. It was fun catching up with them."

"They all showed up at once?" Seeing her felt too good, something to treasure because at any moment it could vanish.

"Yeah, it was nuts. How are you?"

"I'm good. Everything here today is good. I miss you, El." Jack thought "missed" was a drastic understatement, but he never knew how exposed he should allow himself to be.

"I miss you, too, Jack. Seeing you is a nice surprise."

"I hoped you'd like it. I gotta go, though. I'll message you, okay?"

"You better. Bye, Jack."

"Bye for now, beautiful."

The video window closed and Jack exhaled. Eloise always made him feel at peace, and seeing her made the ever-present weight he carried around feel a bit lighter.

CHAPTER 11

J ack looked different to her. He looked focused and tired. His smile was the same, and his eyes still made her heart skip. Jack was still Jack underneath everything that had changed him over the last ten years, but Eloise felt like she only saw glimpses of him. The problem that Eloise saw herself facing was the realization that they'd never be able to be who they were. They had to move forward as the people they were now. Eloise hoped Nickie was right, that their core was still the same. Jack had found a way to save her, and she hoped that she was doing a little of that for him.

Eloise felt her chest tighten and wondered if she'd eventually run out of tears. She didn't want to be falling for Jack, not the old Jack, and not this new one either. Why did he have to make liking him so easy? Everything about him made Eloise happy. The way he remembered the little things like her going back to work. How even from what seemed like a million miles away, he found a way to make sure she knew she was on his mind. Seeing him was overwhelming, but now that his face was gone, all Eloise wanted was to see him again. She wanted to tell Reagan that she was sorry, that this wasn't her plan, and that she'd do everything she could to not love Jack. The problem was, Eloise had always loved Jack, even before she loved Reagan. She couldn't promise Reagan a lie, no matter how badly she wanted it to be the truth. The slow tears turned into an uncontrollable sob, and Eloise stared down at her empty palms, her white gold band suddenly seemed out of place.

J ack tried to video call Eloise once a week, but sometimes it only happened twice a month. Sometimes he got to tell her goodbye, but more often than not, the Wi-Fi would suck so badly that eventually their screens would freeze. They exchanged messages daily and he was always thankful for that. Jack was sitting on the ground outside when he saw Chase texting and it reminded him about a question he'd been struggling with.

"Hey, Chase, do you ever wish time would just freeze?"

"Huh?"

"I love having Facebook and Instagram and even Snapchat. Since I started messaging Eloise those things have been great. But they also show me what I'm missing, you know?"

"Oh." Chase looked up from his phone. "I get that. Allie's always posting pictures of her and my kids and I love seeing it, but I also hate that I'm missing it. Sometimes I think it'd be easier to not look."

"Same. But I love seeing her smile too much." Jack stood up to go get his phone and message Eloise.

I hope you're having a good day.

I am, handsome. Are you?

Yeah, just thinking about freezing time.

Why? Most days I'm thinking about speeding it up. Haha.

I miss a lot while I'm away. It's hard being reminded of that sometimes.

I never thought about it like that, like watching your world pass you by.

Exactly.

I'd freeze it for you if I could. Also, I'm on break so I only have about twenty minutes.

Send me that gorgeous smile.

Jack couldn't take his eyes off the message. How would she react to him wanting a picture of her? Sure he flirted sometimes, but this was bold for him. He should say it was bold for this aged Jack, because the Jack of ten years ago would have no problem telling Eloise exactly what kind of image to send and it'd have nothing to do with her smile.

Jack couldn't believe the photo. God she was beautiful, and she looked happy sitting at her desk. He set the photo as his background, not taking the time to analyze what that meant. He just wanted to see that smile anytime he picked up his phone. She sent *your turn* after her photo. He ran his fingers over his hair, put his helmet back on, then pulled down on his Kevlar. He tried to smile, but it was nowhere as big as the smile Eloise gave him and hit send before he overthought it.

Thank you for making my day, he added after he sent the

photo. He felt weird for wanting her to think he looked good. She had been keeping him at arm's length, but maybe her sending the picture, not questioning it, not asking why, maybe that meant there was hope.

Thank you for making mine.

Eloise set her phone back in her desk drawer as the bell for third period rang, then stood to greet her students. Coming back had been a good idea. She didn't realize that she missed interacting with people until she was doing it again. Teaching may not have been her original plan, but after she started, it quickly became her passion, and it made her feel like herself.

When the bell at the end of the fourth period rang, Eloise had already gathered what she needed to leave. She pulled her phone back out of the drawer and sent a message to Jack.

Leaving work. I know it's getting late there. Be safe.

You drive safe. Message me when you get home.

I will.

Eloise hit send and pulled out of the parking lot. She hadn't thought much about lunch, but decided about half way home that she'd stop and get sushi. She called ahead so that she'd just have to pick it up and felt a pang when she thought about sitting in her house alone. She hoped her real estate agent would tell her she had an offer on the place soon.

The next morning Eloise had an email from her real estate agent about a second showing. He seemed confident that they'd put in an offer that afternoon, and Eloise was thrilled. She needed to message Jack, but first she called Nickie.

"El." Nickie picked up on the second ring. "I'm so happy you called. I'm at work, so if I hang up, I'll call back."

"Okay. My real estate agent contacted me. He thinks I'll have an offer today." Eloise stirred her coffee.

"That's great, El. What are you going to do?"

"Well, that's why I called. I want to go to Colorado." Eloise paced her downstairs, coffee in hand.

"Are you serious?" Nickie's volume left Eloise pulling the phone away from her ear. "El, that's awfully, uh, random."

"I have nothing keeping me here."

"Why not go somewhere where you do have people, family?"

"I can't, Nickie. I love you guys, and I love my family, but when I think about going back to Arizona, I feel like I'm suffocating. I know it doesn't make sense, but I need something entirely new. I went to Colorado once while I was in graduate school and loved it. It's something I did, just me, and I need that. I need to remember that I can be alone. That's also why I'm calling. Do you think if I set up some showings, you and Gage could go look at them with me?"

"Of course, just say when and send addresses. We'll find you something. We've never been, and it'd be amazing to get away. Are you finishing up work?"

"Yeah, trying to. I can pay for your trip. I want animals, Nickie. I want the sanctuary." Eloise swore she could hear Nickie's smile.

"It's about damn time," Nickie said. "And I'm sure being next to Jack's base hasn't crossed your mind?"

"I know. I finally feel like I can do it." Eloise stopped before she started to cry. She had wanted an animal sanctuary for years. It was something she joked with Reagan about at first, and then she got more and more serious about it. He never really cared one way or the other, but said he would do it because it was what she wanted. They were trying to find properties large enough in Houston when Reagan died. It was always Eloise's dream. She just hoped that she could handle doing it without him. She felt like it would heal her, remind her who she was separate from Reagan. "And as for Jack, that's not his permanent place. The Army could send him anywhere."

"Yeah, but for now, pretty convenient," Nickie said. "I gotta go, babe. I'll call you later." Nickie hung up, and although Eloise knew it was because of work, she was still sad the second Nickie's voice was gone. Eloise sat down at her laptop to type a message out to Jack.

> *Good news, I just got off the phone with Nickie.*
> *She and Gage are going to help me find a*
> *house in Colorado. Nickie is a godsend, willing*
> *to fly up there. My real estate agent believes*
> *my house will be sold by this afternoon, and I*
> *couldn't be happier about that. It'll be weird*
> *not being here. Have you ever had something*
> *you thought you'd never lose? That's what*
> *Reagan was, and this house. When we bought*
> *it, I never thought I'd leave. I believed I'd grow*
> *old here, die here. Reagan did too. I just don't*
> *think he planned on it being so soon. I wonder*
> *sometimes if he'd be angry with me for giving*
> *up a place we purchased with the intention of*
> *staying forever. But mostly I think he'd want*
> *me to do what was needed to survive, and I*
> *can't do that here. It's like this house is frozen*

in a time where things were different, better,
and I know I'll never be able to unfreeze it.
Be safe.

Eloise watched her screen, like if she looked hard enough his message would materialize. Finally, it did.

Congratulations. I hope that offer comes soon and
you know for sure that you can move forward. I
obviously didn't know Reagan, but as someone
who cares for you, I can promise, he'd want
you to be happy. Reagan loved you and
because of that, he wouldn't just want you to
survive, he'd want you to flourish. Don't ever
feel bad about that. I'm sure Nickie and Gage
will help find you an incredible house. Do you
know what you're looking for?

Eloise did know what she was looking for, but she wasn't sure what Jack would think of it. She'd never told Jack she wanted a sanctuary. It was a dream Eloise had almost given up when she married Reagan, but a few years before his death, she had started planning to make her dream a reality.

Eloise had been working three jobs back then. She was teaching at the high school, at the college, and working as a tutor. She was slammed all the time. She was driving home from a late class at the college when she saw Rossi. She was tied up in the backyard of a house that looked abandoned. Eloise pulled over and carefully approached her. She didn't bark or act aggressive, so she untied the rope around her neck. She didn't see water or food. When the dog was free, it didn't run, it sat in front of Eloise, waiting. She reached down and patted her head.

"Good girl, good girl," Eloise repeated, while the dog seemed to be thanking her. She had no clue what to do, so she called the Humane Society. After a few weeks and realizing no one was looking for this dog, Eloise decided to keep her. Reagan liked having Rossi around, he grew up with dogs and had been trying to talk Eloise into one for years, but she always said they were too busy. Rossi adjusted to their hectic routine quickly, and that night, when Rossi jumped into their bed, after she clearly thought they were asleep, Eloise knew she wanted to help animals who had no one else. It was a fleeting thought, because she had stopped chasing her dream of being a veterinarian years ago, but the thought grew every time Rossi did something to remind her how big a dog's heart could be.

Yes, Jack and Nickie helped tremendously after Reagan died, but it was Rossi she held while she sobbed the day she got the news. Rossi who slept on the floor next to her recliner each night. Rossi who had spent days covered in Eloise's tears. Eloise would trade everything, including her sanctuary dream that now seemed like it was going to be a reality, to have Reagan back, but if she couldn't have him, she'd keep him alive by helping as many animals as possible. People may think that was silly, but they didn't know the way Reagan looked at a dog. *Could she say all that to Jack?*

> *Shocking, but something you don't know is that I've wanted to open an animal sanctuary for quite some time and that's the property I'll look for. It started a long time ago when I found Rossi, and that's what my heart keeps telling me to do now. I don't think we ever talked about my plans to be a vet. When we were in college together, I was studying biology, but I don't think I ever said why. The sanctuary wasn't something Reagan was passionate*

about. He wanted to do it, because I wanted to. But now, it seems like I have to do it for him. Does that make sense? Like, somehow if I complete the dream he was following for me, he'll know and it'll mean something to him?

It goes beyond that too. I need to be me again. I don't know if that'll make sense either. I wasn't me with Reagan. I was an extension of him. Happens when you're with someone for a long time. You become two pieces of the same person. You lose yourself in each other and that's okay, because you're together. But now, half of me is gone and I have to do something to build that half back. I have to be able to be a whole person again. Somehow, I know you'll get that.

Eloise his send and committed to sitting there until Jack replied.

I do understand needing to find yourself again. I've spent a lot of the last ten years trying to do that. So much of who we are is dependent on the people in our lives. It's hard to even answer the question "who are you" without using words like son, wife, or brother. It can be incredible, though, losing yourself in someone else, falling so deeply that you don't know who you are without them. I can't imagine having that and it being taken. I mean it when I say I wish I could absorb that pain for you. I'd take it all if I could, El.

As far as following a dream to honor someone else, you're speaking to the captain of that ship. I'm in the Army for my brother, remember? I think he knows. I think Drake would be proud of me. I believe Reagan knows too. Knows that you're trying to be the best version of yourself you can while also keeping him alive in your heart. I think an animal sanctuary is an amazing way to find yourself and do something that would mean a lot to Reagan. He'd just want to see you happy, El.

If there's anything I can do to help, just say the word. You're about to make a big move. I wish I were there to help. Seriously, anything you need that I can book, buy, rent, or send from here, it's yours.

Eloise couldn't stop reading Jack's message. She wanted to hug him and scream at him for being so damn helpful and supportive. He was making it impossible to not like him. Eloise had a strong love-hate relationship with Jack, one that was also ridden with guilt. Eloise thought about what it would be like to not answer him. She'd stopped talking to him many times before without a single word. Could she do that again? Would Reagan want her to do that? How much of herself did she still owe her husband?

The truth was Eloise was afraid of what would happen if she stopped talking to Jack. She didn't know if she was to the point of functioning every day without a reason for getting up. She had Rossi. Rossi needed her. She could be enough. It felt wrong to want Jack to call her "beautiful." The way her breath caught anytime her phone went off, too closely resembled betrayal.

Eloise clicked in the box to type and looked at the blank space.

"Do you know I'm talking to him, Reagan?" Eloise said to her empty house. "Do you know all the things I kept from you about us? How close we were? Do you know everything now that you're gone?" Eloise waited for the answers she'd never get. She wanted so badly for Reagan to find a way to tell her that it was okay. Eloise knew she was selfish for wanting his blessing, knew that her guilt came from feeling like she was hiding something from Reagan. In so many ways, she was. She never told Regan what Jack had meant to her, because when she made the decision to stop talking to Jack, she didn't see the point. Why hurt Reagan by describing a relationship the two of them would never achieve? She should have told him, maybe then she'd feel less sick about the whole situation.

> *Thank you. If I need anything, I'll let you know.*
> *Stay safe.*

Eloise was disgusted with herself for sending a one-line message, but she didn't know how to do this. She had no idea how to be close to Jack without being too close. She always knew they couldn't just be friends. That was the whole point of not talking when they were with other people. Eloise still felt like she was with someone else, and to remain faithful to Reagan, she'd have to stop talking to Jack, she just didn't think she could do that today.

One line. She sent him one line. Jack wanted to be pissed, because he understood what she was feeling. He tried to help her and she sent one line. He'd never lost a wife, but he had lost a brother and a mother, and he understood what it was like to feel as if your identity was lost, six feet under with the person you loved.

Jack read Eloise's message three times before he closed out of Facebook Messenger. Something was up with her, but obviously she didn't want to talk about it. He wasn't going to respond to that one line. If she was going to push him away, he'd make it easy on her, and himself. There'd be no begging her to stay. Eloise knew that Jack would be there for her in any capacity. She knew. Jack was not about to tell her that again. If she decided to tell him what had her acting weird out of nowhere, she'd message him again. Jack knew Eloise well enough, even now, to know that if she wanted to talk about something, she'd talk. He just hoped she would talk. He hoped she wasn't done talking—permanently.

CHAPTER 12

Eloise hadn't spoken to Jack in four days. He never messaged her back, and she couldn't make herself tell him that she was confused, that she just wanted to be close to him but didn't feel like she could do that without destroying herself. She couldn't explain that she felt like she was cheating on her dead husband. There were no words for that.

Eloise would go to work, then go home and stare at her phone. She knew he wouldn't respond, not until she did, not after her last reply. Eloise knew all she'd have to say was she got in her own head, that her thinking about Reagan led her to that short response. That'd be all it would take, and Jack, being Jack, would say she didn't have to apologize, and the two of them would go back to talking every day.

Things were never that easy.

Eloise missed Jack. She missed his video calls, his messages, and his pictures. She missed knowing he was okay, and safe. She wanted to be brave enough to tell him that she never stopped loving him. She wanted to say that getting to know him again over these months had caused her love to grow and change. Jack wasn't her first love anymore. Now, he was something Eloise knew most people would kill to have. She loved her husband. She loved Jack. She also hated that Jack was now available to her, because having him meant not having Reagan. Jack wouldn't ever make her say she didn't love Reagan. He'd never tell her not to think about him, so why did she feel like telling Jack the truth meant things with her and Reagan would disappear? That she'd have to bury their memories and denounce their love?

The bell for first period rang and Eloise shook herself out of her thoughts. She'd have to message Jack. She couldn't leave things the way she had before. Not again. He didn't deserve it the first time, and he sure as hell didn't deserve it now. Eloise's students started taking their seats and Eloise closed the drawer with her phone. She'd have to tell Jack she was sorry after work.

When Eloise's last class was over, she pulled up her Facebook app not wanting to wait until she got home. Frankly, she was over the lack of Jack. She'd rather feel guilty about talking to him than be miserable without him.

> *Jack-*
>
> *I wish I had a better reason for not talking to you for four days, but I don't have any good excuses. The last time we talked, I started thinking about Reagan and I'm still so hurt, and lost, and confused, and I know that's not your fault, but I don't know how to keep letting myself get close to you. I don't think a version of us where we're just friends exists for me, and I don't know what to do with that yet.*
>
> *I may not know how to feel, but I know I never want to feel like I do now again. These last four days were hell. Somehow I'm more lost, more of a mess, without you.*

*I'm sorry, Jack. I'm sorry I'm always leaving, and
always a mess. I hope you're safe and I hope I
hear from you soon. Be safe.*

Eloise closed Messenger and walked to her car. She wouldn't
blame Jack if he didn't answer, but she would still pray all the
way home that her phone went off. Eloise pulled into her
driveway and clicked off her seat belt when her phone buzzed.
The Messenger bubble with Jack's face brought with it the first
relief she'd felt in days.

*You never have to worry about not having me. You
have me. You always have.*

*I knew something was up and figured you needed
some space. I won't lie, hearing from you feels
like waking up on Christmas. I've missed you,
beautiful. I'll try and call you soon.*

J ack couldn't stop smiling. He'd spent the last four days
pissed at the world, and everyone around him knew it. It
wasn't safe for him to be on such a rampage, but he
couldn't stop himself. Everything made him mad.
Everyone annoyed him. He was still mad, but he couldn't tell
Eloise that. She felt bad enough. He just wished that sometimes
she thought about things from his side. It wasn't just her who
spent four days in hell.

He thought she would take a day, maybe two. When day three
came and he still hadn't heard from her, he thought for sure their
friendship, or whatever they'd been doing, was done. Eloise was
good at disappearing when things got too hard emotionally, and

Jack was stuck waiting just like before. He was so wrapped up in her that he knew he'd wait forever. He just didn't want to have to.

"She finally wrote back?" Chase said as he walked up to Jack.

"What?"

"Dude, you haven't smiled in almost a week and now you're over here smiling like someone just gave you a thousand dollars."

"She wrote back."

"I said that." Chase patted his friend's shoulder. "I'm glad she did. We were all about ready to sacrifice you in our next mission."

"Wow. Little extreme, don't you think?"

"Not one bit. You've been a nightmare." Chase started to laugh, causing Jack to join him. He knew he'd been a grouch, but a nightmare?

Jack was happy they fell back into their routine without much drama. He thought that Eloise needed to stop getting in her own way, but he knew she wouldn't be able to do that as long as she felt like she didn't deserve to be happy. Jack wanted to be the person who made her happy, more than happy. From the moment he met her, she made him believe the world wouldn't always be dark. He wanted to make her believe that too.

Jack's favorite part of the day went back to waking up Eloise, and he never tired of listening to her sleepy voice. Four days had seemed like a lifetime and now that another four days had passed, Jack was back to believing that a life with Eloise was possible. He waited for Eloise to end the call before walking out to begin the workday. Jack looked up at the sun, and wondered how it could be so bright when it was freezing, unknowing that today would be the moment Eloise was no longer his friend, that it would be the day she became something more.

Jack sucked in the icy air and adjusted his helmet, still examining the sky. He turned as the sergeant yelled for them to load up. Jack watched as they scrambled to grab their guns. Everything in the Army was fast-paced, and usually precise and calculated. It was the rare moments of chaos that Jack reveled in. The brief seconds where soldiers looked like men, when their body language wasn't uniform, those seconds made Jack feel alive.

Jack should have known something was wrong when both Chase and Connor were unaccounted for. Jack yelled for them to get a move on and jumped off the Humvee to see where they were. Jack rounded the corner just as Chase was buckling his helmet. Connor's helmet hung from his hand, his fingers laced through the straps. Jack couldn't peel his gaze from Connor's helmet. *Put it on*, something whispered in his mind. *Put the helmet on, Connor*. Jack watched as the two men spoke back and forth. Connor laughed and for a split-second Jack questioned why. The two of them started pushing one another back and forth. Their smiles seemed to be suspended in the frost of the morning air. Jack was opening his mouth to tell them to stop goofing around when the crack of a rifle sang through the air like church bells but unlike the bells, the shot had no echo. The weight of Connor's body slammed into Jack's chest and knocked him flat on his back. Jack tried to sit up. When he lifted Connor's torso, Jack crumbled.

"What the fuck." Jack's screams should have caused the other men to look, but they had dropped down to return fire. Jack's shrieks were laced with curses, outrage, and anguish. He could hear shots being fired, but he couldn't help. He couldn't move. He felt Connor's blood smeared across his face and neck. He held Connor tighter as the shots continued around them, Jack's screams matching the bullets in noise and intensity.

Jack was still clinging to Connor when Chase and three other men kneeled next to him. Jack assumed the enemy was no longer a threat, but he didn't release his hold.

"Let us help." Chase said as he unclenched Jack's fingers. The three men lifted Connor's body so that Jack could stand, but after he rose Jack took over and carried Connor to the medic tent alone.

Jack thought about how people always said tragedy happened in slow motion. Nothing was slow about Connor being gone. He was there, with his goofy grin suspended in time and then as quickly as a blink, he was gone. Jack placed Connor on the table in the medic tent and whispered to him that he'd trade places with him if he could.

When Jack returned to his own bunk and finally looked in the mirror, he realized the blood and dirt on his face would take scrubbing to get off. Jack wondered who would go to Connor's wife. Who would tell her that her husband wouldn't walk through their door?

Jack couldn't make himself message Eloise, and he couldn't call her either. There was so much he wanted to tell her, but he didn't want to bury her in his own pain. She had enough sadness of her own to last her multiple lifetimes. Was he allowed to be mad at her for that? It seemed wrong, but it also seemed unfair. Unfair that Jack could carry all her shit, but he never felt like she would be able to carry his. Or, maybe he'd never given her the chance. He wasn't sure he wanted to. He didn't like feeling weak or broken. He didn't want Eloise to feel like she had to be strong.

Jack didn't have words for watching Connor's head explode. The words to say that to Eloise didn't exist. He'd lost men, and women, before, but never like that. Chase got the sniper, but that hardly helped. He couldn't put all that into words, couldn't tell her the way it felt when Connor's blood splashed his face.

Jack rolled over that next morning and his hand hit his phone. He didn't have the words, the call would just be silence, but he needed to hear her voice. He dialed Eloise's cell by memory, instead of finding her contact.

"Jack, are you okay?" Eloise's voice cracked and Jack knew instantly that he wasn't the only one buried in pain.

"No. Are you?"

"No." Jack wanted to ask if it was work or Reagan, but he wasn't in a place to maker her feel better.

"Can you talk about it?"

"Can you?" Eloise asked.

"I don't have the words." Jack felt his face getting hot.

"I feel the same way."

"That's why I called. I needed to hear your voice. I needed to hear something that never fails to make me smile." Jack needed to be the selfish one. The realization made him want to puke.

"I'm sorry I can't give that to you, Jack. I'm so sorry." Her sobs carried through the phone and Jack's matched hers on the other end of the line. She couldn't be his happiness in that moment, and he couldn't be hers. They couldn't be the kind words or the loving thoughts. In that moment, the only thing they could do was listen to the other completely break and share in the tiny comfort that they had each other as the hellacious darkness engulfed them whole.

He eventually hung up because he couldn't bear hearing her when he couldn't do anything to ease her pain. Jack looked at the phone in his hand and thought about calling back. It tore him apart not being able to hold her while she cried.

Jack wasn't sure where to go from there. He'd never been that vulnerable before, not even with Eloise. He couldn't take it back or pretend it didn't happen. Whatever line they were trying not to cross had been bulldozed with that phone call.

Jack's fingertips hovered over the call button, Eloise's name still pulled up on his screen. He was never sure with Eloise, he just guessed what his next moves were and hoped she didn't react badly. He was going to message her as Chase walked in.

"First Sergeant said we're heading out," Chase told Jack.

"Now?" Jack stuffed his phone back in his pocket.

"Yeah. I don't know how he expects us to be in the head space for it, but we're going." Chase didn't meet Jack's eyes. "He said this is it. After this, we go home."

"Thank God." Jack had no clue where home was anymore, but if Eloise would let him, he'd call her home. That's what he needed to know. She was buying a house in Colorado, but did that have anything to do with him? She didn't make it seem like it did. Jack stood up, knowing he'd have to think about all that later, after whatever mission they were going on. The look in Chase's eyes confirmed that no one thought they'd survive another loss.

Eloise didn't realize Jack had hung up until her phone started to beep. She wasn't sure how long they'd cried together, but she was certain a shift happened during that call that could never be reversed. She didn't have to wonder if he felt the same way, because she knew that he did. They'd both crumbled, broke, and Eloise knew they'd never be the same. Hours before Jack called, she drove to school, and wondered if Jack had ever been her friend. There was always more between them when they were younger, but now she wasn't sure. Was there ever a line, or were they just tiptoeing through the fact that neither of them had ever drawn one? That was supposed to be her problem to solve that day.

Eloise knew it wouldn't be easy, stepping into Jack's world. He had always meant something, but now she would have to admit that. Now she would have to accept the risk of losing him, risk the darkness coming back if he ever went away for good. Jack was this force, and Eloise knew that's why she'd always kept him at arm's length. The two of them colliding would've been like diving into a black hole, no return, no surviving. Even at eighteen, she knew if she lost Jack, it would've killed her. Eloise walked into her empty classroom and sat at her desk. She got up to go to the bathroom before the bell, as she did every morning. She'd teach three classes in a row before she'd get another break. Eloise should've known something was wrong when the girl's bathroom door was locked. Teachers had their own bathrooms, but most of them checked the bathrooms for students throughout the day. That was how they made sure things like locked doors and students ditching class didn't happen. She pulled her lanyard from around her neck and put the master key in the hole. She pushed the door open and stepped from the hallway carpet to the bathroom tile. The hand dryer was directly in front of her and when she stepped toward it and then to her right, she hit her knees.

Eloise let out a scream that rang through the halls as she scooped Jasmine up in her arms, getting blood all over her clothes. The cuts on Jasmine's wrists were deeper than anything Eloise had ever seen. Jasmine's brown eyes were open, her makeup pristine, her long brown curls covered in blood. Eloise cradled Jasmine's head in her lap, begging and shaking her to wake up, unable to move from her knees. Eloise kept screaming, begging Jasmine to move, begging someone to help her. Eloise's tears fell from her cheeks, then lightly pushed Jasmine's eyelids closed to keep them safe from the salty water. The darkness took over, and the light left in a way that made Eloise think it would never return.

The noise of the sirens played in Eloise's ears long after the ambulance left the school. She didn't have the strength to teach that day, but couldn't leave her students with no one to talk to about Jasmine. She had to stay until each student was picked up.

Eloise sat on top of her desk and didn't try to hide her tears as her students came in. When the bell rang, Eloise's students stayed quiet. The ambulance had come and gone. They were aware that something had happened, but no one was sure what. Eloise thought about Jasmine's parents as she heard the intercom click on. The principal made the announcement of Jasmine's death brief, ending with the fact that the counselors would be available to any student who needed it. All eyes were on Eloise.

"Mrs. Masten," Antonio said. "We don't have to talk about it."

"Thank you," Eloise whispered, tears still streaming down her face. Antonio got up and grabbed Eloise's jacket off the back of her chair, handing it to her. Eloise slipped into it, zipping it up to cover the blood. Antonio sat back down, and Eloise loved him for his small gesture, knowing that right then she didn't stay because her students needed her, she stayed because she needed them.

Eloise didn't message Jack that day. She had no clue what to say. She didn't receive any messages either. Not that she'd checked. After the police questioned her, Eloise went home. She didn't get anything from her classroom. There was no point. Eloise wouldn't be grading tonight. Honestly, she didn't care if she ever saw her classroom again. She'd showered three times and still felt Jasmine on her. The way Mr. Maddux had looked at her as she walked out the door, he knew she wouldn't be back—not tomorrow at least, maybe not ever.

Eloise didn't sleep at all. She was still sitting in her recliner staring at the wall when the sun began to rise, no music, no television, no coffee. She wasn't sure how to break the trance, wasn't sure she even wanted to.

When Jack's call broke through the silence, her trance lifted, just long enough to worry about Jack. Just long enough that she was able to pick up the phone.

Eloise didn't want to push Jack away when she woke the next morning. Much to her surprise, she wanted to pull him to her, hold on to him for dear life. She couldn't tell him all the things she needed to, in a message, because she also needed to feel. Eloise wanted that ache in her hand from writing too long. She wanted to know that every ounce of emotion drenched the physical page.

Her morning had started with Eloise stopping to get coffee on her way to work, and later Jack would tell her that he had also started his morning with some crap that said coffee on the box but tasted like dirt. Years later, Eloise would wonder what would've happened had someone told her that morning, with the exception of losing Regan, if she went to work that day, she'd have the worst day of her life. Years later she knew without a doubt that Jack, too, would say it was the worst night of his.

Eloise shook out her hand and kept writing. She held back her tears so she wouldn't ruin the page. When she finished, she folded the letter and addressed the envelope. She wouldn't talk to Jack again until he read this letter. When Eloise lost Reagan, she stopped living. Losing Jasmine made her realize how incredibly selfish that was. Jasmine had the world at her feet and in an instant, she was gone. Eloise had to live for her, and for Reagan. She had to allow herself to heal, to be happy, to love, because the people she'd lost deserved that version of her.

CHAPTER 13

Eloise never went back to work. She just sent Mr. Maddux an email after not speaking to him for two days that said she couldn't do it. She never looked at her school email after that to see if he'd responded. Her heart felt shredded when she thought about the students she deserted, but if she didn't get out of Houston, any pieces of her that were still good would vanish. This year was dead set on wiping her off the face of the earth. If she didn't escape her tainted house and her now infected school, the torment would devour her and any chance at being okay would be gone forever.

Moving to Grand Junction happened quickly, much quicker than Eloise had originally planned. Before Jasmine, her intent was to finish the school year and house shop with Nickie and Gage. After quitting her job, she went online, found a few houses she liked, called Nickie and they picked one over the phone, which Eloise bought, sight unseen.

She didn't keep anything. Nothing. She posted online that she was having a moving sale and at the end of the day, the things that were left, she donated or threw in a dumpster. What remained from her life with Reagan, Jack had put in storage. Things she had every intention of leaving in that storage unit.

Eloise didn't have to book a flight, because she was going to drive Jack's truck. She left the day after Jasmine's funeral. Eloise was in a robotic mode, not fully aware of her actions until much later. She sold her car and everything except the clothes she wore and one extra set. She drove halfway to Colorado and booked a hotel. Eloise focused the next five days on finding the things she'd need to fill her home. She scoured online stores and made dozens of phone calls. The hotel felt oddly freeing, with only her and Rossi. Rossi officially owned more material items than Eloise, and something about that was funny to her.

Rossi was growing restless, even with being walked twice a day. When she unlocked the door to her new home, it was dark so she didn't bother walking the property. She didn't even have a place to sleep. It had been way too long since she'd talked to Jack, and as Eloise lay down on her new living room floor, she didn't have the energy to care that she didn't even own a pillow.

Jack sat on the edge of his cot, Eloise's letter felt entirely too heavy in his hand. He'd sent her message after message when he returned from his last mission. They were flying back to Colorado Springs today to start the debriefing process before being sent back to the new base in Grand Junction. Connor's death meant that each man in the unit had to see a counselor to determine whether they were still eligible to be redeployed. Jack placed a finger under the envelope flap and slid it open. Eloise hadn't answered a single message, or phone call, and now he was holding a letter that would likely put his heart threw a woodchipper. Why else would she mail him something? If it was good, wouldn't she have messaged him?

Jack closed his eyes and took a few deep breaths before he unfolded the paper.

Dear Jack,

I'm sorry I couldn't make myself message after we hung up that night. I'm sorry I didn't have the words and above all, I'm sorry I couldn't be your light when you needed one. I had to handwrite this letter. I needed to feel the words leave my soul through the pen.

The night you called me, I'd just gotten home from the school. I found a student, Jack, dead on the bathroom floor. Her name was Jasmine. She was in my class and she was a beautiful, young person who still had the world at her feet. Being the one to find her was too much. I literally felt something in me crack.

You had something happen to you too. I know that your soul shattered that day with mine. Somehow, I knew then that you and I would never be the same. There's no returning from what happened to me, and I know you'd say the same. I don't have to know what happened to realize that it will forever change you.

You've always been my lifeline. I can't explain how during every moment that threatens to kill me, you somehow find the words, and that night, the silence made me believe that I could keep going.

I loved Reagan, with every piece of me. Loving you is different. I've loved you for a long time. I pushed that away because I had Reagan, and he was wonderful, but he wasn't there the nights my existence was put into question...you were. I hate saying this. I hate saying I love you. I hate feeling it. I hate knowing that in loving you, I'll never get Reagan back. I know it's not your fault, but I blame you anyway. I blame you and I love you, and I know what I'm saying may push you away, but being able to be the raw version of myself that no one else sees, hell, that no one else even knows exists, is a huge part of my love for you.

If after this you still want to talk, send me a message or write me back. I wish I could be better for you.

I love you, always,

Eloise

Jack was at a loss. He told himself he wouldn't let this happen. He went to check on her, not to fall in love with her. Damn Eloise and everyone's inabilities to tell her no. He hated that about her. The way she always got what she wanted, but he loved it, too, in a way, because it meant she was happy. Eloise would rip him to shreds. God, he loved her. He loved her from the first day she walked into that theater at eighteen, but now it was different. It wasn't just her body or sex or lust, it was friendship and trust. It was months of messages, packages, and phone calls. It was knowing that she'd finally let him in, let him within reach.

Jack couldn't help but wonder what that would be like once he got back. They'd have so much to talk about. He'd go wherever, leave the Army if he had to, be as much in this as she'd allow. He just wasn't sure how much she'd actually allow. If he gave up everything, changed his whole life for her and she pushed him away, he wasn't sure he could live through that. He'd lost Eloise once, but he'd never really had her, or at least that's what he told himself. This would be a relationship, with labels, with attachments. It was something they'd had the entire time, but never said so out loud. Talking about it made it real, and Jack wasn't sure Eloise was ready for real.

Jack looked at the letter in his hand and reflected on what Eloise had said about the words leaving her soul. He needed that too. He carefully folded the letter, stuck it back in its envelope and then in his chest pocket, and went to find Chase.

"Chase," Jack yelled and found him at one of the tables with a few other men. "I need some paper." Jack remembered that Chase kept a couple of notebooks to write his wife. Everyone mostly used social media, but as Jack now knew, there was something about a physical letter.

"Writing Miss Eloise?" Chase stood and Jack followed him.

"She said she loves me." Jack slammed into Chase's back. "What the fuck?"

"Sorry." Chase turned to face him. "You shocked the shit outta me. She said what?"

"You heard me, man." Jack didn't want to tell Chase that Eloise had endured more trauma. He didn't want Chase to bring up the possibility that Eloise only said that because she was hurting and didn't have anyone else. He didn't want Chase to suggest that it didn't mean anything, that she'd take it back, or that once he was home and she had to face her written words, she'd cover them in friendship and destroy him in the process. Jack already felt those things. No, he didn't need Chase to say them.

"What are you going to do?" Chase started walking again.

"Write her back, if you ever give me paper."

"Not what I meant."

"The hell am I supposed to do, Chase? I've always loved her. Always. You suggesting I lie about that?"

"I'm suggesting that you protect yourself." Chase handed Jack a notebook and a pen.

"Will do." Jack turned to leave, but then stopped. "I'll try, Chase, but she's…"

"She's Eloise. After everything you've said, I get it. I just worry about you."

"Thanks, man." Jack held up the notebook and then walked out of Chase's quarters.

When Jack was back to his own bunk, and staring at a blank page, handwriting a letter suddenly felt like an impossible task.

Eloise,

I have to start this letter by saying I wish I could have been there the day you found Jasmine. I feel sick about you having to face that alone. You're always my light, El. Don't ever doubt that. Even when we're both in the dark, it's always you who brings me back.

Something did happen to me that day, and you're right, I'll never be the same again. I've seen a lot of men die, Eloise, but this was different. I was right in it. So close that it could've been me. It's gut-wrenching—feeling like you're drowning in pain over the loss while also taking a full breath because it wasn't you who died. The guilt over feeling relieved is what eats at me.

It's okay to hate loving me. I don't even mind you blaming me. If you need someone to take it out on, if that's what will help you heal, then I can be that for you. I've never been afraid of you loving me, Eloise. I'm afraid of the loss. I never pushed for more, because I knew if we had it and you still left, it'd shred me apart from the inside out. I've never not loved you. I'll be your boyfriend, your husband, your best friend. I'll be anything you want, but you have to tell me what that is, and you have to mean it.

I'm all in, but, El, please, please, I beg you, if you truly love me, make sure that you are all in, too, before you tell me what's next. The love has always been there, beautiful, on both our sides. It's just a matter of what we're going to do about it. As always, the ball is in your court.

I love you, forever,
Jack

W hen Jack's letter finally came, Eloise felt like she could breathe again. She'd read through all the messages he'd sent in between Jasmine's death and waiting for her letter. She had to be hurting him by not replying but waiting was important. She needed him to know how she felt, and for him to tell her where his head was before she could go on answering messages like nothing had changed.

He wanted her to be sure. She felt sure, but understood his concern. Eloise didn't exactly have the best track record when it came to sticking around. Jack's love for her was so extreme that it was uncomfortable. Eloise didn't know what to do with that at eighteen. She wasn't ready for it. She wasn't ready for it when she lost Reagan. But, she felt ready now. Eloise twisted the wedding band on her finger. She didn't want loving Jack to mean forgetting Reagan. She wanted to love them both, cherish them both. She believed Jack could give her that. She wanted to believe Reagan was happy for her. She had to believe that Reagan was okay with Jack, she had to believe that to stay sane.

Eloise was cracked open in a way she wasn't before. It was as though losing Reagan sent a vibration through her body and then finding Jasmine ripped that line wide open. Eloise wanted to bask in her love for Jack. She needed to feel the happiness that came with that. She needed to tie herself to him so that she didn't dissolve into the black hole that lurked nearby. Jasmine changed everything, because Eloise understood now that the guilt and the pain would be there regardless of whether or not she let Jack in all the way.

Before she was afraid of losing herself in Reagan, but now she was afraid of allowing herself to be lost in Jack. She was scared that she didn't know who she was on her own, but Eloise didn't want to be on her own. Nickie had told her it was okay to be a person who loved other people, and Eloise didn't want to be anybody else. She loved Reagan, and a piece of her died the day he did. But, a lot of her stayed, tiny shards of broken glass, glass that Jack had somehow glued back together, and she loved him too. She was done denying that.

Eloise opened her brand-new laptop. Her house was still very empty, but she had bought a bed, bedding, a laptop, and some clothes. She opened Facebook Messenger and found Jack's name.

> *Jack-*
> *I got your letter. I won't pretend I know how this is going to go. I can't promise that I won't have sad days, that I won't miss Reagan, or that I'll ever stop loving him. The fact is I love you both. Right now, in this moment, I love Reagan and I love you. I don't want to hide from that anymore. I pushed it away, because I thought if I said I loved you, it meant I didn't love him, but that's just not true. I've loved you since the first day I laid eyes on you, and for a long time that was suppressed because Reagan was with me and I fell in love with him too. Loving him didn't mean I stopped loving you, and I know now that loving you doesn't mean I stop loving him. I hope I'm making sense, and I hope you can be okay with me having both. If I'm being really honest, I'm hoping that somewhere out there Reagan is okay with me having both too.*

*You said you were all in. I'm all in, Jack. I'll
probably stumble through this. I know I'll make
mistakes. I know it'll be hard because so many
days I feel like Reagan is still here, and there's
going to be times when that's not fair to you.
But, I want this. I want you. I'm absolutely
terrified, but I'm not running.*
Always,
Eloise

J ack sat in Grand Junction and read Eloise's message. He needed to tell her that his unit had returned. She wanted this, him, words he never thought she'd say. Jack was petrified. Giving in meant the risk of losing her if she decided to bolt when things got hard. Telling her no meant he'd already lost her before giving them a chance. Jack hit Eloise's number on his phone.

"Hello." Eloise answered before the second ring.

"Hey, beautiful," Jack said.

"How are you?"

"Reading your message has me pretty freaking happy."

"I'm glad you called. I love hearing your voice."

"Did you notice where I called from?"

"Your cell phone!" Eloise screamed. "I didn't even realize when your name, instead of just a number, came up. You're home?"

"Back at Fort Gunnison, yeah."

"I'm really happy you're back safe, Jack."

"I was thinking, maybe you could come see me." Jack sucked in a breath, moment of truth.

"I'd love to." Eloise didn't hesitate. Jack silently thanked God that she hadn't changed her mind.

"I'll get you a plane ticket. I can email the details to you."

"Actually, I can drive. Then you can have your truck back."

"Huh?"

"I moved. Well, sort of. I bought a house and I drove your truck here. I didn't pack or move anything, per say."

"Wow, El. Congratulations. In that case, I'll text you my address." Jack was stunned. He had never entertained the possibility of her being in Grand Junction when he returned. "I spent a few days in Colorado Springs, but I'm back now. We lost four men on this mission. That's a huge hit. We all had to see a counselor. I still have a few meetings." Jack spoke quickly, as though the negative parts of this could spoil everything else if he lingered on them too long.

"I can't wait to see you," Eloise said, then surprised Jack when she continued. "I can't believe that I'll be able to touch you in a matter of hours."

"I can't wait either. I'll message you the details, and then call you back."

"I'll be waiting," Eloise said before he hung up.

Eloise looked in the mirror for the fiftieth time. She was mad at herself for being the reason Jack doubted her so much. If it took the rest of her life, she'd prove to him that she meant it when she finally admitted how much he meant to her. She checked every detail, her tight moss green sweater, her black pants, her knee-high black boots. She shook out her freshly curled hair and pursed her lips. She looked good and she knew it. She felt a pang in her chest at the thought of wanting to look hot for a man who wasn't Regan. She twisted the band on her finger.

"Please understand, babe" she said to her empty bathroom.

Eloise held her breath when she saw Jack standing in his driveway waiting for her. He looked so different. The eight months apart had hardened him. His arms were much bigger, his face more defined, his hair almost shaved off, and his eyes were even blacker. He didn't smile or look her way. Eloise wondered if he wished he hadn't asked her to come. He definitely didn't look happy to see her.

"Eloise." Jack's voice was a whisper as she stepped out of his truck.

"Welcome home, Jack," she said, looking up at him. He leaned down, stopping just shy of her lips.

"Eloise." When he spoke it this time, her name sounded like a question. She knew he was waiting on her. She reached her hand up and gently stroked his now bare cheek before she closed the rest of the distance between them. For the first time in ten months, Eloise's full attention was on the moment she was in, and not on her past.

Jack had her in his arms and off the ground in seconds, twirling her before he set her down. "You look beautiful. Thank you for coming."

"Well, after talking to you for eight months, it was hard to say no." She took his hand and watched as he looked at her ring. She wasn't sorry she wore it, and she wouldn't say she was.

"I'm really glad you're here."

"Me, too, Jack." Eloise squeezed his fingers.

"Chase would love to meet you while we're back. If you're okay with that." Jack started walking toward his front door, pulling Eloise with him.

"That'd be nice."

Jack stopped at the door. Eloise wondered if he'd ask her to spend the night, but he didn't speak. She could spend every night there and it wouldn't be enough. She locked on his eyes and loved that she didn't see any fear, any hesitation. She didn't drop her eyes, she needed him to know she wanted to be there with him.

"Eloise, if this is too much…" Again, his eyes found her ring. Eloise did nothing but think about this moment since she wrote him that letter. It took writing it for her to realize that they were both afraid of the same thing. They were both so paralyzed by the thought of losing the other, that she wasn't sure they'd ever get to have each other. She kept telling herself to let him all the way in. She had crossed the imaginary line, she opened that door, Jack just had to walk through it. She could do this, she prayed she could do this without pushing him back out again.

"It's not. It's just different, you know? Having you as a friend all these months has been a lifesaver, but transitioning to something else, it's going to take getting used to."

"I'll wait. You call all the shots, okay?"

"You'll just wait?"

"Eloise, I've been waiting on you for over fifteen years. I hate that we're here because of what happened to your husband, but we are here, and I'll never take that for granted. I'll always wait." He leaned down and placed a kiss on her cheek, squeezing her hand as he did.

Jack pushed his front door open. Eloise was seeing a side of Jack she'd never seen, adult Jack, mature Jack. His house was a testament to just how much had changed over the last ten years. Jack walked Eloise through the house, showing her each room. Eloise giggled at how excited Jack got over his kitchen, and she knew he'd be cooking for her tonight just by the look on his face.

After Jack had sent her his address, she started researching fun things to do in the area. She hadn't been living here long enough to know what to do and she wanted to surprise him with something fun as a welcome home present.

Jack opened the door to his guest room, and Eloise realized

that she had no clue where his head was with sex. She had no idea where hers was either.

"I know I didn't ask, but you can stay, if you want to." Jack shut the door.

"I live close, Jack, less than twenty minutes."

"Not the point, Eloise."

"I know." Eloise pushed herself up against Jack, leaning her weight into him. She wanted to kiss him, wanted to remind him again that she was incredibly happy to see him. When their lips touched, she swore she felt him relax.

Eloise pulled out of the kiss and was rewarded with Jack's dancing eyes.

"I'll stay. I have no clothes, no makeup, nothing, but I barely have that shit at home. I'll stay." She had to find a way to make him see that she was serious about this, that she wasn't going to run away.

"Great." Jack's smile always amazed her. He smiled so much when she first met him, but all these years later, it seemed like he kept his smile mostly hidden.

Jack held his hand out and Eloise took it.

"Jack, I have a surprise for you."

"Is it that you want to sleep in my spare room?"

"No." Eloise laughed. "Though I wasn't sure how you felt about sleeping in the same bed."

"Eloise, if one of my options is a bed with you, I choose that, regardless of what the other choice is."

"Okay, so maybe I wasn't sure about how I felt about it."

"Fair enough. I told you, we're taking this at your speed."

Jack walked Eloise to his room last, held the door open, and let her walk through first. She set her purse on a chair he had in the corner and wondered if he'd ever stop being so considerate all the time.

"So, how should we take Junction by storm?"

"Well, now that you asked, that's your surprise." Eloise walked over to her purse and unzipped the outer pocket. She handed Jack the envelope with their concert tickets.

"Rodeo tickets *and* we're going to three concerts? You really outdid yourself, El. Thank you. This is amazing."

"Welcome home." Eloise tiptoed to kiss him. She didn't resist as he grabbed hold of her shirt and fell to his bed, pulling her on top of him.

CHAPTER 14

Eloise and Jack walked into the rodeo hand in hand. Eloise looked exquisite in her dress and boots, and Jack felt good in his black T-shirt and jeans. Every few feet there was something else to see and smell. As they walked, Eloise told Jack that she'd only been to the rodeo once before, with her aunt, and she was happy to find something that she and Jack could share that wasn't a part of who she was with Reagan.

"Do you want to eat first?" Jack asked.

"Yeah, there's a ton to choose from." Eloise pulled his arm toward the tent with the food vendors.

When Eloise and Jack sat down, they had a pile of fries, two fried Snickers, two strawberry margaritas in tall, plastic, guitar-shaped cups, and enough fried shrimp to feed Jack's entire unit. Everything here was fried and delicious.

When they finished eating, Jack went for strawberry margarita number two and Eloise ordered a pina colada. He held her hand again, and when she didn't pull away he hoped it was because she liked his touch and not because she felt that she couldn't.

Eloise stopped Jack at a booth selling towels. She said she wanted to pick out some decorative ones for her new kitchen. The next booth had handcrafted signs and Jack watched as she looked through those as well.

"I don't want the house to be too girly, so you have to help pick stuff out. You're going to live there too," Eloise said as she browsed.

"I have a house, El." Jack wondered where that had come from. There was no slow transition with Eloise, no build up. She went from cautious to balls-deep in what seemed fast to Jack, making him worried about something that should make him excited.

Jack watched Eloise's face fall. He loved the thought of always being with her, even if they stayed just as they were now. Jack had never pressured her for more. Not when they were kids, and he wouldn't now either. Jack would let things go at her pace, always putting the ball in her court. He wasn't doing it because she lost her husband, he was doing it because he always did. As she stood there, decorative towels in hand, watching him stare at her, he wished he could stop being so damn considerate and thoughtful and careful. For the first time, he wished he could dive headfirst into his feelings for her.

Jack remained silent while Eloise shopped, and he knew that after his last comment, she wouldn't dare ask for his opinion again.

Jack didn't want to interfere, not because he didn't care, but because he didn't think it was his place. She had built and furnished a home before, with another man. This home should be hers. She worked for it, had earned it. He wasn't sure why she suddenly seemed upset about that. Jack wanted to be long term, but he wasn't sure Eloise would ever be ready for that. Her ring was still on her finger and he could tell when something reminded her of Reagan. Jack didn't want to push her, but he didn't want to wait forever if she'd never be ready.

That was the hardest part for Jack, he'd already lost Eloise once and wasn't sure he could do it again. He had awful self-esteem in college, something he went to great lengths to hide. He was extremely versed in putting on an act. Jack always smiled and was the social butterfly. He exacerbated confidence on the outside. The real reason he never put a label on them was because he never thought he deserved her. She was too good for him. She still was. At nineteen he knew he'd shatter if she told him no, so he just rode it out. Jack enjoyed every minute she spent with him and when she left there was no discussion, no breakup needed. It about killed him when she left the final time, but it would've been worse had he been referring to her as his girlfriend the entire time. The lack of a label gave his brain the distance he needed to survive her going away.

Now, he would be forced to do the same. Jack would stay with Eloise as long as she'd let him. He would cherish every kiss, and remember each time she let her walls down and allowed him to comfort her. When she left again, or told him to leave, there'd be no need for a breakup or a conversation because Jack wouldn't put a label on them in the first place.

Jack never felt like Eloise wanted him in the forever type of way, but at the same time, he never minded being the guy she called, loved it actually. He and his brother used to joke about it. Drake always said something like "you're what she wants tonight" anytime Jack's phone would ring. Their chemistry was unmatchable, making him crave her in a physical way. She went to him when she was lonely.

Nickie wasn't kidding when she said Eloise was impossible to say no to. Eloise always seemed to get what she wanted, and Jack was fine being what she wanted, even if it only lasted for a while. When they were together, she made him feel like he was the only thing she needed, and right now, if he could help her survive, he would, even if it killed him. He told her to be sure, but hadn't brought up calling this a real relationship, a commitment. Eventually the other shoe would drop.

❤

Eloise guessed she should stop thinking that this would end up going somewhere. Jack kept saying he'd wait, but then would say something like he had his own house. Eloise couldn't risk her heart again for a "maybe."

Eloise had too many bags to carry, so she handed three of them to Jack. They walked out to his truck to drop them off before sitting down for the rodeo. She loved watching the men rope and ride and couldn't wait to have a horse of her own. The metal stadium seats were a bit cold, and Eloise smiled as Jack wrapped his arm around her. A few people gave them looks, but Eloise didn't care. She wasn't sure if it was because she wore a ring and he didn't, or because they were snuggled so close together, or if it was because Jack looked so dark next to her pale skin. Regardless of why, people could shove it.

Eloise leaned up and kissed Jack's cheek, his smile forming under her mouth. He was such a force. He squeezed her in closer.

"Having fun?" Jack asked.

"I'm having a blast. What about you? How do you feel about your first rodeo?"

"I think it's great. I'm excited for tonight."

"Me too." She turned her head up so he could kiss her lips, and for a moment, she forgot her pain and her sadness and let Jack kiss it away.

There was a certain choreography to the rodeo events. Barrel racers, roping, and Eloise's favorite, team roping. Jack cheered when Eloise didn't expect it and she enjoyed watching him almost as much as the riders. The bull riding seemed to be Jack's favorite. He even stood up a few times, grabbing Eloise's arm until the buzzer sounded.

"Do you want to eat or anything before the concert starts?" Eloise asked Jack when the last rider was done.

"I think another drink is a good idea." Jack stood up and reached for Eloise's hand. She took it and stood, smoothing out her dress.

"I may have to grab my jacket out of your truck."

"We can do that." Jack let Eloise head up the stadium stairs first, following close behind.

Eloise grabbed her jacket out of Jack's truck as he opened his console and placed three twenty-dollar bills in his wallet.

"You think we'll drink sixty more dollars?" Eloise asked, poking him in his side.

"You never know." Jack winked and locked the truck. The walk back through the parking lot was more exciting than when they arrived that afternoon. There were a lot more people, and Eloise liked looking at all the different types of boots. There were women in worn boots, boots that said they actually worked while wearing them. And there were women like Eloise, who wore boots because they liked them, or because they thought they were cute, and it had nothing to do with working in them.

Eloise hoped that would change for her soon. She wanted her boots to be dirty and worn. She couldn't wait for the day she not only had a working farm, but then could use that farm to help save animals. The vision she had included using farm work to help finance animal adoptions, but it went beyond that. She wanted to get up early, clean stalls, brush horses, and haul hay. She wanted to hear the crunch of snow and see her breath all winter long as she broke through frozen water troughs. She needed to become the woman she had always pictured herself. She was worried more about that dream now, because Reagan wouldn't be there to help her make it a reality. It was a dream he encouraged her to chase, but now she was on her own and dreaming for the both of them.

Eloise and Jack ended up in almost the same seats, but two rows closer to the stage. Eloise was near giddy with excitement and Jack looked like he'd burst at the first chord. It wasn't long before the lights were off and an enormous circular stage was being positioned in the center of the arena. When the lights on the stage came on and that first note played, the stage started rotating, ensuring that all sides of the stadium would get a view. Eloise had seen it before and watched Jack discover it for the first time, taking in every piece of his marvelous smile.

"This is amazing," Jack screamed over the music.

"Great, right?" Eloise squeezed his hand.

The sets during the rodeo were only an hour long, but they'd be back tomorrow and the next day, so Eloise wasn't sad when the concert was over, knowing sleeping wasn't too far off.

Jack opened the passenger-side door for Eloise before getting in himself. He drove to his house without saying anything, and Eloise found herself thinking about all the ways in which Jack and Reagan were similar, and all the things that made them different. Reagan was more reserved than Jack. Jack was comfortable being the center of attention, at least he always was when they were in college. Reagan was a fixer. When Eloise told him about a problem or how she was feeling, his reaction was to fix it. Jack wasn't like that. Jack was a listener. He never tried to fix or change anything for or about Eloise. She usually loved that about him, but sometimes she hated it too. Jack never pushed Eloise, not like Reagan did. Reagan and Jack weren't afraid to call her out, but they did so for entirely different reasons. Reagan would push her, encourage her to reach a goal, ask for better or for more, and to make Eloise question herself. Jack did it when he thought

Eloise was being an ass. Jack took a more passive approach when it came to criticizing, and Eloise wasn't sure if that would always be a good thing. It was like Jack knew but wanted Eloise to come to the conclusion on her own.

J ack held Eloise's hand resting on the middle console. He liked Colorado. There was a time in his life when he never thought he'd wind up here. It's funny that he was here now with Eloise. She was always the one who got away. He just never knew how to hold on to her. She was always this wild thing in his eyes, this creative and fun girl when they met who just plowed through every obstacle put in her way, and now she was this unstoppable woman. She'd overcome so much and even though he knew she felt broken, he never saw her that way. He just wished he had the courage to say that to her. When they had met, he was scared of his feelings for her. Nineteen-year-old Jack was nowhere near ready for Eloise, for a girl who would turn into the forever woman. That was stupid. He kicked himself daily for that now. He should have held on to her, shouldn't have taken her friendship for granted. Eloise was there for him in a way no one had ever been, so he assumed she always would be, but then one day she was married and ten years had flown by without them speaking.

The little lights lining Jack's driveway were shining bright when they pulled in.

"I'm going to get water. Want one?" Eloise asked Jack as he unlocked his front door.

"Sure, thanks." Jack liked that she seemed comfortable at his house.

Eloise pulled two water bottles out of the fridge and placed them on the counter. Then she opened his freezer and laughed loud enough that Jack had to see what she found.

"Eloise what in the…?"

Eloise held up the ice cream sandwiches and watched as Jack threw his head back in a roar of laughter.

"If we're doing that again, I'm going to have to buy more ice cream." He could barely get the words out.

Eloise looked down at the ice cream in her hand and Jack saw himself at nineteen. The two of them naked and lying in his bed, with an unopened twenty-four pack of ice cream sandwiches. They spent the entire night eating ice cream and having sex. It was glorious. By morning, the box was empty and they were so tired they slept the day away.

"I think we'll start with one each this time." Eloise handed him the ice cream and picked up the water bottles. Jack was still smiling when Eloise skipped from his kitchen to his bedroom, shutting the door behind her.

When Jack opened his bedroom door, Eloise's mood had sobered as she stared at him in the doorway. She set the water bottles on his nightstand and started to rip the paper off her ice cream. They stood there like statues, the bed glaring at them as if daring them to lie down right that instant.

"Reconsidering the guest room?"

"Jack…" Eloise looked at the bed, the window, the door, anywhere other than Jack's face.

"It's okay, Eloise." Jack took a few steps forward. "I'll take the guest room, how's that?"

"Terrible. I'm going to shower." Eloise sidestepped into his bathroom, still refusing to look at him.

Jack placed his hand on the bathroom knob. It wasn't locked. He knew it wouldn't be. Jack wasn't the type to barge in. He wasn't even the type to knock. Eloise knew he'd leave her alone.

Jack knew coming back would be an adjustment, especially after everything they'd been through the last eight months, but he had no clue that it would be so awkward. He wanted to jump her right then, but the voice in his head kept telling him that was an awful idea.

Jack was split in two. Half of him blamed Eloise for being unsure and then there was his own uncertainty. Were either of them ready for a full-fledged, committed relationship?

Jack sat on the bed while he waited for Eloise. He wouldn't bother her when she clearly didn't want him to. He was always good at reading her and that made him smile. Eloise was—could be—a complicated woman, but some things hadn't changed. She still avoided his eyes when she didn't want to talk about something, avoided anything serious, avoided conflict, and avoided her feelings for him. He never told her before how he felt, but it wouldn't have mattered. She never would have gone for it then. He thought it was because she was afraid of the intensity, and maybe she was. He'd tell her this time around, though. He wouldn't waste this second chance. If she wanted to push him away after everything she'd said in her letter, he wasn't going to make it easy on her.

Jack tried no to picture Eloise undressing in the safety of his bathroom. Eloise was never a fling. Even when they were in college, he knew she always cared deeply about him. It was different then, though. They were so young, kids really, and just open about everything. There weren't any secrets, but there also wasn't any pain. Jack's pain grew out of losing his brother, starting with when he dropped out of school and the scars he had now were the reason for his seriousness when he'd never been the serious type.

That was partially an excuse. Jack had grown up, and he had to believe she saw the changes in him over the last ten years.

They were similar in that way. Their smiles not as bright, or as frequent. The darkness in their eyes deeper, and the lines in their faces betraying their true feelings. Jack had been through much more than she knew, because he spent so much time focused on her problems.

Eloise flung open the bathroom door stopping Jack's thoughts and walked out wrapped in a towel. Jack was sitting on the bed, flipping through the channels.

"I left everything out here." She looked at him without turning toward him, then started unzipping her bag. Eloise had nothing when she arrived earlier that day, but she and Jack had stopped at her house before the rodeo so that she could pack an overnight bag. Jack looked at her by the bag now, and thought Eloise would ask to go home, but she stayed quiet as she pulled clothes out.

"Right." Jack placed a hand over his mouth so he wouldn't laugh. He stood up, threw the remote on the bed and walked over to her, touching her shoulder lightly to turn her to face him. "Eloise," he whispered as he kissed her. Eloise melted into him, clutching the towel so hard she thought her fingers may rip the fabric. Jack wouldn't push her, but she could stop him. Jack felt Eloise take one deep breath through their kiss and then she released the towel.

Jack's hand dug into her wet hair, pulling her body into his, her dampness leaving icy water marks he could feel through his clothes. He pulled back, abruptly breaking their kiss. He looked at her body and she stood there, mouth slightly open, letting him.

"God, Eloise, ten years and you've barely changed." He pulled his shirt over his head and Eloise stepped up to touch the tattoo on his chest. He knew she'd always loved that tattoo.

She pushed his shoulder and he laughed under his breath, knowing she wanted him to turn around. He turned slowly and stopped as she ran her fingers over the ink. She pressed against his back and ran her hands down his arms before nudging him again so he'd face her.

"You were always a sucker for tattoos." He leaned down and kissed her collarbone. "We can stop." Jack looked her in the eye. "We can stop and it won't change anything."

"I want this. I want you." Eloise placed her hand on the back of his neck, pulling him to her. "I've never *not* wanted this." Jack knew that was the truth. Right or wrong didn't matter, Eloise and Jack wanted one another since the first day their eyes met and no amount of time had changed that. It started because of the physical attraction, but that was only part of what had the two of them standing there ten years later.

"How about you get dressed, I'll shower real quick, and we'll eat more ice cream?" Jack picked up Eloise's towel off the floor. Eloise frowned and then bit her lip, her eyebrows squishing together as Jack held out her towel.

"What?" She wrapped the towel around herself. "You don't want this?"

"I do, believe me I do, but not like this, not some quick thing we do in the heat of the moment. I know you don't believe me, and I know that version of me you used to know wouldn't have said this, but I want you. All of you, not just the sex, not like before. I want the real thing, and I don't think this would mean that for you. Not yet." Jack rubbed a hand over his hair.

"Oh." Eloise bit her lip and looked away from Jack. He felt awful that she looked like she was about to cry. She was about to sleep with someone who wasn't her husband, and he said no. Jack had never said no before, not once. Eloise would frequently text him in the middle of the night, usually after a horrible day and ask, *wanna have sex,* and he was waiting for her at his apartment. It never mattered what he was doing before that, or if she woke him up, or if he had plans, he'd be there when she arrived at his place at all hours of the night and early morning. Eloise sat on the bed, looking at the floor. Jack considered sitting next to her, considered reassuring her, but his body turned away from hers. He sauntered to the bathroom shutting the door behind him. He'd never told her no.

Jacked turn the water on, and stripped off the rest of his clothes. How could he tell her no? She couldn't think of a single time he'd ever told her no, about anything, but especially not about sex. Unlike Jack, Eloise didn't give a care in the world whether or not he wanted to be alone, something he was reminded of the second she barged in without knocking.

"What the hell, Jack?" Eloise screamed at him through the glass shower door.

"I was in here asking myself the same question." He continued to lather soap over his body. Eloise wouldn't be able to see anything through the foggy glass.

"You've never told me no."

"Another thing I, too, was just telling myself." Jack let the water run down his face.

"Jack, this isn't funny."

"I know, I mean I don't know, it's a little funny. Plus, I meant what I said, El. I'm in this for the long haul and I just don't know that you are." Jack could see her circling the small space between the shower and the door.

"First off, how dare you tell me some bullshit like that. I told you I was all in. I said it, Jack. Second, since when was this not about sex for you? That was always who we were. We were the friends with benefits, the sex anytime, anywhere people. We'd send pictures and videos and if we were within five feet of each other and not at work, we were naked. Hell, Jack, sometimes at work we were almost completely naked."

"It's always been more, and you know it. We were just always too scared to admit it." Jack stood under the water. He was ready to get out, but wouldn't until she left.

"I wasn't scared, Jack, but I knew you weren't boyfriend material."

"I never slept with anyone else when we were messing around, never."

"Neither did I, but that's not the point."

"It's one of the points."

"Maybe so, but we were going in two different directions. You really think we would have made it through me graduating, Drake dying, you dropping out, you enlisting, me moving. My God, Jack, we had everything working against us."

"We'll never know now, will we? Oh, and don't forget my mom." Jack's anger climbed up his throat, threatening to erupt. He tried to swallow it, but it only grew.

"What?" Eloise stopped pacing the bathroom.

"My mom. She's gone too. We probably wouldn't have made it through that either, Miss Pessimistic."

"Jesus, Jack, I'm so sorry, I didn't know." Eloise stepped up to the glass with every intention of opening the door.

"Don't, El. Just let me finish taking a shower." Jack watched her hand slide down the glass. Letting her walk out of the bathroom and shut the door was near impossible, but he did. He wasn't sure what else to do, so he slowly counted to twenty before shutting the water off.

Jack walked back into his room and saw the tiny ball of Eloise underneath his blankets, a sure sign that she didn't want to talk this out. That right there was always her problem. She couldn't just face something, just have that blowup, scream, get it all out. No, not Eloise, she had to give him the silent treatment until her mood changed because God forbid they actually talked through anything serious. She liked to blame him for not being boyfriend material at nineteen, but she was no prize back then either.

Jack was too mad to try and reason with her, so he got dressed, not bothering to hide himself while doing it. If she looked, he didn't care. It wasn't like she hadn't seen it all anyway. He imagined he hadn't changed much either. Jack climbed into his bed, kicking one leg out of his covers and faced his back to Eloise. If she wanted to avoid him, he figured two could play that game.

CHAPTER 15

When Eloise rolled over the next morning, it was early. Jack's back was still to her and she outlined his muscles with her eyes as she watched his shoulders rise and fall. She felt terrible about last night and would have to apologize. It wasn't Jack's fault that Reagan was gone, and it certainly wasn't his fault that she kept him at arm's length. She supposed she was always that way. Jack was, too, when they were younger, but it didn't seem like he was now. Or, maybe it was just her always pushing him away. She used to think they weren't capable of being serious back in college, of being the people they'd have to be for their relationship to endure time, but maybe he was and she'd just missed all the signs.

Eloise put herself as close as she could to his back and wrapped one arm over the top of him. She felt him stir, and when she was pretty sure he was awake, she put her mouth to his ear.

"Jack, I'm sorry."

Jack rolled over to face her, looking in her eyes before wrapping her up in his arms.

"It's okay, El. I'm sorry too. I shouldn't have thrown my mom at you like that." Jack released her and she shifted her body until she was comfortable.

"What happened?"

"After my brother died, she just sort of lost it. She'd always had a bit of a drinking problem, you knew that. It got a lot worse when Drake died. I was at work one day, not even two weeks after I dropped out, which also really hurt her, and I got a phone call that she'd been taken to the hospital. She took a shit ton of pills, which she washed down with enough alcohol to kill a horse."

Eloise rested her hand on Jack's arm, scooting in a bit closer to him.

"You were right, about what you said before, about saying I'm sorry," Jack continued. "I'm sorry leaves the expected response of 'it's okay,' and nothing about death leaves you feeling okay."

Eloise wrapped her arms around him, promising herself she'd be better for him, be there for him like he had been for her. Jack's pain was almost worse, because he had kept it bottled up inside him. When Eloise lost Reagan, she had a chance to mourn with people who mostly supported her—her mother, uncle, and Nickie. And Jack.

Jack had no one when he lost the two people who made up his family.

Eloise just held Jack and neither of them said anything for a while, until Jack pulled back and moved some of Eloise's hair out of her face. He leaned down and kissed her.

"Thank you, Eloise."

"Jack, I can be your person, too, you know. You've been so good to me these last few months. You've been the only thing holding me together through all this. But, you've never once opened up and just let me be that for you."

"Eloise, don't get mad, but you weren't really in a position to be there for me before today." Jack kept his hand on the side of her face, his fingers stroking her cheek.

"Fair enough. I'm sorry, Jack." Eloise moved from under his hand and kissed his cheek. "I can be there now."

"You've always been there, El. That's what I wish you'd understand. Regardless of what's said or not said, or the amount of time that passes, I know you, I've always known you, and you've always made me better." Jack pulled her on top of him and wrapped his arms around her so she couldn't move.

"You, too, Jack. I know you don't believe it, but your positivity when we were kids, God, Jack, I was so broken, so lost when I went to college, and you put me back together. I don't know if you ever knew that." Eloise fell into his embrace, her head on his chest.

"I knew you were searching for yourself, and I thanked God every day that I was the one to find you." Jack squeezed his arms tight for a split second before loosening them again. "I still think we should take this slow. There weren't expectations before, you were right about that last night. I think at some points we both wanted commitment, but neither of us took the chance. I'm taking the chance now, and I think we just need to get settled and let the intensity of me getting back mellow out, and then see where your head is at."

Eloise thought about where her head was. It hurt to admit that it had never left Jack. It was easy to ignore her feelings for Jack when she had Reagan. It was easy to justify her choice in marrying Reagan when he was alive. Eloise didn't like thinking she'd made the wrong choice, because she didn't like thinking of her marriage to Reagan as wrong. With him gone, though, that thought crept up a lot. The one that said she could have spared herself a lot of pain had she never ended things with Jack. The thought that she may have loved Reagan, but only chose him because he was safe, because he was a sure thing when Jack wasn't, yet, it was Jack who was with her now.

"My head has always been with you, Jack. I loved Reagan. I

love Reagan. I won't pretend I didn't, and I won't say he wasn't an incredible man and husband, because he was. But, you always stayed in my thoughts. I didn't talk to you because I knew there was a line that I couldn't cross being married, and talking to you would have made it too easy to step over."

"I get that. I don't blame you for putting your marriage first."

"Thank you. And I meant what I said. I *do* want this. But I understand your hesitation, and when I'm ready to let all the way go"—Eloise followed Jack's eyes to her ring—"you'll be the first to know." Eloise rolled over to get up and Jack smacked her butt. "Hey."

"Slow, doesn't mean sloth speed." Jack laughed.

"Get up, get ready, let's go get breakfast." Eloise pulled her shirt over her head and threw it at him, twirling as she did. If he was going to make her wait, she was going to enjoy every minute of teasing him. When Eloise shut the bathroom door this time, she felt as if she were floating and drowning all at once. Jack made her come alive, but the guilt she felt was ever present and frequently reminded her that she had a husband. She had her chance to be with Jack before and didn't take it, and all she was doing now was betraying her husband.

Eloise was washing her face at the sink when she heard the door open. Her eyes were closed and she was rinsing off her soap.

"Is it too late to take it back?" Jack whispered next to her ear.

"What changed?" She reached for her towel, eyes still shut, and patted her face dry. Jack ran his hands up her still bare sides.

"When you walked in here, I got to thinking." He kissed her neck and brought his right hand up to her nipple. Eloise sucked in a hard breath. "I could wait for you to be ready and do that in misery. Or, I could fuck you in this bathroom and anywhere else you'll let me until you're ready, and that just sounds more fun." Jack tugged at her nipple, making her ride the line between pleasure and pain, which Eloise loved.

"And if I'm never ready?" She would have banged his brains out last night, but he said no. He made her think twice instead of just going with it then, and now the roles were reversed and Eloise wasn't sure what to do. Seconds before he walked in there, her guilt was taking over. What if he was right? What if they needed to wait? Jack dropped his hand and turned her around.

"When was it not about sex? Isn't that what you said?" Jack's eyes burned into her soul.

"You reminded me that it was always about more, remember?"

"But it was about that, too, the chemistry, the physical attraction, the inability to stay away from each other." Jack's mouth slammed into hers.

Eloise immediately grabbed his arms, running her hands down them and smiling through their kiss. Jack pulled back and Eloise's face fell.

"What now?" Eloise tried to slow her breathing.

"Can we do this?" Jack's hands found Eloise's waist and drew her into him.

Eloise hated this. He loved her, she believed that. He'd loved her for a long time, and now here she was offering herself to him again and he was hesitating, again. Eloise couldn't take no, she couldn't handle any more pain or disappointment. Maybe tomorrow she could, maybe then she'd be stronger, but right now all she could think about was every time Jack had said yes. When she'd coax him into following her into the shower or talk him into screwing her senseless somewhere completely inappropriate, like Drake's bed. And, as much as he loved her, she longed for him. Lusted over him. She wanted to him to touch her, to remind her how crazy good they were together, and in that instant, she realized that if that was all she could ever give him, if it was always just sex to her, it wouldn't matter. If she was never ready, it didn't matter, because he had always loved her, and he was always going to love her. Jack may not see her epiphany as the answer, but Eloise knew if she wanted to keep him at arm's length emotionally and wear her wedding band until the day she died, while destroying him sexually, he wouldn't stop her.

"We've done it before," Eloise whispered, knowing full well it was a lie. It wasn't that they didn't get emotionally attached, it was that both of them were masters at pretending they didn't care. If she did this, there'd be no going back. Yet, in this moment, with him standing there looking at her like he was, she didn't care. She'd probably care tomorrow. She'd definitely care when the guilt crept up to shame her for sleeping with someone who wasn't Reagan. She'd care when, like countless times before, their relationship stopped and she was left alone again. That was really the only way this could end. Life had told them again and again that it wasn't meant to be no matter how many times they found their way back to each other. But instead of being smart, instead of protecting her heart, instead of staying loyal and faithful to her husband—because even though he was gone, she still felt married —instead of saying no like her brain was screaming at her to do, Eloise placed her hands on Jack's chest and pushed him back just a step, then hit her knees.

Eloise tugged his silk shorts down, taking his boxers with them. She watched his eyes widen as she grabbed him, stroking up and down, never breaking eye contact.

"El." Jack sounded nervous to her.

"You came in here for this, so let's do it." She pushed him into her mouth and found extreme satisfaction in him throwing his head back. Jack used to tell her that she gave the best blow jobs and she'd be interested to know if that was still true. When he wrapped his hand in her hair, she knew that he wanted her to stand, but she didn't, instead she started massaging his balls. When he tugged her hair after a few minutes, she stood, knowing he'd pull her to her feet if she didn't. He didn't say a word before he scooped her up and walked out of the bathroom.

"You're gonna be the death of me." He groaned against her neck before tasting her skin. "You drive me insane."

Eloise didn't play fair when it came to Jack and she loved using that against him.

"It doesn't matter." He moved away from her neck and looked in her eyes as if he could read her mind. "It never mattered to me because it meant I was being used by you, and having you in any form is always better than not having you at all." Jack threw her on the bed a little forcefully, but she didn't mind. She knew Jack was well aware of her preference for rough. "You were right. I did walk into the bathroom to fuck you and deal with the conse-quences later, but probably would've chickened out had you not went for it."

Jack pulled his shirt over his head and crawled up the bed to hover over her. Eloise lay perfectly still. She knew he was about to take control and she was happy to let him have it.

"Tell me you want this," Jack ordered, not an ounce of worry in his voice.

"I want you." Eloise watched as he untied her sweatpants.

"Lift," Jack said, and Eloise lifted her hips so that her bottom half was off the bed. Jack pulled her pants off, leaving her lace panties on, just like she knew he would. "Down." Eloise complied. Eloise smiled at Jack because of how surreal this was, the two of them naked together, after all the time that had passed.

"What?" Jack lay next to her, surprising her.

"This. Us. I never thought this would happen again." Eloise climbed on top of Jack, pushing her panties into his cock. She moved her hips against him. She reached down and pulled her panties to the side, but kept them on.

"I love it when you ride me," Jack said as Eloise positioned herself to take him.

"I know." She pushed down and then pulled back, again, and again, teasing him. She kept this up until he grabbed her ass and slammed her down, hard. Eloise let out a moan and Jack gripped her tighter, thrusting faster.

"Jack," Eloise whispered. "Jack."

"Yeah, beautiful?" He raised his eyebrow. Damn him. He knew exactly what she wanted but was going to make her say it.

"Rub my clit." She dug her hands into his chest.

"God, I love it when you say that." He rubbed her clit in circular motions. "I don't know how I went so long without this."

"Neither do I." Eloise told the truth. She loved how Jack knew exactly what she wanted. There was a shyness in sex with Reagan that was never there with Jack. He knew all her kinky secrets, most of which he'd helped her discover. She needed this more than she realized. Jack made it so easy for it to be about sex. Eloise didn't want to make love, and she didn't want to be treated like something breakable. She wanted to feel alive, to ride the line between pleasure and pain. Eloise looked down at her nails digging into Jack's chest before her world exploded.

"Jesus, Jack." Eloise rolled off him, completely out of breath, and laid her head on his chest.

"Miss me?" Jack kissed the top of her head, making her wonder if she should go back to her own house now. Eloise wasn't ready to *not* be Reagan's wife, and to devote herself to Jack meant she'd have to give up that part of herself. She couldn't help but wonder if loving Jack, if sleeping with him, meant her love for Reagan was less somehow. Did wanting Jack diminish what she had with her husband? She felt like she should know the answer by now, but she didn't, and she wanted so badly to have both.

"My vagina apparently did." Eloise laughed and then yawned. If she was going to move, it would have to be soon or Jack would have them going for round two.

"I'll take it." Jack laughed with her. "You staying?" Jack asked as if he could read her mind. "If you do, I promise that we can go back to being friends with no benefits if that's what you want. We can put ourselves back in our own boxes and hang out our signs that say *off-limits*."

Eloise knew that Jack was trying to help her not feel guilty, trying to reassure her that this didn't have to mean anything. He was always concerned with how she felt, so much so that he often disregarded how he felt, and she hated that. He said he wanted this to mean something, but he'd pretended it didn't if she asked him to. The problem was Eloise wasn't sure she wanted to go back to the way things were before, and she wasn't sure they should keep doing this either. This was a have-your-cake-and-eat-it-to scenario, so instead of arguing, she didn't comment at all, she simply snuggled in closer to Jack.

The next morning, Eloise felt the guilt before she opened her eyes. She wouldn't call it regret. She didn't regret sleeping with Jack, but she did feel like a cheater. She told herself how irrational that was, because Regan was gone, but it didn't help. The problem now was where did they go from here? Jack told her it didn't have to mean anything, so for now, she was going to treat it like it didn't. She'd never be able to go back to not banging him at every opportunity. They didn't just open that door, they ripped it off its hinges.

"Good morning," Eloise said when she felt Jack move.

"Morning, beautiful." Jack kissed her cheek and started to get up. "I'm gonna go make some coffee, so we can get going." He pulled his shorts on. Eloise didn't ask for coffee, and Jack didn't offer, but she knew he'd bring her some. That was the thing about Jack, he just knew. Little things like coffee, and monumental things like her desperately wanting him but not being ready to take her ring off. There were so many things that never had to be said, because he knew without asking.

Jack walked back in a few minutes later with two coffee cups and a yogurt parfait for Eloise.

"Breakfast." Jack handed her the two items.

"Thank you, handsome." Eloise set the yogurt on the nightstand and started sipping her coffee. "Jack."

"We don't have to talk about it, El."

"Maybe we should. We never talked before and that didn't really get us anywhere."

"I don't want to talk about it. I don't want to go into all the reasons we shouldn't do this or talk about commitment versus no strings attached. I don't want to. I just want us to drink our coffees and then go about our day."

"Why?" Eloise was worried. They never talked after when they were young. They had a lot of sex, a lot, but they had a ton of fun, too, and that was enough. He was asking for that now, and she pondered what he said about going back to friends. Did he actually mean that?

"Because, El. We aren't going to reach some conclusion. We've always been good at living in the present together. Let's just do that. Talking means risking this ending when you decide you aren't ready or I want more than you can give me."

"So we just avoid being adults altogether."

"God, I hope so."

"We can't undo what happened last night."

"Don't worry, El, my body is here for you to use anytime. You say the word. This isn't about stopping. This is just about enjoying what we have without pressure for more. That's always seemed to work for you."

"Okay, Jack." Eloise couldn't say anything else because if she did, she'd cry. He was so sure before. He told her he wanted the real thing and now he was backpedaling? What was she supposed to do with that? Jack was scared she'd bail, and Eloise couldn't really blame him. He'd always wanted more, but Eloise had always kept him just out of reach and that was safe. Back then, Eloise didn't have to think about what this all meant and she didn't have to dread the day it'd inevitably end.

J ack watched Eloise finish her coffee, not saying anything else. She was worried, he could see it on her face, but he couldn't go down that road with her. He wanted to believe every word of the letter she had written to him, but that desire was shattered when she showed up still wearing her wedding band. His only options now were to leave her to finish grieving on her own and move on with his own life, or continue having incredible sex with his best friend. Number one wasn't even really an option. Jack had known Eloise over fifteen years and even after a decade apart, he hadn't ever moved on.

Jack couldn't understand why she didn't want more from him, why she never had. He understood her choice now, she'd only recently lost her husband. But what about before? Would she ever want him for real? Their connection was real, he felt that in the depths of his soul, and yet he always ended up feeling like he wasn't good enough. Jack felt better with her around, and he wasn't about to walk away now that he had her back in his life. He just wasn't sure how he'd survive the two of them continuing to collide. Jack tried to picture them together in five years, in ten, in twenty. Would she still be wearing Reagan's ring? Would they just go through life never talking about anything that had the potential to push them apart? Would he give up on commitment for mind-blowing sex? Would that be enough for him? Just being around her, having incredible sex, and continuing to say they were friends? Eloise was his best friend, the best and closest friend he'd ever had. She knew him, and not in the way people meant it when they said someone truly knew them. Eloise had access to the depths of his soul. The way they both just said exactly what was on their minds made him think he could live a life like that with her. She was exposed, and so was he. They never tried to hide from each other. Having Eloise in that way, in a way he knew no one else had her, that could be enough.

CHAPTER 16

J ack wasn't ready for a twelve-hour day. As he drove through the gates of the base, he spotted Chase making a beeline for him. He parked his truck and thought about Eloise waiting at his house for him to come home. He'd told her that he wouldn't be able to talk much, if at all, during his shift and that he'd also have to be ready to leave at a moment's notice, which could come any day, at any time. Eloise said she still wanted to stay with him. She had her house but explained to Jack that she wasn't finished decorating it, and all of that could wait as long as he was home. The best part of his morning came when she'd said, "If you're going to disappear at two in the morning, I want all the time I can get."

"Did you get the call?" Chase asked as he jogged the rest of the distance.

"Not yet." Jack was barely done speaking when his phone started ringing. "This is Brennan," Jack answered.

"We're meeting in three minutes. This is your eighteen-hour notice."

"Yes, sir." Jack hit the end button. "I got the call now."

"Me too. You make number five. Me, You, Jonsey, Leaf, and

Stewart." They turned to head toward the meeting, Jack right behind Chase. Jack cursed in his head. They just got home. Eloise was sitting in his damn living room.

Chase and Jack walked through the door and took their seats. Their first sergeant stood at the head of the table.

"You five are leaving within the next eighteen hours. This is a rescue mission, should be a quick turnaround." Beckett looked over the paper on his clipboard.

Jack listened carefully as Beckett explained their travel plans and gave them the details on the missing soldiers.

After Jack's squad was dismissed, he walked outside to call Eloise. All five men were on the phone within seconds of leaving their meeting.

"Hello." Eloise sounded excited and that made Jack smile.

"Hey, beautiful. How's your morning going?" Jack hated himself for being the one who was going to ruin her day.

"It's been good. Rossi and I have been raiding your fridge. I hope you don't mind."

"Not at all. Make yourselves at home."

"How's your day going?"

"That's why I'm calling, El. I'm leaving."

"What?"

"I have to go on a mission. I leave in like fifteen hours. But I shouldn't be gone long."

Eloise didn't speak.

"El, you still there?" Jack looked over at Chase, who seemed about as excited as Jack was to be having this conversation.

"Stay safe, Jack." Eloise's words were barely audible.

"You can stay at my house if you want, El, while you're moving things into your own house. This won't be like before. I won't be able to contact you."

"How long?" Eloise sniffled and Jack knew she was crying.

"I don't know, El." Jack felt like time was going in slow motion, every pause of Eloise's—an eternity.

"Just come back, Jack." Eloise hung up without another word.

Jack stared at his phone, cursing the fact that he couldn't go to her, couldn't promise that everything would be okay.

When their plane landed, Jack's squad hit the ground running. The mission had been discussed repeatedly over the hours on the flight and now everything was in motion without missing a beat.

None of the men spoke, and every step was calculated. There was no time to make changes once you landed. You did all your thinking before your boots hit the dirt. Obviously, things went wrong, adaptations had to be made, but changes happened in the moment and only when forced. When it was possible to follow the plan, they followed every detail. Jack looked to each man, men he'd known for years. He'd go to any length to keep them safe.

Jack found himself running ahead to assess the wounded, soldiers who'd been stuck under heavy fire for almost two days. Jack heard the helicopter above them and knew things were about to get wild.

Jack stopped at the first wounded man he saw, his uniform soaked in blood. Jack ripped open the man's vest, then unzipped his medical bag. He started stuffing the soldier's holes with gauze, and tried not to think about how he had lost so much blood that he didn't even wince from the pain. Jack moved from soldier to soldier, examining them and doctoring them up as quickly as possible.

Hours later, the wounded were loaded up, the gunfire had stopped, and Jack's unit was headed back to the base. So many of his missions came down to pushing forward, to giving more when he had nothing left to give, to his body saying no but pushing past that, because he had no other choice.

Jack was beat. The mission lasted mere hours, but he felt

more exhausted than he did after being gone six months. Walking onto the overseas base, Jack felt all eyes on his unit. The staring men were clean shaven, showered, and didn't smell like dried blood and death. Jack looked at the four men with him, facial hair, sweat stains, hair covered in dirt, and no one wanted to think about their smell.

Jack and the men walked straight to clean up, but only because they wouldn't be allowed in the chow hall looking like they did. They were greeted with less staring in the chow hall, but seeing as how they weren't showered, people still gave them long looks. Jack shoveled in his food, barely swallowing before pushing in the next forkful.

After he ate, Jack walked to the showers. He watched as the mud that caked his hair and skin swirled down the drain.

When Jack found a good enough Wi-Fi signal, he pulled up Facebook. He saw that Eloise was online and instead of typing out a message, hit the video call button.

"Jack, hi," Eloise answered, smiling so big it made Jack's heart skip.

"Hey, beautiful. How are you?"

"I'm fine. How are you?"

"I'm okay, back on base now. I'll be back in the States tomorrow."

"Rossi and I can't wait to see you."

"I'll call you when we finish on base."

"Sounds good. I got all moved in, so maybe you can stay with me? See the house?"

"I'd love that."

On the flight home, Jack found himself thinking about the last ten years. He'd seen six transfer services while deployed. He'd traveled to places he would've never visited as a civilian. He had met people who became his family, and learned more skills than college would've ever taught him. It was hard to think about his service without thinking about the people he'd lost over the years. As a medic, Jack always blamed himself when someone died with his hands on them. As close as he was with the people he worked with, no one was always there. People left, transferred, died, were promoted, there were all sorts of reasons for someone being there one minute and being gone the next.

Everyone handled their time in the service differently. Some, like Jack, talked to their loved ones every chance they got. Some talked to their families the least amount, sometimes not at all. It was hard to handle being away from the people you loved, and for some people, it helped to keep the two worlds separate. He saw men and women worry that their families didn't stop living, because their spouses had to move on in a way similar to separation or divorce. When a soldier was gone, a wife or husband was left handing everything at home. He saw people stressed beyond belief over not seeing their family again. The biggest fear, of every person Jack had worked with, wasn't something happening to themselves, it was something happening to their family while they were too far away to do anything about it. Jack hadn't had to worry about that for years. When he first enlisted, Drake was already gone and his mom didn't live long after. When Jack was alone, he focused on the routine. When he wasn't working a shift, he ate and he worked out. He went to the gym obsessively, because there wasn't much else to do. Jack spent any remaining time doing laundry, which always took most of his day off, because you had to wait for working machines.

Jack dated after Eloise stopped talking to him for good, but nothing serious. Jack had always felt like Eloise had a part of him that no one else could. He could've let someone else in, but no matter how much he tried, he was never able to give himself to someone in the raw way that Eloise had him. It was less of a choice with her and more of the naturalness of their relationship.

He and Eloise had that openness without trying, and with everyone else, Jack felt like he was forcing it.

One woman came close once, Trinity, and Jack sometimes wondered if he should tell Eloise about her. She had reminded Jack a lot of Eloise and he always felt bad about that. Their relationship didn't work out largely due to Jack constantly questioning if he was with her for her, or because she reminded him of what he didn't have. The last time he saw her was two years ago.

"Is there someone else?" Trinity had asked, crying.

"Not in the way that you think." Jack couldn't look at her. "You deserve more than I can give you, Trinity. I loved someone, a long time ago, and I never stopped. And I thought with you, I had moved on, but I haven't, and that just isn't fair to you." Jack couldn't make himself tell her that she made him think of Eloise, that the two of them were similar in so many ways. That would have caused unnecessary pain, or at least that was what he told himself.

"It's not fair for you to spend the rest of your life alone over a woman you can't be with." Trinity had wiped her tears.

"Not a lot has ever been fair when it comes to Eloise." Jack stifled a smile. He hated that Eloise still had that power over him, the power to make him smile, even in the entirely wrong setting.

"So that's it then? You're just throwing away our last three years? We could be happy, Jack. I get it. I'll never be her, but that doesn't mean we can't build a wonderful life together."

"I'll never regret knowing you, Trinity. You're amazing. I know I could have a good life with you, a great one even, but you deserve someone who loves you like…"

"Like you love her," Trinity finished for him.

"Yeah." Jack had waited for her to get mad, to flip out, to scream, anything that would shake him out of his own head. Anything that would make him believe he was sacrificing a life of happiness with her for a life of solitude. Trinity never got angry.

She had simply dried her tears, grabbed her purse, and walked out of Jack's house, his life, like so many women had done before, including Eloise.

♡

Eloise was going nuts just sitting at home waiting for Jack to call, so she left and went to get coffee. She was nervous about him coming and going on missions. She didn't know how she'd handle it, but no matter what she felt, she had to stay strong for Jack while he was away. It was odd, because she had no experience with the military, but something in her made her think he'd need her strength and reassurance when he was gone.

When Eloise still hadn't heard from Jack, she decided to drive up the mountain. The Grand Mesa was one of the main reasons she had chosen to move to Colorado. When the leaves changed colors, people came from all over the country to see them in their vibrant yellows and reds. The pines and the aspens covered the mountainside and Eloise wasn't sure how many lakes covered the Mesa, but it was a lot. She had pulled over to look at one of the lakes when her phone finally rang.

"Hello."

"Hey, beautiful. I'm all done here on base. I'll be heading your way soon."

"I ran up the mountain, so I'll be like forty or so minutes. I'm sorry."

"No worries. Waiting for you is one of my favorite things to do."

"Bye, handsome." Eloise laughed.

"See you soon," Jack said and then hung up.

When Eloise pulled up to her house Jack was waiting for her. Jack met her as she cut across the gravel driveway.

Jack met her as she came to the front of his truck.

"Hey, beautiful." Jack took her wrists and pulled her into him, finding her lips with his. Eloise smiled against his mouth and wanted to live the rest of her life in that moment. "I missed you," Jack told her as they separated.

"I missed you, too, handsome. I'm so glad you're back." Eloise couldn't stop looking at Jack's face, in his eyes. Eloise felt right, complete when she was with Jack, but those feelings were always followed closely by her guilt.

Jack waited about two seconds to tell Eloise he was starving. They didn't have options up in Mesa. There was one place to eat, aside from the ski resort, but it was a homey place, one that didn't care what you were wearing or if you got up to refill your own drink. Jack took Eloise's hand and walked her to the passenger side of his truck. He opened the door and waited until her seatbelt was on before he shut the door and went to get in on his side. The restaurant was empty, likely due to the time of day. They sat themselves and when their food was delivered, Jack shoveled in chicken fried steak like it was his first meal in days, making Eloise wonder if it actually was.

"How do you feel about being back?" Eloise asked once Jack was finished with his plate.

"Good. It always takes a few days, adjusting, even with short trips. But I feel good."

"What makes adjusting hard? You didn't seem to mind much the last time you got back, even after being gone all those months."

"I've gotten very good at internalizing." Jack took a sip of his tea. "Things are always different, changed, when we come back. Even when we aren't gone long. It's hard to explain, but it's like pausing a movie on live TV, but when you come back, the credits are rolling and you can't rewind."

"It's all the things you miss?" Eloise kept eating between sentences.

"It's more the realization that life goes on without us."

"Us?"

"We all basically feel some version of the same thing coming home. At least, in my experience we do."

Eloise set her fork down and reached across the table and took Jack's hand.

"Life has to go on, Jack, we can't pause it. You all have a life, too, when you're gone. A life we know little to nothing about. I know it's probably not the same, but it is hard for the people left behind too." Eloise squeezed his fingers. "I can promise, at least on my end, all I think about when you're gone is you coming back."

"That's the crazy part. I love what I do. I never thought I would. I never wanted this. I did it for Drake. But over the years, the Army became my identity. I can't imagine being anyone else. I was robotic before you. I could leave, not care how long I was going to be gone, and do my job, laser-focused. You changed all that."

"I don't like the thought of you being on a mission unfocused."

"Not the point I was making, El."

"I know, and thank you, Jack. I'm happy it's me distracting you and not someone else."

"It almost was once." Jack said.

Eloise wasn't sure she wanted to know where this was going, but she was also happy at the blunt honesty, maybe they'd find the people they once were after all.

"Someone else?" Eloise lifted her fork and took another bite.

"I haven't seen or spoken to her in two years. Her name was Trinity. We were together three years, she even lived with me. She was the closest thing I ever had to something serious, besides you."

"I don't need to know about your relationships, Jack. I was married, for God's sake. What you did the years we didn't speak isn't really my business." Eloise took a long drink of her water.

"It feels like it is. I know what you were doing, who you were doing, the ten years we were apart. It feels right that you should know the same. We always knew before."

"In that case, did you love her?"

"Not in the way you loved Reagan. I cared about her. She reminded me a lot of you, something I never told her. That's ultimately why things didn't work. I didn't think it was fair to be with her solely because she made me think of you."

"I hate to say you're right. Why did you hold on so strongly? I mean you could've married, had a life with someone." Eloise pushed her plate away and Jack stacked everything neatly like he always did.

"I tried, but I never connected with anyone in a way that compared to you. You set the bar pretty damn high, El."

"You shouldn't have compared at all, Jack. Had I done that, I never would've married Reagan." Eloise regretted the words the second they were out of her mouth. "I shouldn't have said that. I just meant, you can't blame future partners for the things past partners put you through, you know? Trinity should have had a chance, separate from anything to do with me."

"That was always the problem. There was no separate from you. You were infused into every thought, every action. Maybe it was the way I grew up, no father, a mom who spent my life in a constant cycle of addiction and trying to get sober. All I really had was Drake. I lost you and then I lost him, and it wouldn't have mattered who I met, El, because they weren't you."

"I never thought like that. I never compared Reagan to you. I couldn't. You would've won." Lying seemed ridiculous at this point.

"Why then, El? Why'd you leave?" Jack's eyes were on his tea glass.

"Do you remember when I took your photos for my photography class?"

"Fondly," Jack said, and they both smiled.

"I knew that day that I was in love with you." Eloise thought about meeting him in the photo lab and taking his pictures. She remembered everything about that day. Jack showed up in a white T-shirt and jeans, with a black flat-brimmed hat. She had him sit, stand, hold a football, pretend to throw it, all sorts of poses, and he did exactly what she asked. They hadn't known each other long then, just a few months. Jack always showed up for her, always, no matter how many crazy things she wanted from him. He never wavered or complained. That day she took his photo for almost two hours and not once did he rush her. When she was done, she set her camera down. They didn't have to speak to know what they both wanted. When Jack twisted the lock to the door, and turned to face her, the second her eyes hit his, she knew she was in way over her head.

"Okay," Jack said, motioning his hand for her to continue.

"I was scared. I used to say it was because you weren't boyfriend material, or that you were a player, or that you didn't want commitment, but you and I both know that those things aren't you, weren't you then either." Eloise looked at her hand on his. "The truth, Jack, was that I wasn't sure what I wanted. I didn't have control over loving you, but I had control over what I did with those feelings."

"And you chose to fight them like hell?" Jack started to pull his hand away, Eloise felt it shift, and then he stopped himself.

"Yes. That, and ignore them."

"I still don't understand why."

THE MAN BEFORE YOU | 191

"I've always needed to be in control, Jack. Something you know about me. I hate not knowing, I hate surprises and the unknown. Plus, we were young. I guess I just wasn't ready for something so permanent."

"That second part is bullshit. We were permanent *and* serious anytime we were together for five years, El. And, after you stopped talking to me, you were engaged, what, ten months later?"

"Jack." Eloise watched as he took his hand from hers, scrubbed his hands down his face before taking her hand again. "It was a risk I couldn't take. Reagan was safe. He was dependable, predictable. You were this wild and free spirit, no strings, no pressure. You were fun, we were fun, but when I pictured my future, I pictured someone like Reagan." Eloise swallowed. She hated admitting to him what she knew he'd always thought. She didn't think he was good enough. Tears swelled up, making her face feel heavy. She was grateful that the restaurant was empty.

"Did you not think I would've done anything to make you happy?"

"I think I did know, but I also didn't want you to sacrifice who you were to give me the life I thought I wanted. I was dumb, Jack, honestly. It was way more about me overthinking and struggling with what I thought I was supposed to be doing versus what I wanted."

"You thought people would judge you for being with me?" Jack took his hand away and pushed his chair back. Eloise swore she felt the vibration of his force in the wood floor beneath her feet. "Why? Because you had a supportive mom, and I had an alcoholic mother? Because there's no way the partying black kid would ever amount to anything? We would've faced challenges, all couples do, but I never would've pegged you for the judgmental type."

"I found a lot of reasons to push you away when I should have been holding you as close as possible." The disappointment in Jack's eyes made Eloise hate herself. She picked up her glass and held it to her cheek, hoping the coolness would stop her hatred from knocking her unconscious. "I was so terrified of not having a plan for my life, and Reagan had plans and ideas that made me feel like I was living the life I was meant to." Eloise stood and walked around the table. Jack leaned back so she could sit in his lap. Eloise put her face in his neck. "I always believed you'd do great things, and you have. I'd picture you out in the world, make stories up in my head about what you were doing with your life. Not a single day went by where I didn't think about you. I never – look at me, Jack – I never would've given weight to what anyone thought about any of it. I knew who you were. I loved who you were. I love who you are. I'm sorry, Jack."

"It was a long time ago, El. It's okay." He rubbed his hand up and down her back.

"I should have done things differently back then." Eloise inhaled the scent of Jack before kissing his neck.

"Maybe, but everything happens for a reason." Jack laughed and squirmed a bit. Eloise forgot how ticklish he could be.

"You really believe that?" Eloise wiggled her nose, now tickling him on purpose.

"I have to." Jack squeezed her, both arms wrapped around her waist.

"Me too." Eloise knew Jack would be carrying her out of the Wagon Wheel whenever they decided to leave, but this time she wouldn't be angry and she wouldn't be pretending.

CHAPTER 17

Eloise took her keys out of her purse. Her house had three bedrooms and an actual bed, a new one of course. She opened the door and watched as Jack took in his surroundings.

"It's great, Eloise. You did good." He smiled and set his backpack on the floor at his feet.

"Let me give you the grand tour." She giggled. The living room and kitchen were open and fairly large, Eloise had filled both with furniture and appliances. She walked through the kitchen and opened the door. Jack followed her into the master. The other three bedrooms were on the other side of the house.

"Are you going to show me outside?" Jack yelled from one of the rooms after a few moments.

"Whenever you're ready."

"I'm ready." Jack was in shorts and a T-shirt, looking handsome as ever. Eloise was thankful she was in a new house. Now that they were sleeping together, it would've felt too much like cheating if she and Jack were in the house she shared with Reagan. Eloise stood from the couch and grabbed Jack's hand.

She was most proud of the property she managed to find and couldn't wait to see what he thought of it.

Eloise opened the sliding glass door in the dining room and stepped out onto the porch. They were surrounded by a fenced-in backyard with three huge trees. It was landscaped with gravel and had two long flower beds.

"Is the sanctuary why you wanted to buy a horse property?" Jack kneeled to pet an excited Rossi.

"Yeah. I wanted to have a property where I could take in rescues. I started looking in Houston. I don't know if I told you that. Reagan was on board, but only because I wanted it. We had just started looking at properties and then..."

"Hey, it doesn't have to be a sad thing." Jack kept scratching behind Rossi's ears.

"I know."

"You bought this place for him?" Jack dropped his hand from Rossi to look at Eloise.

"No. I bought it for me, but with him in mind."

"That makes sense." Jack said. Eloise started across the yard and Jack matched her stride.

"I'm not honoring him in the way you honor Drake; though, Reagan deserves that. It's more that I thought about him and decided I needed to do something that was mine. I needed to take the step toward moving on."

"I'm proud of you, El. That's not just any step, it's a big one." Jack opened her back gate. "Now show me the barn."

"When are you planning on getting horses?" Jack asked as Eloise pushed the barn door open.

"Soon, I hope. I want goats, too, and maybe a pig or something." Eloise flipped the lights on.

"I like seeing you so happy." Jack started to walk the perimeter of the empty space. Eloise loved the exposed beams in the roof and the way the light crept in from the random holes in the wood walls.

"I've always wanted this, well for a long time. I just never really thought it would happen."

"Your sanctuary?"

"Yeah. It was always hard to picture, and now I'm trying to do it on my own."

"You're not on your own, El. And, someday in the near future, you'll have your sanctuary."

"I did think about that while choosing this." Eloise had thought about it a lot. There was already the barn as well as three lean-tos that could hold hay or be fenced in for smaller animals like goats or pigs. The ten acres wasn't enough for a huge sanctuary, but it was a start. Eloise had talked to her real estate agent about the fifty-acre lot behind hers and would purchase that as soon as she could.

"I think it's great, El. Are you planning on going back to work?" Jack pushed the window open at the back of the structure and looked out.

"No, not right away. I used the life insurance money to buy this place and I have enough left not to have to worry for a while, until I decide what to do." Eloise came up behind him and wrapped her arms around his waist.

"Well, now that you live close, I'll help anytime I can."

"Thank you, Jack. I know I'll need it. There's a lot to do before I get animals and even more to do after they're here."

"So I'm manual labor?" Jack turned his head to face Eloise.

"Essentially." Eloise tiptoed and kissed Jack's neck. He turned in her arms and looked surprised to Eloise as she stepped away from him. His surprised morphed, a smile spread across his face as she jumped into his arms and wrapped her legs around his waist to kiss him.

Eloise stood on the porch the next morning watching as Jack unloaded bales of hay that she had bought the afternoon before. He wore jeans, boots and a cowboy hat that he got from God knew where. He looked incredible, his muscles flexing with every toss. He was stacking the barrels under the lean-to closest to the barn and it looked like he laid a tarp underneath and planned to put a second one over the top of the pile. Eloise wondered where he learned to be a cowboy. He was such a city boy when she knew him. Reagan was the cowboy, the man who was always handy.

She slipped on her muck boots and walked out to him. "You're out here early."

Jack stayed at his house a lot, because it was easier for him to get to and from work, but on his days off and most evenings, he was at Eloise's.

"I wanted to get all this out of my truck."

"I didn't know you did cowboy stuff." Eloise crossed her arms over her chest.

"Turned on?" Jack's hand covered his smile.

"Just surprised." Eloise's eyes glanced upward.

"I'm not really a cowboy. I'm all city. You know that. But, I can figure stuff like this out, if it'll help you." Jack tossed another bale.

"Thank you, Jack. It really is good to have you back."

"Good enough that you're going to cook me breakfast?"

"I think I can manage that." Eloise leaned in closer to him and he bent down and brought his lips to hers. Her chest still hurt every time they kissed, her guilt ever present, but she liked kissing Jack, she had always liked kissing him.

Jack had all three lean-tos stacked with hay within a week and Eloise had found two horses she was interested in, six goats, some chickens, and even pigs. She was supposed to go look at the horses this afternoon. She wasn't sure what to look for, so she called her uncle.

"Hey, Uncle Jim. I have a question for you." Eloise moved through her kitchen, wiping down counters as she spoke.

"Shoot, kid. How are you anyway?"

"I'm good. I'm sorry I haven't called in a while. I've been so busy with the move."

"I'm thrilled to have you close again. You'll have to come visit soon."

"That's why I'm calling actually, well, sort of. I found two horses that I'm about to go look at and I wanted to see if you'd come with me? I'm not sure what to look for. That was more Reagan's thing." Eloise rinsed her rag and hung it over the faucet to dry.

"Why are you getting horses?"

"I have the land for them now. Plus it's something I've wanted to do for a while. Reagan and I were going to do it before. We had started plans but then…" Eloise still couldn't say the words.

"Okay, okay. I remember you wanting horses. I mostly just mean why now, but you have the location so it makes sense. I remember teaching you to ride."

"Me too. The months I lived with you are still some of my favorite times." Eloise didn't want to go home from college, so after her first year she moved in with her uncle and got a summer job. He taught her all kinds of things, including how to ride.

"Me, too, Eloise. And, of course, I'll go with you. Want me to meet you in town?"

"No, they live out toward you, so I'll pick you up." Eloise leaned against the kitchen island, the tile cold on her forearm.

"Okay. Do you need a trailer?"

"No, my friend Jack will take his truck and the trailer I have here."

"So prepared. I'm proud," he said. Eloise loved him even more for not asking about Jack. Truth was he probably didn't care. Eloise's uncle was a solitary man, and he never pried.

Anytime they discussed anything personal, it was because Eloise brought it up. He had a lot of insights that Eloise valued, but she was happy that he never pushed her to discuss things she wasn't ready to.

"Thanks, Uncle Jim. We're going to leave in a few minutes and I'll see you soon."

"Sounds good." He hung up first and Eloise wondered if he'd ever met Jack. She honestly couldn't remember. He'd met a lot of her friends while she lived with him. He lived an hour out of town, though, and Eloise always told him she was sleeping over at a female friend's house when she'd stay at Jack's.

Eloise was just about done with breakfast when she heard Jack stomping the dirt off before coming through the front door.

"Right on time. I just made your plate." Eloise set Jack's plate on the table and started making her own.

"Thanks, mind if I strip these clothes off?"

"Are you showering? I can put your plate in the microwave." Eloise watched as Jack pulled his shirt over his head and headed toward the bathroom.

"Yeah, thank you, El. I'll be right back, eat quick, and we can go."

"Okay." Eloise grabbed Jack's plate and set it in the microwave. She stood at the little island in the kitchen to eat her breakfast.

Everything in Jack's life was continuing to change at a pace that was difficult to keep up with. As he hopped in the shower, he was amazed at the amount of dirt that washed down the drain. He'd been showering dirt off for three weeks now, but the amount of grime his body held kept amazing him. He washed his body twice, making sure the water ran clear before stepping out to dry off. Eloise had seemed to fall into a routine again and Jack couldn't be happier about that. She cooked and did the cleaning. Sure, he did the bulk of the outside chores, but he really didn't mind. He enjoyed being outside and the calm of everything. Being here with her was so different from being overseas. People always wanted to know what it was like being deployed, but the job, training, workouts, and hours didn't change much. It came down to comforts. It was fucking nice being in his own bed, or in Eloise's, and being in the same time zone as her. Jack didn't have to worry about freezing his balls off or dying of heat exhaustion in one-hundred-and-thirty-degree weather from sweating his asshole off. Being home was pleasant.

When they pulled in, Jack couldn't believe the number of horses. He had no clue how she'd choose. Eloise had said she wanted at least two, but she was already plotting out loud how many she could safely haul in the trailer, and how many she could realistically care for at home.

"I think you should get females, especially if you want multiples," Jim told Eloise.

"Okay, should I get any males?" Eloise asked as Jack grabbed her hand.

"Let's see what this guy has and go from there." Jim was suddenly all business, ready to talk horses.

"Bringing him was a smart idea," Jack whispered to Eloise, knowing Jim was obviously in his element.

"Horses are his entire life." Eloise squeezed Jack's hand, he was happy that he could share this moment with her. He figured he was different from Reagan, but guessed they were the same in their willingness to do things that made her happy. He was here because Eloise wanted to do this, but he was also enjoying it. He was there for himself too.

Getting the five horses back to the house wasn't hard with Jack and Jim both helping. Eloise had their stalls ready days before going to pick them out and they looked right at home by that evening.

Eloise's favorite was the one she told Jack she'd call October because her golden mane reminded her of fall. The all-black horse was Jack's favorite, and Eloise told Jack he could name him, the only stallion. Eloise said she wasn't sure what she'd do with him, but her talked her ear off about breeding.

"Do you want to stay for dinner?" Jack asked Eloise's uncle as they walked into the living room.

"Sure. If that's okay with you both," Jim answered before sitting on the couch.

"Of course it is. You can stay the night, too, if you don't want to drive back tonight." Eloise said.

"I don't want to cause too much trouble."

"Please, after today, you can move in. Besides, the guest room is all made up." Eloise pointed in the direction of the room her uncle would stay in.

"Thank you, Eloise. Today's been a great day."

"Thank you." Eloise told him. On the way to meet him, Eloise had told Jack she believed her uncle was lonely sometimes, and that he wished he had more people around. She told Jack about living with her uncle and that she'd always admired his more solitary lifestyle, his ability to be alone. He had courage that most people didn't. Being alone with your thoughts could be dangerous.

The next morning, after Eloise's uncle left, she and Jack went back to bed. Jack loved falling asleep and waking up to Eloise, but there was still a moment in the morning where he knew she thought she was waking up to Reagan. It lasted only a few seconds, just before she'd open her eyes. Her lips would creep into a small smile, and her face looked absolutely at peace. Jack referred to it as her short window of guilt-free bliss. He never commented on it, but when she realized each new day that Reagan was still gone, and Jack was in her bed, her face would fall for an instant and she'd whisper to Reagan that she loved him, and that she was sorry.

Jack was getting, in his opinion, too comfortable with Eloise. He touched her any second he could, and though Eloise never flinched or told him to stop, he always wondered what she was thinking as he kissed her, ran his fingertips over her body, held her hand, or smacked her ass as he passed. Jack never believed he'd be in a position to touch her again. He spent almost every minute waiting on the other shoe to drop, waiting for her to push him away.

As they stood in the store parking lot that afternoon, Jack thought about Eloise's not so secret obsession with sex in public places. This wasn't exactly the seats of a movie theater, but he'd take it. Eloise opened Jack's passenger side door and Jack came up behind her. Eloise was conveniently wearing a dress, and when Jack slid his hand up her leg and then between her thighs, Eloise sucked in her breath as Jack kissed her neck. Eloise didn't move, but she did giggle as Jack moved her panties aside to play with her. Eloise didn't last long before she turned to face him, crashing her mouth to his. Jack picked her up, shut the passenger door, opened the back door, and laid Eloise across the seat, with, by his estimation, only three people stopping to stare at them.

When they got back to Eloise's, much later than originally planned, Jack helped her carry in the groceries and then the two of them decided to eat and watch a movie. Jack woke up, still on the couch, to his phone ringing. He moved carefully, as to not wake her, and took his phone into her room, shutting the door.

"This is Brennan."

"We need you back, Brennan. I'm sending five of you out as

soon as we can get a flight cleared," Beckett said. Jack pulled his phone from his ear. It was just after three in the morning.

"Yes, sir," Jack said and then hung up. When Jack opened Eloise's bedroom door, she had turned over on the couch. He took a moment to be in awe of the fact that he was standing there, in her living room. He still couldn't believe that he could walk right up to her and kiss her, and it was real. He didn't want to wake her, but couldn't leave without saying goodbye. Jack sat in front of Eloise, placing his hand on the top of her head.

"El." Jack lightly moved his hand across her face. "El, wake up." Eloise started to wiggle and made some sleepy noises that made Jack laugh. "Wake up, beautiful." Jack leaned down and kissed her cheek.

"Why?" Eloise groaned, still refusing to open her eyes.

"I've gotta leave." Jack barely got the words out before Eloise shot up.

"Now?" she said, bolting upright and rubbing her eyes.

"Yes, right now." Jack scooted closer and Eloise climbed onto his lap.

"Will it be long?" Eloise sniffled, as if trying to stop her tears.

"I don't have the details yet, but when I do, I'll call. Anytime I can message or call, I will. If I don't, it's just work, El, and I will the second I can, okay?" Jack kissed the top of her head.

"I know, Jack. Can I drop you off?"

"You don't need to go out at this hour. I can drive."

"Please. I don't want to beg, but I will." Eloise told him.

"Okay, beautiful. We should get going then." Jack squeezed Eloise before she climbed off him so he could stand.

Eloise dropped Jack off at the entrance to the base, instead of going through the steps to drive in. They kissed and Eloise only let a few tears fall in front of him, which he wiped away. Jack waved before turning his back and jogging toward the building where he'd meet the other men.

When Jack walked in, Chase was there and so was Jonesy, but whoever the other two men were, weren't there yet.

"Do you know where we're going?" Jack asked Chase as they waited.

"Kuwait," Chase said. Jack noted the purple bags under Chase's eyes and hoped he was doing okay. It was never good to be leaving when your head was somewhere else.

Egan, still considered the rookie of the unit, walked in next, followed by Stewart, who shook everyone's hand. Jack was relieved that he was there. Somehow, he always felt safer with Chase and Stewart around. Jack always liked Jonesy being in the mix, but he was still adjusting to working with Egan.

After Beckett shared all the details of the mission, Jack stepped out to call Eloise. He hoped she fell back asleep, but figured that probably wasn't the case.

"Hello," Eloise answered.

"Hey, beautiful. I can't talk, but wanted to let you know that I shouldn't be away too long." Jack wished he never had to leave her crying alone.

"That's always good to hear," Eloise said. "But anytime away from you is too long."

"I'll contact you when I can." Jack wanted to tell her that he loved her, that he'd come back to her. He wanted her to know that she'd never have to be alone again, but he said none of those things.

"Stay safe, Jack." Eloise whispered and Jack could hear her muffled sobs. "I need you to come home."

"Home with you is the only place I want to be," Jack told her. "Talk to you soon."

"Talk to you soon, handsome," Eloise said and Jack hung up the phone.

Jack slid his phone into his pocket and jogged to find Sergeant Beckett. The men always gave Sergeant Beckett a letter for their wives or other family in case they didn't come home. This would be the first time Jack would be giving Beckett a letter to guard. Jack wanted to let Beckett know that Jack would write it on the flight over, and double check his medical bag before they took off.

The flight was silent. Jack wrote and sealed his letter, and then was in and out of sleep like the men around him. After they landed, Jack had barely settled in his bunk before Stewart was calling his name. Apparently, they'd be wasting no time before pushing out. Jack's unit was there for the aftermath of something that had happened a couple of days ago. Sergeant Beckett didn't tell them much, only that their job was to help where needed and fix up as many soldiers as possible.

Jack was drained as he collapsed into his bunk days later. This entire mission was rushed and chaotic. He had patched up everyone he could, then said a quick thank-you to the universe that none of the people he had to heal were from his group of five. When Jack walked back onto the base, he looked at the men at women examining him. He always did this, and even after what felt like thousands of faces, he was still surprised. Every single time. They were all soldiers with a common understanding, but soldiers left, and soldiers stayed, and the ones who left never came back looking the same.

The entire mission only lasted six days, including travel, but it had seemed much longer. Sometimes there were moments during a mission where you could exhale, but this wasn't one of those times. Even debriefing after the mission felt rushed. The men were loaded onto a plane without much warning to head home, and before Jack had time to call Eloise at a decent hour, he was back in Colorado. Jack put his key in Eloise's front door, trying to be quiet, because it was two in the morning. He pushed Eloise's bedroom door open, then said her name once as he reached the edge of her bed. Jack shook Eloise just slightly, repeating her name.

"Jack," Eloise said, a bit too loudly, as she sat up in bed, throwing her arms around him. "You're home." She started kissing him, pulling him into bed as she did.

"I'm home," Jack said as he covered Eloise's body with his own.

CHAPTER 18

J ack had been staying at Eloise's more and more since returning from his last mission. He was almost always up before the sun, now that Eloise had her horses. There was a never-ending to-do list between feeding, brushing, cleaning stalls, watering, and everything else that had to happen on the property that had nothing to do with animals. Jack tried to get a few things done before work, but did most things after his shift.

On Jack's days off, they had their routine almost down to a science. She was always up about an hour after him and by the time she finished making breakfast, he was getting out of the shower. They'd eat together and then go back to doing what had to be done, sometimes together, sometimes separately.

With the exception of when he was with his unit, Jack couldn't remember the last time he had this much structure in his life. Usually when he was on leave, he was either lazy or crazy, either sleeping the days away, or not sleeping at all because he was partying. Truthfully, the lack of structure when he had more than a day off sort of drove him insane. He didn't miss it like he thought he would. Eloise cooked most of the meals, but Jack usually made dinner a few times a week, just because he wanted to keep up with his cooking. When Jack was in the kitchen, he felt at ease, cooking being the only thing that helped him relax.

"Jack, can I ask you something?"

"You can ask me anything." Jack shoveled in his breakfast. He was mentally ticking off the things he had to finish today.

"Do you ever regret enlisting?"

"Are you a mind reader?"

"What?"

"I was thinking about that earlier. About being a chef." Jack smiled, keeping his eyes on his plate. "I'll never regret joining. I love my life. Sometimes I wonder how things would be if Drake hadn't died and we opened our own restaurant. But, I have to believe that everything happened the way it was supposed to. It always comes down to believing that so the what-ifs don't kill me. Besides, I love this, Eloise. I don't feel like I'm missing out on anything."

"I want you to have the things you love too."

Jack wanted to say that he had all the things he loved, but he bit his tongue. Instead, he walked his empty plate to the sink and rinsed it off. He felt Eloise at his back, wrapping her arms around him, tipping up on her toes to whisper in his ear.

"You make me happy too," she said, kissing his cheek, which made Jack think maybe she could read his mind.

When Jack walked out of the house, he knew the day would be hotter than the previous ones and he couldn't wait for it to start cooling down. Being in Colorado had been something he liked a lot more than he thought he would. The Grand Mesa was a gorgeous mountain and when it was in full bloom, like now, the reds and yellows would take your breath away. Eloise kept him so busy, largely because there would be snow soon and if they didn't finish her to-do list, things would have to wait until spring.

Jack was always surprised at how hard Eloise worked around

here. He did the brunt of the outdoor chores, but she was always willing to help when he needed it. She'd hold tools, help him carry things, do anything he asked, and he knew it was because she was proud of this place and wanted to be able to take care of it, with, or without him. Jack hoped there'd never be a *without him*, but he was also happy about her newfound independence because that was part of finding herself again.

Today Jack was painting the fence he'd been putting up around the property. It would take days, maybe longer, but Eloise wanted a perimeter fence, so he would make sure she got one. When it was too dark to see, he finally packed up his supplies and headed toward the house. Eloise would have dinner ready and was eager to wrap her in his arms.

"Hey, handsome," Eloise said as Jack walked in the front door.

"Hey there, beautiful," Jack said as he removed his boots.

"I hope you're hungry. I ran to the farmers' market today and bought salmon."

"Sounds delicious." Jack walked over and kissed her lips. "I'm going to shower."

"I don't suppose you have room in there for me?"

"I don't care where I am, there's always room for you." Jack reached around her and shut the oven off, kissed her again, and said, "We'll reheat it," as he threw her over his shoulders. Eloise squealed the entire way to the bathroom, a sound Jack wished he could record and listen to anytime he was sad.

They ate dinner, still naked, and when Eloise flashed her give-it-to-me smile, Jack didn't have to ask if he was sleeping at his house tonight.

Jack snuggled around Eloise, content. He didn't sleep with her every night, but the nights were getting more frequent. He always let her ask, or rather tell, him to sleep in her bed. He never assumed, but loved when Eloise did want him there and he never questioned the nights she didn't. He was doing things her way, even if it killed him.

Jack woke to Rossi barking her head off and jumped out of bed just as Eloise said his name, scared. He pulled jeans on, stuffing his feet in his shoes, no time for socks, and headed toward the door.

"Stay there, El," Jack said as he walked out. The pounding on Eloise's front door worried

him. He didn't know anyone who would come here this late without any warning. Jack cracked the door open and was shocked when he saw Chase. "Eloise, you can come out." Jack yelled before opening the door and letting Chase in.

"What the hell are you doing here?" Jack closed and locked the front door. Chase was pacing the living room when Eloise walked in.

"Eloise, this is Chase. Chase, Eloise." Chase waved and then turned and continued his circular motion.

Jack flipped on some more lights and wondered how Eloise would react to Chase's bloodshot eyes and literally smelly clothes.

"Hi, Chase." Eloise looked at Jack. "The spare room," she answered his unasked question.

"Thanks, beautiful. I'm going to get Chase settled and then I'll come to bed, okay?" Jack's way of indicating he planned to explain.

"Okay, handsome. Nice to meet you, Chase."

"You, too, Eloise. Thanks for, just, well, thanks." It wasn't like Chase could say "thank you for not freaking out about the hour or the fact that I look homeless."

"Sure, Chase." Eloise smiled before heading to her room

"Chase, what the fuck? Why are you showing up like this?" Jack whispered the second Eloise shut her door.

"I didn't know where else to go, Brennan." Chase ran his

hands over his face and slid down the wall, sitting on the floor.

"Chase, what happened?"

"Nightmares. Cold sweats. What hasn't happened. Allie went to stay with her mom. She took our kids, *my* kids, man." Chase was crying now and Jack had no idea what to do, so he just listened, kneeling in front of his friend. "I can't stop seeing it. I can't. I try, but it's always there. Shit, I blink and it's there, but you seem fine."

"I have nightmares, too, Chase," Jack admitted. What he didn't say was that Eloise knew he had nightmares. There were countless nights she'd shake him awake, his screams waking her, to remind him that he was safe, that she was there, and that he was just dreaming. The nights he had nightmares, if he wasn't already in her bed, he ended up there. Eloise never tried to get him to talk about it, she'd just wake him up, or unlock her door at an ungodly hour, remind him he was okay, and then hold him until they both fell asleep. He loved her so much for those nights. "Have you talked to anyone, Chase?"

"Have you?" Chase shot back.

"I've talked to Eloise." Jack sat down on the floor now. Eloise never pushed him, and as he told her pieces of his tours, he realized talking to her helped because the weight wasn't just his anymore. She helped him carry the pain. "She encouraged counseling, but I can't make myself go. Maybe someday. But, she's a good listener. She doesn't try to fix it, she just hears it."

"You don't think it's too much for her?"

"She hasn't acted like it is."

"I've never talked to Allie about anything we've seen. Never. But I've never been like this either. This bad. Connor really messed me up. But Allie does try to fix it, she just doesn't know what she's working against."

"Why'd she leave, Chase?"

"I think I started scaring her. When I refused to talk to her, or anyone, she said she had to be sure the kids were safe."

"She's not wrong." Jack hated to say it, but he also knew how quickly the things Chase was experiencing could end up hurting people or himself.

"I know." Chase wiped his nose with the back of his hand. "I gotta get them back, Brennan. I lost it when she left, when my kids left. I can't live like this. It'll kill me if she doesn't come back."

"Let's get you help first." Jack looked toward Eloise's door, knowing that as soon as he made this offer, there'd be no going back. "Stay here, Chase. You can stay here, and get help. I'll help you find it. You get better, Allie will come back."

"What about Eloise?"

"Eloise has known the same kinda pain. She'll understand."

"You don't want to ask her first?" Chase's eyes looked like his heart may stop if this plan didn't work.

"She'll understand," Jack said as he stood. He left Chase sitting as he got him a towel and pulled out a pair of his basketball shorts and a T-shirt. "Get up, man." Jack showed Chase to the spare bathroom and handed him the clothes and towel. "Clean up, try to sleep, take the room next to the bathroom, the bed's made. Don't stress about the nightmares. Eloise has heard me scream plenty of times." Jack decided to admit this so that maybe Chase would actually sleep. "You aren't gonna scare her away."

"Thank you." Chase embraced Jack. The hug was quick, but it was enough that Jack knew Chase came here because he needed someone to save him. Jack just hoped he could be the one to do it.

"Sleep, Chase. I mean it. We'll call around and find a good group tomorrow. You and me. And we'll call Allie and let her know you're here."

"I can't do this without you."

"You're not gonna have to." Jack stepped out of the bathroom doorway so that Chase could shower.

Eloise was reading when Jack opened her door and joined her in her bed.

"He's taking a shower. I gave him some of my clothes and tomorrow I'm going to find him someone he can talk to. A group or a counselor. I'll have to drive him, so you may have to do some of the things outside for a few days."

Eloise reached out and took Jack's hand. "I can do that."

"Do you have questions?"

"No, Jack, no questions. He can stay as long as he needs to. I've had that look in my eyes before. He clearly needs you."

Jack knew she'd understand. He didn't expect her not to want an explanation. Knowing Eloise, maybe she already knew.

Eloise put her head on Jack's chest. "Sleep with me."

"No place I'd rather be." Jack placed a kiss on the top of her head.

Chase didn't wake them up screaming, and Jack took that as a win. He was still crashed when Eloise finished making breakfast and Jack had completed all the outside chores. Jack said a quick thank-you to God that Chase showed up the night before a day off. Chase was in no condition to go to work, but he'd been going and that confused Jack. He must have been keeping it together at work until Allie and his kids left. Jack would have to ask to be sure but didn't see another explanation.

"Should I wake him up?" Jack asked Eloise as she made their plates.

"I say let him sleep." Eloise handed Jack his plate. "He probably needs it. He might not have felt safe to sleep before." Eloise broke her eye contact with Jack.

"Sleep it is." Jack smiled and started eating, Eloise sitting across from him. "What's on the agenda today?"

"I have to go pick up another dog. I told them I can't take any more until we adopt at least three out. I also have to go buy feed. You?"

"Get Chase set up. Show him around here. If he's here, he can help." Jack thought it'd be a good way to keep his mind off things, being outside with the animals definitely wouldn't hurt. "You need help with the feed?"

"They'll load it at the store, but you guys can unload it for me once I get home," Eloise said. "It'll be nice having extra manpower."

Between the dogs, the horses, the pigs, chickens, and goats, and more animals all the time, food was no light task. The Humane Society called when they had an animal that needed fostering. Sometimes Eloise had room, but more and more lately she didn't, and Jack knew she always felt horrible about that. Animal control would occasionally call, too, when they had to take neglected animals from people. Eloise never said no to abused animals, not even when she didn't have room.

Jack and Eloise had recently talked about buying the property behind hers, which would give her sixty acres. She wanted Jack to take a section and build a restaurant on it, but Jack wasn't sold yet.

"**M**orning." Chase walked around the corner and into the kitchen. Eloise thought he looked sad and a bit embarrassed at being there.

"Good morning," Eloise and Jack said together.

"How'd you sleep?" Eloise asked Chase.

"Best I've slept since we got back." Chase sounded honest.

"That's great. You stay here as long as you want." Eloise turned to make Chase a plate.

"Thank you, Eloise," Chase answered as she handed him a coffee mug and then his plate.

"She's a pretty good cook," Jack said. "Almost as good as me." He winked at Eloise.

Having Chase there would prove to be almost as good as having Jack there. It was nice that Jack would have help around the place. Over the next few days, Eloise realized that Chase, like Jack, would do anything she asked and always asked for more to do. Jack had driven him to all of his therapy sessions and group meetings over the last two weeks, and it seemed to be helping. At first, Chase made Jack swear that he'd keep everything a secret and Chase continued going to work, even with Jack encouraging him to put in for leave. Chase finally had the conversation he'd been avoiding and though he was no longer deployable because of it, he seemed more at ease, more sure that he was going to be okay. Eloise also knew that Chase called his wife every day and with each passing day, he seemed more confident in his marriage working out.

"She just needed you to talk to her," Jack said to him after he hung up with his wife and was grinning from ear to ear.

"At the time"—Chase looked up to Jack—"that was a lot easier said than done."

"I get that," Eloise chimed in, and she did. She got that all too well.

Chase had started leaving her money on the kitchen table two weeks ago, even though she repeatedly told him he didn't need to. That day, Chase had started making calls to set up his counseling closer to his house. Chase only lived about a half hour away, but he told Jack having to drive that distance all the time would get old. He planned on meeting his wife back at home in two days. He frequently said he missed his wife and his kids and had been saying "I think it's time" a lot more often.

Eloise was elated Chase was feeling better, getting help, and that his wife seemed supportive and wanted to save their marriage, but Eloise would still miss him. She'd gotten used to

Chase, just like she'd gotten used to Jack. She liked the three of them drinking coffee in the morning together. She loved to watch Jack and Chase outside, taking care of all the animals and fixing random things, goofing off like two teenagers the entire time.

When they returned from Chase's house, Eloise knew Jack would want to finish up the chores for the day, but she had other ideas. Having Chase around had been great, but it had also caused Jack to pull away from her physically. Emotionally, things had been better than ever, something Eloise credited to his meetings. But, Chase was always there, so Jack hadn't been naked as much as she'd like. They'd hold hands and kiss, and Chase realized there was something going on, but they didn't go all out like they had been prior to his arriving.

"He's just going through so much, I don't want him to feel like we're throwing it in his face," Jack had said after Chase had been there a week.

"I get that. I just— It's hard not to be all over you." Eloise smacked his butt, and his eyes went wide as he dramatically opened his mouth in what Eloise assumed was supposed to be shock.

Now that they were back home—and Chase was safely at his home—Eloise wasn't wasting any time.

"The chores can wait." She stripped slowly, making a show of it.

"Don't have to tell me twice." Jack ripped his clothes off, not aiming for sexy at all, which made Eloise laugh hard.

"The couch, Jack," Eloise said once her laughing subsided. Jack said nothing, just threw her over his shoulder and then down on the couch, making her laugh again.

Jack spread Eloise's legs wide and kneeled in front of her. She wanted him to sit down so she could ride him, but he started kissing every inch of her and she was more than okay with that happening first.

CHAPTER 19

The weeks after Chase left evolved into months before Jack had time to process. Jack didn't want to admit that he needed help with all the work around Eloise's place. Chase's absence made him think long and hard about hiring an extra hand. Jack thought about how to find someone as he kept himself busy outside and hid from Eloise. Jack had been avoiding her all weekend. He had received his orders two nights ago and wasn't ready to break the news. Things had been going so well between them, the animals had mostly settled in, and Eloise was planning to take new rescues within the next few weeks. She had even considered hiring a hand to help Jack after he brought it up, since he was still working full time in the Army.

Jack had to tell her today. She'd be pissed if he kept her in the dark until he was saying goodbye.

"Hey, El." Jack sat at the dining room table while Eloise washed dishes, looking out the window at the chickens.

"Hey, you. I was thinking we could do spaghetti for dinner tonight." Eloise dried her hands on a towel and went to sit by Jack.

"That'd be great. I've got to tell you something first, though, and I want to do it now, so I don't lose my nerve." Jack rubbed his hands together, looking down at them instead of at her.

"What is it?" Eloise reached out and took his hands.

"They're sending me back." Jack finally met her eyes.

"What?" Eloise blinked, keeping her eyes closed.

"I have to go back. I'm being redeployed." Jack caressed his thumb over the back of one of her hands.

"What do you mean you're going back?" Eloise was fighting tears as she spoke. "You can't go back."

"I have no choice, Eloise."

"People always have a choice." Her eyes opened in a flash and Jack saw a fury in them he'd never known before.

"Not in the Army they don't. You knew this was a possibility." Jack had been on two short missions since returning, but this would be different, and by the look on her face, Eloise knew that.

"Not after four months I didn't!" Eloise yelled as she stood, the chair tipping over as she stormed off to her bedroom.

Jack was right behind her and caught the door just as she was slamming it. "Eloise, we have to talk about this. You can't just disappear."

"Me disappear? Are you kidding me? You're the one about to ship off again for another God knows how many months. You just got home."

Jack couldn't hide his smile at her mention of home, and her confused look indicated that she had no clue what he found funny in this mess. "Eloise, we'll message each other just like we did before, it'll be okay. We'll get through this."

"Jack, I don't know if I can do this. What if you get hurt?" She sat down on the edge of her bed and Jack took a seat next to her. He reached for her hand and she started to pull away but stopped.

"We've already proved we can make it through deployment.

I'll be fine." Jack brought her fingers to his mouth and kissed each of their tips.

"As friends, Jack. We made it through that as friends." Eloise watched as he turned her hand and placed another kiss on the inside of her wrist.

"Were we just friends?" Jack kept kissing up her arm.

"No. But, now we're so much more. I can't imagine going back to not touching you for six or more months. What if you don't come home?"

"You can't think like that. No one can think like that. Do you hear me?" He let go of her arm and grabbed her face to make her look him in the eye. "I will come home, and you have to believe that the entire time I'm gone. No matter what. Do you understand me? It's knowing that you're here waiting for me that will bring me back."

"Okay."

"Promise me, Eloise."

"I promise, Jack. I'll wait for you, and you will come back to me."

"No matter what."

"No matter what."

Jack tugged Eloise into him and prayed that his promise found its way into her heart. If he was being honest with himself, he didn't think she was ready to go back to having a strictly conversational relationship with him. It would be so different now that he'd been in her bed, or her in his, for the last four months. She'd take him to the base in two days and just thinking about kissing her goodbye nearly made him cry. All she'd done since he told her he was leaving was cry. He couldn't believe she still had tears left.

Jack sat alone in the living room and thought about the first time Eloise came to his house, and the first time he'd seen her new home. It seemed like a lifetime ago. It felt like he had always been with Eloise and her animals. He never wanted that to change. Everything had been going so well. She was opening up to him in ways he didn't think she'd ever be able to, and now he had to leave again. He felt as though him leaving would make all their progress disappear. Once Eloise was alone again, she'd forget how great they were together.

There was still no label and that terrified Jack. He wanted to believe that this was something to her, a real relationship. He couldn't place all the blame on her, he hadn't asked for a label either. It didn't bother him until he got the order to deploy. What if this time was like all the times before? Great sex between two friends. Yes, he and Eloise were connected in more ways than that, and open and honest with each other in every way. But they'd been that before and she still left. He had to ask her before he left. He had to leave knowing they were committed to each other, that she saw this as more than sex with an old friend. He had to make sure she knew how much he loved her.

The night before Jack was set to leave, he and Eloise decided to go out to dinner. Jack watched Eloise get ready with precision. He could die a happy man having seen her in the near backless green dress, one that made her eyes stand out, and black heels.

"We can't go out with you looking like that unless you want me to fuck you on the table." Jack finally spoke after almost an hour of just watching.

"Do it. Maybe if you get arrested, they will let you stay," Eloise shot back. "I got you something." Eloise gave him a small smile. She walked out of the bathroom and Jack followed her into her bedroom. She opened the top drawer to her nightstand and pulled out a small leather thing that looked like a wallet. "Here." She handed it to him.

Jack opened it and was greeted with Eloise's smile. It was a pocket-size photo album. Eloise by herself, Jack and her together, Rossi, a few of Eloise's other animals that she knew Jack favored, and a final picture of Eloise blowing him a kiss. Jack closed the book and held it close to his chest.

"This is perfect, El. Thank you." Jack reached for her, pulling her to his chest. "I love that I'll have this with me."

"When you get there, turn the pictures over." Eloise leaned up to kiss him, and he wondered what she wrote on the backs of the photos she'd chosen.

Jack waited until after dinner and they were back home to talk to Eloise about giving their relationship a permanent label. The thought terrified him, because there was still a chance that she'd say no. Jack didn't want to leave without her being his girlfriend, a term that didn't seem enough to him. Eloise felt like so much more than a girlfriend. He'd always known that he was meant to be with her, but there was no term for the person you were born to love. He could call her a soul mate, but the guys in his unit would have a heyday with that, so girlfriend would have to do. If she'd have him.

"El, we need to talk about something before I leave in the morning," Jack told her as they both lay down in her bed.

"Spit it out." Eloise's voice sounded cold, which only added to Jack's worry, but he had to resolve this, now or in the morning, so he figured he'd better get it over with.

"Okay." Jack took a breath. "I want this to be something. I didn't want to bring it up, because I said the ball was in your court, but now I'm about to leave again, and I have to know before I go that we're on the same page."

"You can call this whatever you want to call it, Jack. A relationship, a girlfriend-boyfriend thing, a friends with benefits thing. This can be whatever you need it to be."

"How do you see me, Eloise?"

"As my saving grace, my light, the best friend I've ever had, my lover." Eloise paused. "You're everything to me, Jack. We tiptoe around this, even though we've both said we love each other. I don't know how to not love you, and I don't know how to stop feeling bad about loving you."

"I love you too. Always have." Jack rolled over and kissed Eloise. "You're all those things to me too. But..." Jack started to laugh a little. "How about we say girlfriend, because all that is a mouthful."

"Okay, *boyfriend*," Eloise said, and playfully punched Jack in the arm.

Eloise was focusing on ignoring the pang in her chest that was no doubt there to remind her that she was betraying her husband by moving on. She wished she knew when that feeling would go away. Would she ever not feel bad about being with Jack? Would she always feel like loving Jack was wrong?

The morning after Jack left, Eloise felt frozen. She was back in a recliner, which made absolutely no sense, seeing as though she shared her bed with Jack, he wasn't dead. He was coming back. He promised. Eloise had to get up, she had animals depending on her, and based on all the wind throughout the night, they'd be cold and hungry.

When Eloise stood, it took her a moment to find her balance. Eloise couldn't deny how much life Jack breathed into her and when he was gone, the empty dark that Reagan left her with was free to take over. The only thing that forced her to put her boots and jacket on was knowing that the animals had to eat. She reached down and rubbed Rossi's head. The look in her eyes was one that Eloise assumed was worry. Did Rossi know how broken Eloise was when she was alone?

The second Eloise stepped outside, she lost her breath. The cold air smacked her in the face, but instead of being annoyed, she smiled. Eloise could feel Jack's arms around her, and she took a deep breath to breathe in the cold, and to allow the feeling of Jack to blanket her. She felt fabulous and thinking about that made her feel even better. Jack was gone. But Jack was coming back. The cold snapped the darkness away, it brought color to her cheeks, and by the time she was done with the outside chores, her fingers were so cold she couldn't close them. Eloise made coffee and sat outside, still freezing, but afraid to leave the cold, afraid that it was her new protector and if it left, too, all hope would go with it.

It took her a few days to admit it, but she needed someone to help around her place. Eloise could do all the chores, but it was hard to keep up with everything Jack did and everything she had always done. Jack probably wouldn't like having someone around while she was here alone, but she didn't have much choice. She was at capacity, in the process of buying the fifty additional acres, and already had a waiting list going for when that property was ready for animals.

Jack and Eloise were back to messaging every chance they could, and calling when their schedules allowed. The days mostly flew by for Eloise, because there was so much to do, which she was thankful for, because even when she woke up feeling paralyzed, she had to keep moving forward. Eloise wasn't sure if she should worry that she hadn't heard from Jack. He warned her that it may be a while before he'd be able to contact her again, but never told her what amount of time was too much. She decided that no news was good news after calling her friend from college whose husband was in the Navy.

"Yeah, yeah, don't even stress," Phoebe said over the phone. "I once went six months without talking to Tony."

"Six months!" Eloise swallowed. "How did you manage?"

"He loves it, honey. Loves it. I can't take that from him."

"I can't lose Jack." Eloise closed her eyes to keep herself from crying.

"I know, Eloise. I get it. I worry myself sick, too, but you can't stop because your guy has a dangerous profession."

"Reagan didn't have a dangerous profession."

"Exactly," Phoebe said, then paused. "You can lose someone at any time, in all kinds of ways. The best thing you can do is cherish them when you have them, love them with your whole heart. Don't let yourself think about the what-ifs because you'll drive yourself insane. Just keep Jack close to your heart and believe he'll come back to you."

"Thanks, Phoebe," Eloise whispered, still trying not to cry.

Eloise and Phoebe had met in college, and hung out some, but were mostly just friends online since graduating. Eloise thought Phoebe would think she was crazy when she sent her a message on Facebook and asked if she could call her out of the blue. Phoebe ended up being sweet about everything and Eloise was happy to know someone who understood what it was like to need someone that loved you, but still chose to leave.

After Eloise hung up with Phoebe, making plans to start calling each other weekly, she decided to call her uncle and see if he knew anyone who would want a job. Her uncle knew a man named Jesse who he thought would like a gig.

"He's old, El," her uncle said on the phone. "But he'll work harder than any young guy you could find."

"I don't mind old."

"He's got a few sons, three or four, I'm not real sure. He'll bring them when he needs extra hands, but he won't expect you pay 'em."

"Okay, whatever he needs. I just need someone who can pick up the slack. I got offered a job, teaching a night class one day a week at the college, and I really want to take that, which means I'll need the help even more than I already did."

"That's great. Congratulations. How's everything else?"

"I miss Jack, but it's good." Again, Eloise was thankful that she knew her uncle wouldn't ask anything further. They talked a few more minutes before saying their goodbyes. Eloise agreed to meet Jesse the next morning at a coffee place overlooking a lake. The water and the mountains were the reasons Eloise loved this place so much. Mountains, pine trees, and the ever-changing colors, it was one of the most beautiful places she'd ever been.

"'Ey, you must be Eloise," Jesse, head-to-toe cowboy, said as he stuck out his hand to Eloise. Eloise stood before taking his hand.

"I am Eloise. Nice to meet you." She sat first, and then him.

"It's nice to meet you too. Thanks for meeting me. What kinda work you needing?"

"Well, I run a farm and a sanctuary, or I'm trying to. It's just starting out. But the animal shelters keep me at capacity with horses, goats, sheep, and just about any other livestock that is mistreated or left behind. Pigs too." Eloise took a sip of her coffee. "The pound has me at capacity with dogs. I don't take cats. Had to draw the line somewhere. I just need someone who can clean pens, feed and exercise animals, give baths, buy feed, haul hay, just help run the place, the actual work part. I do all the records, meetings, adoptions, and the like."

"You need the manual labor."

"Yes. I've been doing it, but it's too much. I'll still help. I'm also going to start teaching again, just one night a week, but even being gone that much will make a difference to the animals." Eloise didn't know why, but she added, "I had someone to help, but he deployed. It'll be a while, months, maybe a year, before he's back." Eloise's eyes shifted down to her coffee.

"Hey," Jesse said. "Don't worry, honey. What I can't do, my boys can. We'll have that place running like clockwork before you know it."

"Thank you. I don't think I really knew what I was getting myself into." Eloise didn't want to cry in front of this stranger, so she stopped thinking about how hard it had been since Jack left. There was so much work to be done and she felt a bit stupid now for moving to a place where she didn't know anyone in order to try and heal herself.

"Some of the best things in life are overwhelming." Jesse patted the back of her hand. "When should I start?"

"Tomorrow, or if that's too soon, Monday."

"Tomorrow is fine. Will you be available to show me around?"

"Yes." Eloise dug through her purse and pulled out a notebook and pen. She wrote her cell number and address on it and handed it to Jesse. "If you have any trouble finding it, just call."

"Great. Thank you for meeting me."

"Thank you." Eloise stood and got her things ready to leave.

Jesse reached out and squeezed her wrist. "He's gonna be okay."

And in her heart, Eloise believed him.

Jack didn't wait until they landed to read through Eloise's photo notes. He read them on the plane, and then wished he didn't, because they left him smiling like a fool and based on their faces, the men around him noticed. The first photo of her said *I love you, always*. The next one of them kissing said *I'll think about your lips every day*. The ones of the animals had funny quotes, as if the animals wrote them themselves. The final photo, Jack's favorite, was of Eloise blowing him a kiss and it said *I'll never run again. I'll always be your light*. Jack slipped the photo back in its plastic and stuck the book in his chest pocket.

It took Jack over a week in the Middle East to find good enough Wi-Fi to send Eloise a Facebook Message. He looked at his photo album every day, and worried about her doing all the work around her place alone. The idea of leaving the Army was something that scared him, but leaving Eloise scared him more.

> *Hey, beautiful. I finally found some Wi-Fi. How have things been going?*

Jack kept the chat window open on his phone while he ate, hoping Eloise would answer before the Wi-Fi took a dump.

> *Hey back, handsome. Things here have been great. I actually hired someone to do all the things you did. Don't freak out, he's nice.*

He's nice. That was pretty much the only part of Eloise's message that Jack had retained.

Jack wouldn't describe himself as a jealous man, but springing a random dude on him when he was basically in another world had him a tad stressed. He should have hired someone. He and Eloise had discussed it, but Chase came and then time got away from him. He saw it now. Had he met the new guy before leaving, he wouldn't be feeling like he couldn't breathe.

> *How'd you find this mystery man? Is he qualified?*

Jack imagined Eloise laughed when she read his message. Jack was nowhere near qualified, and neither was Eloise, but the two of them had figured it out.

> *He's worked for my uncle before on odd jobs. I think I'm going to have him stay with me. His*

*wife died a couple years ago and he moved
into an RV park after selling his house.*

Jack couldn't believe he'd been gone less than two weeks and some guy was already moving in. What on earth was Eloise thinking? She never said the guy was anything more than a worker, so Jack didn't have an actual reason to be worried.

*He's just working for you, right? I want you to be
safe.*

Jack's couldn't believe he was asking her if she was having a relationship with Jesse. She'd told him what he meant to her, so why was he still questioning it?

*He's in his sixties, Jack. He does have sons, four of
them, but don't worry—you're the only one I
want.*

Jack instantly felt relieved. He hated himself for questioning her and knew at some point he'd have to trust that she'd stay. It wasn't fair to her for him to continually doubt her. He wasn't thrilled about five men at her house all the time, but if they were nice and were helping, then he would support Eloise. He was happy that she wouldn't be alone the entire time he was gone, that she'd have people around to keep her busy.

*I'm glad you have help, El. I just worry about you,
but I trust you and I love you.*

I love you, too, handsome. Stay safe.

Jack read the message that was attached to a photo of Eloise and then updated his phone's home screen with the new photo before stuffing his phone in his pocket. He wanted to hit the gym before bed, and it was getting late. As Jack walked toward the equipment, he thought about Eloise's picture. His life had changed quicker than he ever imagined was possible. He remembered what Eloise said about Trinity deserving a chance that wasn't based on Eloise. He supposed Eloise deserved that same chance. Jack didn't want to ruin this by blaming Eloise for things she did years ago. Jack pulled his phone out, looked at Eloise's delicate face, and promised her that he would be better, because she deserved his best.

CHAPTER 20

Eloise sat at her desk grading essays when the doorbell rang. She wasn't expecting anyone, and assumed it was the mail, so she continued to read the essay she was working on. The doorbell rang again. Maybe she needed to sign for something. She pushed her desk chair back and stood up. When she turned to face the door, she saw the black SUV parked in front of her house and the sleeve of an Army uniform. Eloise froze. If she didn't open the door this wouldn't happen. This could not be happening. No matter what she said to herself, no matter what, Jack is coming home. Eloise took a deep breath and one step forward to open the door.

The two men facing Eloise didn't say anything. She pushed the screen door open as well and the men stared at her. She'd be damned if she was going to speak first.

"Ma'am," the man on the left said. "Are you Eloise Masten?"

Eloise nodded. If she spoke she'd cry, and she refused to let these men see her break.

"Miss Masten, may we come in for a moment?" the man on the right asked.

Eloise looked up at his chest. His name was Forester. Eloise nodded again and stepped back. She didn't say anything as she walked into the living room and sat down on the couch. The men followed, but didn't sit. They stood in front of her, powerful, steady. Eloise looked at the other man's chest and read his name, Cooper. Rossi came in through the dog door and took a stance between Eloise and the two strangers.

"We're here because of Jack Brennan," Forester spoke first.

"Jack," Eloise whispered so quietly she wasn't sure she actually spoke.

"Yes," Copper answered. The two men eyed each other, as if they should have gone over the plan one more time before coming here. Cooper reached into his chest pocket and took out a folded piece of paper. "We're here because of this letter." He didn't open it. "This is kind of out of our wheelhouse, ma'am. Most people have next of kin. Brennan didn't, and after a while his sergeant read this"—he lifted the paper—"and it basically said that if anything happened to notify Eloise Masten. You, ma'am."

"After a while?" That was the only thing Eloise heard. How long had it been? She didn't question the lack of contact. He told her messages may not come, depending on where he was and what he was doing. She just waited for him. Like she promised she would.

"He's been gone three days, ma'am."

"Is he...?" Eloise couldn't make herself say the word. No one deserved to lose someone who brought them back to life.

"We're not sure," Forester finally spoke. "Sergeant Beckett has letters like these for all of his men. Most are written to wives or other family, but Brennan's was written to Beckett and only said to notify you."

"What the hell do you mean you're not sure?" Eloise was seeing red now. *Not sure. How in the hell could they not know whether a man was dead or alive?*

"His unit ran into some trouble and he's missing. That is all we're at liberty to say," Forester said.

Eloise forced her tears back. She would not cry in front of these men. "You can go."

"You don't have questions, ma'am?" Cooper didn't look at her as he spoke.

"Of course I have questions, idiot, but you just told me you wouldn't tell me anything. You came here to tell me you know nothing. I knew nothing before you got here, so I'm not entirely sure why you're here." Eloise was furious. She had no clue if Jack was alive or dead and no one was going to tell her anything more than he was missing. "Did he instruct you to tell me if he dies?"

"Yes, ma'am." Cooper glanced at her, but Eloise looked away.

"Great, so come back if you find out he's dead. Get out of my house." Eloise knew it wasn't their fault, but she didn't care. She couldn't keep looking at them. The two soldiers gave each other a quick glance and turned to leave.

"I'm sorry, ma'am," Cooper said as he closed her front door.

The second Eloise heard it shut, she lost it. These were different tears than she shed for her husband, because they were cloaked in the not knowing. When Regan died there was no waiting, no question. It was horrible and it destroyed her, but she wasn't left to wonder. Was Jack being tortured? Was he afraid? Was he dead? She may go her entire life not knowing.

Eloise kept her phone in her hands all the time. She knew she wouldn't get a message from Jack, but she held it anyway. She told herself that eventually the message would come, and she'd need to be there when it did. She promised him no matter what, so that's what she was holding on to now. She wouldn't give up on him. He would come home.

Eloise opened up Facebook Messenger.

Jack-

*Two soldiers just left here. They don't know where
you are, and they wouldn't tell me anything. I
know you won't get this message, but I had to
send something. I don't know what to do. I
can't picture a world where you don't come
back to me. I know I wasn't sure, and that I
spent a lot of time confused, but I was
mourning. You understood that. You've always
understood me, even when I didn't understand
me. I'm sure now, Jack. More sure than I've
ever been. Please come home. I love you.*

Eloise went through the days and nights like a zombie. She
didn't speak to anyone she didn't have to. Her college class was
moved to an online format so that unless her students had a question, she didn't have to talk to them either. She fell into an obses-
sive cleaning habit. Every inch of her house was sterile, Jack's
house too. Everything except Jack's room. It was just as he left it.
She couldn't make herself go in there. Just like when her husband
died, anything that reminded her of him was off-limits. Except
Jack wasn't dead. She would not let herself believe he was. She
kept her phone close and her promise to him even closer.

Eloise panicked anytime her phone went off, but it had been
four days since the soldiers came and still nothing new about
Jack. When her phone buzzed in her hand, she jumped so high she
almost dropped it.

Eloise call me. I need to know you're still okay.

I'm fine, Mom. I'm not calling you.

Eloise wasn't calling anyone. This was very much like when
she lost her husband. She refused to call anyone then either. She

wouldn't answer her phone, so her mom should be happy she got a text back. Just like before, the banging on her door was ever present, but this time it wasn't people she knew. It was wives, wives of other soldiers who also worked at Fort Gunnison. She was still working, albeit online, so she wasn't sure why everyone was so worried. With Regan she wanted to die. She quit doing anything that meant she was living—work, shower, change clothes—but with Jack, she wanted to live, she wanted him to live. It was impossible to interact with the people in her life, to explain that she was living for the both of them until he came home. She was being robotic, methodical, they'd think she was crazy. Maybe she was.

After days of living on autopilot, Eloise had an idea. Jack was alive, he had to be, so she'd stop acting like he wasn't at home. She'd stop sleeping on the couch and sleep in her bed, or go to his house and sleep in his, they'd spent a lot of time together in both. She'd go in his room and allow herself to be surrounded by him. His scent was still present on his sheets and pillows, and hers too. She fell asleep in his bed, still clutching her phone.

Eloise woke up to thirteen text messages, ten of which were from Nickie. One was from her uncle and two from her mom. They were all the same thing, only worded in different ways. *Eloise, are you okay?* She sent a group text to save time.

I am fine. I'm just trying to stay busy.

Eloise fired up her computer while the coffee brewed. She scrolled through her "Jack" file, opening each message that she had screenshotted, reading them carefully. She loved reading them and being able to see their evolution in the words. Friends to lovers over the course of eight months during his first deployment and then again over the two months before he went missing. She opened her text messages next. Those were some of her favorite messages. They were quick, intimate, and flirty, and all from when he was home. She felt so stupid for not questioning where he was sooner. More than two weeks had gone by before the soldiers came to her house, but she didn't know that not hearing from him during that span was abnormal. Unlike him, she hadn't done this before, and he always made it sound like there was nothing to worry about.

The days and nights were a blur to Eloise. She never slept, and almost never ate. If Jack didn't come home soon, she'd probably die. Not in a dramatic way, in a very literal way. She was worried about him to the point of it affecting every aspect of her life. She couldn't think straight, but the routines seemed to get her through.

Eloise found herself out before the sun, cleaning stalls and feeding animals. Jesse would do all the work for her, the deal was he'd pick up Jack's work, but she couldn't go through the days without those chores. If Eloise had the animals to depend on her, it would keep her from turning back into the woman who wore the same pajamas for multiple days and basically lived in her recliner.

Jesse fit into Eloise's life as if he'd always been there. She didn't know him well, but she liked him. He was probably near retirement, but worked harder than most twentysomethings. He'd show up extremely early, which didn't matter now that Eloise never slept. Before Jack went missing, Jesse would call Eloise at four or five in the morning and she'd roll over in her bed croaking "hello" over the line.

"I'm on the way," Jesse would say.

"I'll unlock the door," Eloise would answer before hanging up. She'd climb out of bed, barely opening her eyes, unlock her back door, and then climb right back into bed. By the time she'd get up, Jesse, like Jack, would have the outside chores done and coffee made and be waiting on Eloise to fix breakfast.

Now, knowing that Jack was missing, Eloise was up long before Jesse ever called and would have about half of the outside chores done before he got there, most of which was done using a headlamp. He'd finish them up and she'd cook breakfast. She was thankful that he'd sit with her at the table to sip coffee and eat, same as before, because without Jesse, she would never get out of bed and no one would know. Her family and Nickie were used to Eloise barely answering their texts at this point.

Today, Eloise was out in the goat pen when Jesse drove up. She had pulled the trimming stand out because it was time to cut their feet, something she couldn't do without Jesse's help.

"Morning, Eloise." Jesse waved from her front gate as he stepped out of his truck.

"Hey, Jesse. You wanna do this now or after breakfast?" She nodded to the stand.

"Let's knock it out." Jesse reached into the bed of his truck and pulled out his tools before heading over to Eloise. She grabbed the first goat with a rope collar and leash and led him to the stand, he struggled, but not enough that Jesse had to step in. Eloise held the goat while Jesse grabbed his tools, then she wrapped her arms around his neck to hold him tight as Jesse pulled up leg by leg to cut the hooves.

"Any news?" Jesse asked after three of the goats were done.

"Nothing yet." Eloise secretly hoped he'd stop asking. If there was news, she'd tell him. He meant well, though, so she wouldn't ever say that to him.

"I'm so sorry, Eloise. You know if you need anything, I can do it. If it's anything too crazy, I'll get my boys over here." His oldest had just turned thirty and his youngest boy was nineteen. They had all been out to the property to help before. It was Jesse's four sons who had finished painting the fence that Jack had started. Jesse's oldest, Ethan, owned the only grocery store in Mesa, but he never seemed to mind coming to help his dad.

"Thanks, Jesse. You've been a godsend. I think the biggest thing I have right now is I need to get another trailer load of hay. I can't load and unload all that alone." As much as Eloise wished she could do everything alone, she could barely lift a two-string hay bale. She couldn't imagine loading up the entire trailer alone. Before, Jack would always do it, but even he usually had help. Most of the time it came from Chase and other guys in his unit.

"I can bring the boys out tomorrow if you'd like and we can get that done for you."

"Thank you. I can meet you there and pay the guy."

"Sounds good to me, say eight?"

"Sure, I'll call him tonight and let him know we're coming."

"Well, these guys look loads better," Jesse said as he finished the last goat. Eloise watched as he folded up the stand and stuck it back in the tack shed. "What else do you have to do today?"

"Well, now that I know I'm going into town tomorrow, I'll get all the checks written, make the payments I need to. Uh, I told the neighbor I'd run them over some eggs today and then just the usual stuff." Eloise wiped her hands down her jeans. "I was thinking that once I close on the additional acres, we could build a guest house. You could move here fulltime, if you wanted, and so could your boys. You all help so much that all the driving back and forth is silly."

"You sure?" Jesse removed his hat and waited for her response.

"More than sure." Eloise stepped forward and embraced Jesse, not realizing how much she needed a hug.

"He's going to come home, honey. I know it."

"Me too. I just miss him."

Jesse release her, grabbed the wheelbarrow, and stacked two bales of hay in it as Eloise stood watching. "I'm going to take this down to the cows and then I'll be around if you need anything."

"Thanks, Jesse." Eloise watched him head down to the open

field where she kept six cows. She had never really wanted cows, but Jack thought they were a good idea. He said they could sell them if they ever needed money. Well, he said Eloise could if she ever needed money. That was the thing about Jack, everything belonged to Eloise. No matter how hard she tried to include him, he never acted like any of this was his. Part of her loved him more for that and part of her was terrified by it. Maybe he wasn't ready to be responsible for all the baggage that came with Eloise.

Eloise loaded up six big buckets with dog food and waited until she could hear Jesse.

"Jesse, will you help me feed the dogs?"

"Yes, ma'am," Jesse yelled from the goat pen as he stacked the wheelbarrow back against the wall.

The kennels were another project that Jack had completed. Eloise had started her sanctuary with dogs. Six of the eleven dogs she had now were probably never leaving, but she'd do her best to find them all loving homes. In the beginning, Eloise wanted to be able to take on all rescues, but she had to start somewhere, and the vet in town said dogs were the animals that she saw dumped the most. Eloise was equipped for ten dogs, but she told the vet that she needed a break when Jack left. Anytime someone dumped their dog, usually meaning they dropped it off at the vet and never picked it up, the vet called her. Eloise kept a small fenced-in area in the back for Rossi to get a break from the rescues when she needed it and to have for any dog who needed to be separated. Most of the time, all of the dogs wanted to be running the property.

Eloise opened each kennel door and the dogs sprinted out as if it were Christmas. While they ran off some of their energy, she and Jesse cleaned out each kennel before adding the new food and topping off their water. Opening the kennels each morning was one of Eloise's favorite parts of the day. She would let the dogs run as long as they wanted. If there weren't mountain lions and coyotes nearby, she wouldn't make them sleep in kennels, but had to for their safety. The entire property was secured, so they weren't going anywhere during the day. She hadn't had a problem with them and the other animals, and she hoped it stayed that way.

"Thanks, Jesse."

"You got it."

"I'm gonna go make breakfast. I'll yell when it's done."

"Thank you." Jesse headed off toward the chicken coop to check for eggs as Eloise went back into the house.

It was the tiny moments, scooping dog food, chatting with Jesse, cleaning out kennels, that kept Eloise from drowning. She told herself repeatedly that she had to keep moving forward. She missed Jack, but this limbo she was living in was hell. She'd wake up in a cold sweat and screaming, the nightmares too much to bear. She had nightmares before, about Reagan, but somehow these seemed worse. No matter how hard she tried, Eloise couldn't stop picturing Jack making her coffee. Simple. Smiling. A moment that she prayed wouldn't have to become a memory.

Eloise wrote Jack at least one message per day since finding out he was missing. Messages she prayed he'd eventually read. Sometimes she wrote more. It was hard not to write to him about every aspect of her day, hard to talk herself out of sending him messages all throughout the day. Mostly, she wrote him when she was alone, after the chores were done and Jesse was asleep in one of the guest rooms or back at his own place, when her house was too quiet and her mind too dangerous.

Nickie and Gage were supposed to arrive tomorrow, and Eloise wished she'd told Nickie to wait until Jack was safe to visit, but it was too late to ask her to change her plans now. Ethan would bring groceries from his store, and if she asked, he would probably even cook while Nickie and Gage visited, and that took some of her stress away. Her friends would be understanding about her mood, her lack of desire to host, but she felt horrible that they'd have to.

The next evening, Eloise's house was buzzing with excitement. Ethan had cooked, and Gage had been helping Ethan's brothers—Kyson, Markham, and Bryke—wash dogs for most of the afternoon, which Nickie was getting a kick out of watching. Jesse stayed close to Eloise, protective of the young woman he'd come to love.

"You let them all stay here?" Nickie asked as she and Eloise picked up the kitchen after dinner.

"I like them here. They keep it from being so quiet, and besides those three other bedrooms just sit empty. Jesse had his boys put twin beds in two of the rooms for when they all end up here at once. It works, for now."

"You basically adopted an entire grown-ass family." Nickie laughed, looking in the living room at Eloise's makeshift family.

"Well, Jesse lost his wife a couple years ago, and he and his boys help so much around here, sometimes sunup to sundown, so it occasionally makes sense for them to stay here. I'm actually thinking about building like a guest house or something for them to stay full time. If they want to."

"Don't take this the wrong way, but you sound a bit crazy."

"I feel a bit crazy, Nickie." Eloise wasn't lying about that, but what she didn't say was that she didn't care if she sounded crazy. Jesse and his boys made Eloise's days easier. She slept better with one or more of them around. They were nice, and they made her laugh. One thing Eloise believed in her bones since losing Reagan was that she loved having people and animals around that she could help. If it was up to her, Eloise would never be in an empty, silent, house, ever again.

CHAPTER 21

J ack had no clue where he was, but was positive it wasn't where he wanted to be. He wasn't sure what happened. He remembered being shot at or something exploding, but his memories were really fuzzy. He'd been in and out of consciousness and had terrible nightmares about being captured. He wasn't sure what was real and what was imagined. His throat burned and begged for water.

Jack tried to focus his sight. His face and chest were killing him, and his arms felt numb. He reached up to rub his eyes, and then screamed as he touched raw skin. Jack's hands and arms were numb, and the oozing burns made him feel like he was going to pass out, so he quit looking. He'd have to do something for these wounds or he'd bleed to death.

All Jack thought about was getting home, and back to Eloise. She must be worried sick. He had no idea how long it had been since he sent his last email. She told him no matter what, she wouldn't give up on him, and he had to believe that. He had to find people. Lost. If he was lost that meant they had crashed, right? Was he in a helicopter? He had to have been. He wished he could remember who was with him.

"Brennan. Brennan is that you?" The voice sounded far away, almost as though Jack was making it up.

"Hello?" he screamed to the sky.

"Brennan."

Jack stood and looked in all directions, turning around three times before he finally saw someone walking toward him. His vision was still blurry, and before he could make out a face he was being embraced. Pain soared over him like fire and he let out another scream.

"Stewart. Stewart, are you okay?" Jack stepped back. He knew it was Stewart without being able to focus his eyes. "What the hell happened?"

"I have no clue. I woke up somewhere over there. I can't remember shit, except that our helicopter went down."

"Well that's more than I remember. I didn't even know we were in a helicopter."

"Yeah, I remember going out in trucks and then the heli-copter going down. I'm not sure when or why we went from the trucks to the helicopter, but then it got shot down. Jack, you're in rough shape. The adrenaline is keeping you going right now, but those burns are going to need attention, like now."

"How many people were with us?" Jack ignored the comments about his burns. He couldn't feel his arms or the left side of his face, and even though he felt his chest move as he breathed, something was wrong there too.

Stewart closed his eyes, as if trying to force himself to remember, then rubbed his forehead. "Jonesy. He was with us. Do you remember the school, Brennan?"

"Yeah, as soon as you said Jonesy, it hit me." Jack, Andrew Jones, and Hugh Stewart had set out in a Humvee to secure a school under fire. On the way, they broke down and were in some iffy territory. They radioed for help and were sent a helicopter.

They got on, and only made it a few minutes before being shot down.

Jack turned his back to Stewart. He didn't want him to see him choking back tears. Jack couldn't get the image of Jonesy out of his mind. The blood across his uniform and his face nearly unrecognizable before the helicopter even hit the ground.

"He didn't make it, did he?" Stewart asked. "Jonesy."

"No." Jack didn't turn around. "The pilot either." After giving himself a few minutes to get it together, Jack turned to face Stewart again. "We gotta get help, we have to get out of here."

"There ain't shit out here, Brennan." Stewart rubbed his eyebrow, and then shook out his hands before pulling down on his uniform. "Where do we start." Stewart cleared his throat. Jack thanked God that Chase was at home with Allie and his kids. Chase was great to have in sticky situations, but Stewart was just as good.

"We've gotta check the helicopter." Jack's eyes went wide. Checking the helicopter meant facing the two men's bodies who they considered brothers. "I can do it."

"Together," Stewart said. "We do everything together, and we get our asses out of here together."

"Right," Jack said, then turned toward the helicopter, Stewart following closely behind him. "We get them out first." Jack stopped at the front of the helicopter.

Stewart came around to pull out the pilot and laid him carefully on the sand. Jonesy was harder to watch and Jack found that he couldn't look him in the face as Stewart laid him next to the pilot. Stewart looked around at what was left of the helicopter, then pulled Jonesy's dog tags off and stuffed them in his pocket, followed by the pilot's.

Stewart returned to the helicopter, then stuck his head out, holding three bottles of water. "Looks like this is all we got for water. We have a few bars in here, but nothing else for food. The radio is shot."

Jack had no clue what to do. He'd led men and women for almost a decade. He'd been in some situations that would make people question how he was still alive. In all his years, though, he'd never felt this hopeless. He had no idea where they were or which direction to go. Three bottles of water and a few protein bars wouldn't get them very far in this heat. Jack didn't say anything as Stewart motioned for him to sit down. Jack's adrenaline was rapidly being replaced with worry and agonizing pain.

Stewart pulled the first aid kit out and sat next to Jack in the sand. Neither of them said anything as Stewart covered Jack's arms and face in cream and lightly placed gauze over the top of his open burns. Jack hadn't looked at his wounds since the first time, he couldn't. Looking made them real. Looking gave the pain he'd been ignoring power. Instead, Jack continued to pretend his arms, his hands, and his face were fine. With each new bandage, Jack knew how *not* fine he actually was. He could feel liquid oozing from the left side of his face and both his arms were drenched with new and dried blood and what looked like puss. He concentrated on his pain, not long enough to give in to it, just long enough to know for sure that he could still feel the parts of himself that had been in flames. Jack knew because of his medical training that his arms and hands were bad, could kill him if they didn't get out of here soon. He couldn't see his face, but the fact that he couldn't feel it made him worried. He could feel one spot, the area that was dripping, but otherwise felt numb.

Jack found some comfort in the fact that Stewart looked mostly unwounded, with the exception of a few scrapes. Jack knew that if they made it out of this alive, his Army career was over. He couldn't even grip a water bottle. Stewart had to hold and pour it in his mouth for him, but Stewart never commented on that and for that, Jack was thankful.

Jack had to keep his head on straight, because even injured and much worse off than Stewart, Stewart still depended on him to get them out of this. It was their training, ingrained in them, following orders. Jack knew Stewart needed that security now more than ever, and he'd give it to him until his last breath.

"We gotta move." Jack struggled to stand, and Stewart helped by supporting Jack's arms. "Get anything out of there that we might be able to use. If you aren't sure, take it. You never know." Jack could give the orders, but it was up to Stewart to see them through. It took everything Jack had to keep standing. Stewart went through the helicopter a third time, then returned with Jonesy's overstuffed backpack.

"I can't carry them both." Stewart said the thing they both knew.

"I know." Jack's eyes shifted to the bodies in the sand. "Let's find a way to drag them. I can't hold or carry them, but I can pull them if we can strap them around our waists." Jack promised this and even if it was the last thing he did, he would make sure those two men didn't rot in this desert.

"I trust you." Stewart stuck out his hand and Jack shook it. An unspoken pact. All or nothing. They were getting out of this together, or dying together.

The heat was beyond anything Jack could remember feeling. Jack chose a direction and Stewart counted their steps out loud. Each time he saw anything, a bush, a tree, a rock, he said that out loud too. Jack matched his steps to Stewart's voice. Jack was struggling not to fall over and had to stay laser-focused on the sound of Stewart's voice to ignore how badly each step, each breath, hurt. If it wasn't for Stewart and of course Eloise, Jack would've lain down in the sand and died in the middle of the desert.

Jack's arms and face were burning, and he had to consistently remind himself not to touch. He focused all his attention on Stewart's counting, trying not to let the pain take over. The dressing was already soaked through with blood, and Jack knew he'd pass out if he didn't stop bleeding soon. It wasn't gushing, and he was thankful for that, but it was enough that over time, it would kill him. This would probably kill Eloise, too, the not knowing, if Jack's body was never found. He at least had to give her that. If he was going to die, it needed to be in a hospital, in a place where someone could explain to her what happened to him. Jack couldn't think about water or heat. He couldn't think about his wounds or being covered in his own blood. He had to focus on being alive, on staying alive. He promised her he'd come back. He told her no matter what, and no matter how badly the blisters were on his feet, or the burning in his throat, or how bad the scorching on his arms and face became, he had to keep walking.

"Let's stop, Stewart." Jack quit walking. "Just for a minute. Drink some water." Jack unstrapped the pulley system they'd created from around his waist and Stewart did the same.

Stewart pulled a water bottle out of his backpack, drank half, and poured the rest in Jack's mouth. Jack sat, but Stewart stayed standing.

"Jack, we haven't seen or heard shit in hours."

"Someone is looking for us, Chase." Jack hoped that leaving was the right choice. They could've stayed with the plane, but honestly if Jack hadn't forced himself to move, he didn't think he'd still be breathing.

"We don't even know how long we were unconscious. Who the hell knows how long it's been since we went out."

"That doesn't matter, Chase. One day or fifteen. The second they knew that helicopter went down, they were going to find us."

"I know that. I just can't do this to Emma." Stewart sucked in a strangled breath.

"You won't." Jack had to believe that Stewart would get back to his wife and that he would get back to Eloise. Jack knew

Stewart was in pain, but being medically trained, he knew he couldn't do anything for broken ribs. Stewart shouldn't worry about not seeing Emma again. Jack knew that even if he didn't make it home, Stewart would. He had to.

Jack told himself they'd have to start moving again soon but wasn't sure he could. Jack looked up at the sky and told Drake that he needed him, begged his brother to help them out of this, before his world went dark.

E loise was curled up in a blanket watching *Blue Bloods* when her doorbell rang. It was way too late for visitors. She got up slowly, unsure she wanted to know who was here and why. Before she reached the door, she peeked out the side window. The black SUV was back, the vehicle of death.

Eloise concentrated on not passing out. She couldn't stop staring at the vehicle. The windows were tinted so black that she couldn't see any movement inside. No one got out. Still, Eloise held her breath. If Jack was dead, she'd die and not in a metaphorical way. Whoever was here would give her the news and she'd die on the spot because she knew her heart couldn't take anymore. When it broke today, it'd be broken for good.

Eloise dropped the blanket around her feet and opened the door. It was the same two men as before. She pushed the screen open without a word and they walked past her and into the living room, her following them this time. No one sat down. Eloise swore she could hear her heart pounding.

"Miss Masten, we're here because of Sergeant Brennan." Cooper stared at her, but his eyes didn't seem sad. *Do soldiers delivering death notices get sad?*

"I know that." Eloise could barely get the words out.

"He's been found. He's on his way to Germany. It'll be a while before you hear from him."

"He's alive?"

"Yes, ma'am." Cooper was doing all the talking.

Eloise hit her knees. She sobbed into her hands, unable to speak. Jack was alive. He was coming home. He told her no matter what and she believed him. She believed him even when no one else did. Endless hours of waiting. Jack was alive.

"I need a damn phone!" Jack yelled and a nurse came rushing over.

"Are you okay, sir?" She checked his monitors.

"I need to make a phone call. Please get me a phone."

"Sir, we can't let you make a call, you should be resting. Besides, it's very late."

"Please. Listen to me. I have to make a call. The woman I love probably thinks I'm dead. She's already lost one husband, please don't let her go on believing she's lost someone else."

"Okay, sir, calm down. I'll get you a phone." The nurse returned a few minutes later, set the phone on the bed next to Jack's body, and picked up the receiver and held it to his ear.

Jack recited Eloise's number from memory and watched the nurse dial. Both his arms were wrapped from shoulder to fingertips in white bandages. The way Jack felt now, he had no idea how he'd made it. The pain, even with medication, was so intense he always felt like he would puke. He blamed the adrenaline for him living. Stewart tried to keep his wounds clean the days they were lost, but they got infected anyway. Jack was thankful that they put him in a medically induced coma to scrub them clean, but once he woke, he felt as though his body were on fire and that hadn't gone away.

"Hello?"

"Eloise." Jack's voice was a whisper.

"Jack! Thank God it's you." Eloise started to cry.

"Eloise are you okay?"

"Me? I'm fine. Are you okay? They wouldn't tell me anything."

"I'm okay, beautiful. I just had to hear your voice. I needed you to know I didn't leave you."

"I never thought that. Not once. No matter what, right?"

"Right. No matter what." Jack knew they had to have found his letter. Eloise may not know the details, but she definitely knew something happened.

"When can you come home?"

"It'll be a while. I've got some healing to do here."

"I'll be waiting."

"Eloise, I love you. You just have to know that I love you and when I get home, I'll never leave again."

When she remained silent after a few moments, Jack said, "I love you, beautiful. I'll call when I can."

"I miss you, Jack," Eloise whispered.

"I miss you. Talk to you soon." Before she could answer, he turned and the nurse hung up the phone.

"She must be pretty important," the nurse said as she stood.

"She's everything. I just don't know how I can make her deal with this."

"What do you mean? You're going to live."

"Live yes, but both arms, my hands, and half of my face will be one big scar," Jack said.

"Well, the good news is one side of your face won't be."

"Very funny." Jack couldn't help but think about his tattoos. A lot of them would be ruined now, and the only reason he even cared was because Eloise loved them. Stewart was able to keep his arms and hands mostly wrapped, but his face had stayed pretty exposed. His uniform had also burned into his skin, mostly his chest and back, and again he said thanks for not being awake when the doctors dealt with that.

"I'm serious. Scars are minimal in my opinion. You've got your sight, all your limbs, your life, a little fire damage is something any girl can overlook."

"Thank you. And, thanks for letting me call."

"Sure. You let me know when you want to call again. Get some sleep."

Jack closed his eyes and thought of Eloise. Thought of running his hands through her silky red hair, gazing into her green eyes, and touching her porcelain skin. He didn't want to picture what touching her would be like, or think about how nothing would ever be the same. He focused on that fact that she never gave up on him. She'd wait for him. That meant everything.

It took an hour after Jack hung up the phone, but Eloise finally stopped crying. The call was short and she didn't feel like she really knew anything more than she had before. She heard Jack's voice, though. It wasn't strangers standing at her door. It was him, on the phone, promising her that he was okay.

Eloise got out of bed. It was only three in the morning, but Jesse wouldn't mind. She needed someone to listen to her, to make her believe the happiness that came after hearing Jack's voice.

"Knock, knock," Eloise said as she cracked open Jesse's door. She was wrapped in a blanket and holding a flashlight and knew he'd think she was crazy for waking him up at this hour, but he wouldn't be mad.

"Come in, darlin'," Jesse called, already shoving his feet into boots. He must've fallen asleep with his jeans on. "You okay?"

"Jack called." Eloise felt her eyes swell up again and she couldn't believe she had tears left. Jesse stood and wrapped her up.

"That's great." He squeezed her tight before releasing her. "I'll make some coffee."

Eloise smiled as she watched Jesse start out the door. That was exactly what she needed. Jesse would sit and listen to her cry and worry. He'd sip coffee while she played a thousand different scenarios in her head about Jack coming home, and he'd reassure her that everything would work out. And, somehow, when Jesse said the words, Eloise would believe them.

CHAPTER 22

The waiting was the hardest part for Jack. He knew he had a lot of healing before going home, but currently, he couldn't even sit in bed without assistance, and that was not promising. Eloise must be a wreck. He couldn't believe she was going through loss and pain, again, but this time completely alone. He hoped Nickie was there, or her family, or even the guy she hired, anyone who would remind her that things would get better.

Jack never expected to come as far as they had. When he showed up after Reagan, he thought he'd get his friend back, and that was enough. But now, now, everything had changed. This was their second chance, their chance at what was supposed to happen all along. Some things were meant to be, Jack knew that better than most. But he also believed that people were put in your life for a reason. He wasn't what Eloise needed before, they both had growing to do, but now, he knew he was what she needed. He believed that. Jack never believed he was good enough for her, especially not at nineteen. Sometimes you met your soul mate before your soul was ready. Jack was just thankful that his soul was going to get another chance.

Jack and Stewart had nearly died from heat exhaustion and dehydration. They had carried the two other men for nearly ten miles, and everyone who came in his room made a comment about that.

Jack's main thought when he came to, after Eloise, was why it took so long for the Army to find him and Stewart. Stewart told him the radio on the helicopter had been destroyed and that when the helicopter was shot down, it flew significantly off course before hitting the ground. The Army dispatched units immediately, but they had no real idea where to start looking. Units went to the last known location of the helicopter and worked their way out in circles. Jack and Stewart had put a lot of miles between themselves and the helicopter, so when units found the crash site and didn't find any bodies, they were back to continuing to search in all directions.

"I should have thought to leave our direction along the way." Jack told Stewart after a few days in the hospital. He felt stupid for not doing something so basic, something they'd been trained to do.

"I didn't think of it either. Honestly, we were both hurt, disoriented, dehydrated, hell, Brennan, we're lucky we were able to walk away at all."

"I'm sorry, Stewart. I'm sorry for not taking better care of you."

"I'm alive because of you, Brennan, because you didn't give up. I kept walking because you did. You didn't give up on us."

"You didn't give up on us." Jack stuck out his bandaged hand, but Stewart didn't grab it as he once would have. Instead, he put a hand on Jack's shoulder, still much lighter than he ever would have before.

Since Jack called, Eloise jumped back into life full force and teaching face to face. Jesse and his sons had the place running like clockwork, just as he promised.

"Will this job be ending when your man comes back?" Jesse asked that morning over breakfast.

"Not unless you want it to." Eloise sipped her coffee. "We've doubled in size since Jack left, and he was injured pretty badly, I don't know what he'll be able to handle alone. Regardless, he'll need help."

"Great. I like it here. My boys like it here," Jesse said.

After buying the additional fifty acres, Eloise had started plans for a cabin to be built so that Jesse could move to the farm full time. There would be additional rooms in case Jesse's boys wanted to be there too.

"I'll hire them, full time if they want the job." Eloise had been thinking about this for a while. She wasn't sure if Jesse compensated his sons or not, but he was old and getting older, and if a couple of them, or all of them, wanted to stick around, she didn't mind paying them. Things were better than Eloise could've hoped for. The adoptions were going great, and she sent in new grant applications almost every day, plus, most of the businesses in town donated to her operation. She'd never be rich, but she'd be happy, and that was worth everything to her.

Kyson had started training dogs and building a separate set of kennels so people could board their dogs, and that would also bring in income. Markham had taken full control of the cattle, and Eloise didn't mind that one bit.

"Thank you, Eloise. I'll talk to them when they come up this afternoon. I'm sure they'll all take you up on it. Ethan, he has the store, you know, but he may still want the job and just drive back and forth. The other three, though, they'll likely jump at the opportunity to live and work here."

"Great. We can extend the cabin if we need to. I've liked having people around." Eloise meant that. With Reagan, it was always just her and Reagan. And for a while, it was the same with Jack. But, when he left this last time, Eloise realized that she could be alone, she could do it. She just didn't want to. She loved making breakfast for all the guys, loved talking to Jesse over coffee and laughing with his sons over the animals and the chores. She liked that it was never quiet, that boots could always be heard crossing the floor, and that the food bill was insane.

T he first day of Jack's physical therapy felt like a complete joke to him. The therapist kept telling him to trust the process, but he didn't know how to do that when the process was so freaking slow. The only good part was that Stewart was still around and at least the two of them could talk. The nurses let Jack call Eloise once a day and he lived for those phone calls.

"Hello," Eloise answered. Jack was thankful that she always picked up. It didn't matter what time he called or what she was doing, she picked up the phone.

"Hey, beautiful," Jack said.

"Hey, handsome. I didn't know it was you. It's a different number."

"I'm in the physical therapy room. They left, so I took their phone."

"You're going to get in trouble." Eloise laughed. "But I'm glad you called."

"It's their own fault for leaving me unsupervised and I talked a nurse into dialing your number. How are you?"

"I'm fine, Jack. The real question is, how are *you*? I take it you started physical therapy today?"

"I started coming to the physical therapy room to talk today."

"What?"

"They don't let me do anything yet."

"Does it hurt?"

"No, it's just slow, it's like they don't even trust me to grip stuff on my own. I'm very babied."

"Can you grip stuff on your own?"

"No. I try, but it doesn't work." Jack answered her truthfully, but left out that he couldn't open or close his fingers, and was speaking to her on speaker because he couldn't hold the phone without dropping it. "I may not ever get full use of my hands. They're hopeful, though."

"Then you should be hopeful, too, Jack."

"They're still grafting skin. Long ass process. I can't close my hands."

"I wish I could see you," Eloise whispered. "I wish I could make you forget all the terrible things, even if just for a while."

"I do too," Jack said. "They won't keep me here long. The doctor said I can travel two weeks after the grafts are done. I'll get sent to an in-patient rehab in the States. I'll fly you to see me, if you want, once that happens."

"Wherever it is, I'll be there."

Jack closed his eyes, and repeated those words to himself. *Wherever it is, I'll be there.* He honestly couldn't believe she said it. Eloise, his, finally, after years of waiting.

"I can't wait to see you, beautiful. I just hope you can still look at me." Jack thought about the two weeks he'd been here. Two weeks and he was still getting new skin. He knew he had an extremely long road ahead of him, but that road was bearable if he had Eloise.

"I crave the day I can look at you. You will always be handsome to me." Jack knew her words were honest, that she didn't care what he looked like, that she only cared that he was alive.

"Thank you." Jack wanted to tell her that the sight of him wasn't the only thing that worried him. He wanted to explain that his life was over, the life he knew. He couldn't be a Ranger, couldn't be in the Army anymore, and that was terrifying. Jack had spent that last ten years in a strict routine, a cycle that he was comfortable with and felt he had control over. That was gone now. Before joining the Army, Jack knew he was walking a thin line between being a lost wreck and the man he was now. Everything about the military was a struggle, a challenge, but the routine was comforting. Jack knew who he was as a Ranger. He *was* his job. He had to be this specific person all the time, because there were always eyes on him. Who would he be when no one was looking? *Eloise would be looking*, Jack reminded himself. She deserved the best version of himself he could be.

"El," Jack said after a few moments of silence. "I need you to promise me something else."

"Anything."

"I need you to promise me that you'll remind me who I am when I feel lost. I don't know who I am without the Army, El. You knew me before...before I became this version of myself. Just don't let me forget that I'm still in here somewhere."

"I promise, Jack. I'll always remind you who you are and how much I love you."

Eloise knew that would be an easy promise to keep. Jack had done the same for her countless times, especially when they were younger and she'd have her meltdowns. It took Eloise a lot of years to perfect keeping her emotions in check, but Jack had seen that side of her and loved her anyway.

You just feel things intensely, Jack would tell her. *There's nothing wrong with that.*

But Eloise knew it wasn't normal to feel like such a disaster.

"I gotta go, beautiful." Jack broke through Eloise's thoughts. "I'll call you soon. Thank you for sticking with me."

"Always," Eloise said. "Always, and always, handsome."

When Jack disconnected the call, the door swung open. He was relieved no one caught him sneaking an extra phone call. The man who entered was in a wheelchair, and the man following him was missing his left leg. Must be their therapy time, Jack thought as he stood up to leave.

"Hey, man, you new to the group?"

"Group?" Jack asked.

"Support group. We meet in here once a week."

"Oh, no." Jack moved closer to the door. "I just came in here to steal the phone." Jack turned to face the men, remembering that he had no reason to be rude. "I'm Jack Brennan." He stuck his hand out, then pulled it back when he watched the man's eyes fall on his bandages.

"I'm Samuel, Sam Wilkes," the man in the wheelchair said. "And this is Nolan Brooks." Jack turned his gaze to Nolan.

"Nice to meet you both," Jack told them.

"You should stay. We'll start soon. It's a small group, usually about eight of us."

"I don't know," Jack said. He wasn't sure he was ready to talk about what happened to him, or admit all the things he didn't remember about those days.

"Just listen," Sam said as though he could read Jack's mind. "You don't have to talk."

"Okay. Can I invite a friend?" Jack asked.

"The more the merrier," Sam said.

"Can you dial for me?" Jack nodded toward the phone, thinking Stewart could probably use some support himself.

"Of course." Sam picked up the phone and waited for Jack's instructions.

As more vets filled the room, Jack hoped he'd made the right decision in staying. Stewart showed up, so Jack knew he was in this for the long haul now. He wasn't going to bail when Stewart had the guts to show. Nolan spoke first, sharing that he'd just been fitted for his prosthetic earlier that morning.

Jack didn't speak, but he did listen to each story, each heartache and hardship. The things that united the men and women in the room, went beyond service. It wasn't just the tragedy either. It was also the triumph. It was the stories that included the silver lining, from the people who had already come out on the other side emotionally. Jack didn't believe he was there yet, and from the look on Stewart's face, neither did he.

Jack was relieved later that week when they told him they'd be shipping him to the States the same time as Stewart. Traveling with Stewart would make everything a lot easier to handle. Stewart had been a rock through all of this, and Jack knew that at some point he'd have to make sure Stewart was handling every-thing as well as he put on.

The nurses helped Jack pack his things, but he only truly cared about his letter and photo album from Eloise. Anything else could be replaced.

"Thank you, Chanel. I honestly don't know what I would've done without you these last two months." Jack watched as Chanel tucked the letter and small book carefully in his bag.

"Don't mention it. Just message me when you get settled and you're back with your girl." Chanel made sure Jack got his phone call every day. She brought him the good food and even talked his occupational therapist into incorporating cooking during sessions a few times. She was an angel.

"I will. I promise. And, if you ever find yourself in Colorado, you're welcome at Eloise's anytime. She'd love to meet you."

"I'd love that." Chanel hugged Jack and for the first time in two months, Jack felt like everything really would be okay.

There was no reason for Stewart to have stayed with Jack, not medically anyway. He could've gone home shortly after getting to Germany, but chose to stay with Jack. He wanted to see him through, see him all the way back home to Eloise. Stewart's wife Emma wasn't thrilled about it, but Stewart repeatedly told Jack that she understood.

Jack and Stewart boarded the plane and Jack's exhaustion hit him like a freight train. In his defense, he was one quite a bit of pain medication and sleeping a lot more than usual.

"I talked to Chase this morning. He's gonna meet us there." Stewart tightened his seatbelt. "Emma too."

"That's great man. Are your kids coming?"

"No. Just Chase and Emma. It'll be good. I think we need a few days focused on us. We didn't get much before we shipped out again." Stewart said.

"Eloise said she's coming."

"You don't believe her?"

"I do. I just don't know if she should come." Jack's eyes shifted down to his arms.

"Jack, she ain't gonna care about that shit."

"I know. I know she won't. I just hate that she even has to deal with it, you know? She's been through so much." Jack's eyes found Stewart's again.

"Let's just get there, get through today, and then we'll worry about what happens when our women show up." Stewart laughed a little and Jack did too.

CHAPTER 23

The plane landed in Maryland just before dark. Chase had spoken to Emma again she'd be there early the next morning with Chase. Jack hadn't said anything else about Eloise and though it sounded silly, he kept quiet so he wouldn't jinx anything.

The new hospital room was bleak. Jack flipped on the light and his eyes grew wide at the sight of Chase sitting on his bed.

"Aren't you supposed to be here tomorrow?" Jack dropped his stuff to hug Chase after Chase stood.

"Aren't you supposed to be resting?" Chase asked. "Emma and I caught an earlier flight. She thought it'd be fun to be here when Stewart landed."

"Did Allie come with you?" Jack walked around Chase to sit on the bed.

"No. She wanted to come with Eloise. I guess they've been talking on Facebook since I stayed with you."

"Sounds like Eloise. How have you guys been doing?" Jack toed his shoes off.

"We're a lot better. She still struggles with a lot. She understood me needing to come here so that's something and her wanting to come too says a lot. She keeps saying she needs me. I think she's happy about my medical discharge."

"And you?"

"I love her and my kids more than anything on this earth, but I can't help feeling like I let everyone in the unit down. She gets it when it's you. You and Eloise helped me when I had completely lost myself. She knows that without you guys, we would've never worked our stuff out. She knows I'd probably be dead." Chase flopped down in the chair by Jack's bed.

"This life brings a lot of demons." Jack yawned. "I'm happy you two are working through it. You didn't let anyone down Chase. Hell, I'm proud of you for realizing that you weren't in the headspace to be deploying anymore."

"Thank you, Jack. Thank you for everything."

"Anytime." Jack yawned again and shook his head. "I hate to do this to you, but I'm about to crash. Can you help me call Eloise first?"

"You got it." Chase pulled out his cellphone and punched in the numbers as Jack said them before putting the phone on speaker.

"Hello." Eloise answered after the third ring.

"Beautiful."

"Handsome!" Jack smiled at the excitement in her voice. "How are you?"

"Just settling into this place. I'm hoping I don't have to stay too long. They should be able to set me up with a physical thera-pist near…"

"Near home. Home, Jack. You can say it. You are coming home, to me."

"Yes. Home. There should be places I can work on therapy closer to home."

"When should I leave?"

"Eloise, you don't have to come here. You can wait for me

there if you want to. It won't change anything. I want you to do what makes you comfortable."

"Jack, you're insane if you think I'm not going to see you the second I can."

"Just don't feel guilty if you decide not to come. I love you either way."

"You can love me when I get there. Did you send me a ticket?" Chase nodded and mouthed the words *email* and *Allie*.

"Yes. Chase said he emailed it. You'll get here the same time as Allie."

"That's great. Tell him thank you for me." Eloise sounded excited and Jack was ecstatic about that. "He's a good man. Chase. I think Stewart is my new favorite though."

"Are you kidding me?" Chase yelled into the phone.

"He is. He definitely saved my ass." Jack laughed as Chase pretended he was going to hang up on Eloise.

"Don't worry Chase." Eloise giggled. "You'll always have a special place in my heart, but I'll always love Stewart for saving Jack, because I need him. I need you, Jack."

"I guess I get that." Chase said to Eloise.

"Back at you, beautiful. I'll see you soon. I love you, El." Jack followed.

"See you soon, handsome." Eloise hung up the phone.

Eloise had two bags by the front door and slipped off her flats for muck boots before walking out to find Jesse, who was brushing down a horse. Eloise saw his sons out near the dog kennels.

"Jesse," Eloise yelled before she reached him.

Jesse looked up from the horse, then set the brush down. "Hey darlin'. What can I do for you?"

"Jack called." Eloise stroked the horse, looking in its eyes instead of Jesse's. "I have to go to him. It puts a lot on you and your boys. I don't know when I'll be back."

"No worries there. We got this. Ethan will drive out every day, like we talked about, and the other boys can stay here with me, if that's still okay. We'll make sure things stay running." Jesse put his hands on Eloise's shoulders. "Don't worry about things here. Jack is your priority."

"Thank you, Jesse. I'd be completely lost without you."

"Happy to do it, hon." Jesse dropped his arms. "Travel safe."

Eloise started back toward the house to grab her bags and she stood at the door watching as Jesse called his son's over, likely telling them that she'd be gone a few days, maybe longer. None of them looked disappointed or inconvenienced to take on the place while she was away, and that made Eloise feel a lot better about leaving.

When Eloise's plane landed, she got her bags and went straight to book a rental car. She was sure Allie was somewhere doing the same. She'd never met Allie, but felt like she knew her because of all of their Facebook messages.

Eloise drove to her hotel first. As she was checking in, she heard her name.

"Eloise, is that you?" Allie said from behind her.

"That's me," she said, turning to face the voice. "Allie?"

"The one and only." Allie smiled and stuck out her hand for Eloise to shake. "Seems our men planned this."

"I think Chase booked everything." Eloise didn't want to tell her that Jack probably couldn't type on a phone. "It's great to finally meet you off the screen."

"You, too, Eloise. I was planning to drive over there after I dropped my stuff off and freshened up. Do you want to go together?" Allie stepped up to the counter to check herself in.

"I'd like that. Thank you." Eloise opened her wallet and took out five dollars to give to the teenage kid once he took her bags to her room. After she zipped her wallet closed, she held up her room card so that Allie could see the number. "Knock when you're ready."

"You got it, girl. See you soon."

"See you soon." Eloise repeated the phrase she had said more in the last few days than ever in her life. She stepped into the elevator and hit the three. The room was big, much bigger than she needed. Chase sure knew how to pick them. Eloise stripped down and took a five-minute shower. She had no idea how quickly Allie would show up. Eloise tried not to think about the last time she and Jack were in a hotel, or anytime they'd been in a hotel. She wasn't sure it was safe to feel happy, not yet.

Allie knocked thirty minutes later, and Eloise let her in saying, "I still have to put on my shoes."

"You look hot," Allie said as she walked to sit on Eloise's bed.

"You're one to talk." Eloise scanned Allie's long blond hair, dark jeans, and low-cut shirt. She had on a pair of heels that would break Eloise's ankles. Eloise was about six inches shorter than Allie and instead of jeans, had chosen a green dress, one she knew Jack liked, and a pair of brown, chunky wedges. Eloise's red hair was curled in loose ringlets and looked even shorter than usual. The women were far from similar looking, but both gorgeous in their own right.

Eloise grabbed her purse and the two were out the door. She was so nervous she didn't think she'd even be able to follow GPS to the hospital, so Allie drove. Eloise had never seen Jack weak, and that scared her. Jack was always strong. It wasn't just his build, and it wasn't his slightly cocky attitude. It was the way he never put himself first. He'd suffered so much loss, but he never put his hurt above Eloise's. He went out of his way to take care of her, even at his own emotional expense. Eloise prayed the entire drive that she'd have the strength to be that for him now.

"I'm Mrs. Carroll and this is Mrs. Brennan," Allie said to the nurse at the check-in desk. Eloise didn't open her mouth the entire time, afraid she'd say something wrong. Allie had been an Army wife for almost ten years. She knew Jack and Eloise weren't married, so she was likely trying to avoid any issues.

"They're the last door on the right, just down that hallway." The nurse pointed as she spoke, and Eloise smiled but still said nothing.

"Thanks, Allie," Eloise said when they were about halfway to the door. Eloise was taking in deep, steady breaths, trying not to be sick or pass out. She had no clue why she was so nervous. Allie looked excited.

"I got you, girl." Allie threw her a smile, but paused when her hand grabbed the door handle. "When he left, we weren't on the best of terms, well, you know that. I was worried sick when he was gone. Worried that I'd never get to fix what I'd broken. You know about that, too, not having enough time. I just... I have to... I love him."

Eloise placed a hand on Allie's back, now knowing that she was just as nervous. "He loves you Allie. Jack told me he doesn't blame you. Not for one second." Eloise squeezed the top of Allie's shoulder.

"Thanks, Eloise," Allie said, then took a deep breath and pushed open the door.

Chase sat next to Jack, who was in bed and covered in bandages. Allie, seemingly forgetting her nervousness, ran to Chase and he stood just in time to catch her. She wrapped her legs and arms around him and between their kissing and their inaudible words to each other, Eloise knew she was blushing. The door shut behind her, and she figured Chase and Allie had left to make out somewhere else. The couple Eloise assumed was Stewart and Emma sat neat the window hand in hand.

Eloise didn't run to Jack. She barely breathed. One side of

Jack's face was covered in gauze, but Eloise could still tell he'd put on a little weight. She couldn't see skin from his shoulders to his fingertips. He had a T-shirt on, but Eloise noticed the bandages on his chest.

"Hey, beautiful," Jack whispered. "Stewart, Emma, this is Eloise. Eloise this is the man responsible for me not being dead and his gorgeous and thoughtful wife."

"Hey back, handsome." Eloise finally took a step forward. "It is so nice to meet you both." Eloise said as the couple stood and shook her hand. "I cannot thank you enough for bringing him back to me."

"He brought me back too." Stewart said.

"And I can't thank him enough for it." Emma said. "We're gonna go and let you guys catch up." Emma took her husband's hand. "See you in a bit."

"See you guys." Jack said as Stewart and Emma left the room.

Eloise stopped at the edge of Jack's bed, trying to take in every inch of him.

"How are you feeling?" Eloise struggled to get the words out.

"I'm doing great, seeing you. It took a lot to get this shirt on, but Chase managed. I refused to see you in a damn hospital gown."

"I wouldn't have cared."

"I would've." Jack lifted the arm that was closest to Eloise, brushing it against her hand. Eloise tried not to pull away from the feel of the bandage. She was trying to hold it together. She didn't want to break down when Jack needed her to be strong, but seeing Jack was overwhelming. As if he could read her mind, Jack said, "It's okay to cry, El. This is a lot. A lot of change for you, for us, in a very short period of time."

"I just want to be strong for you." At that, Eloise's dam broke. Her cries were likely being heard down the hall, but she didn't care. She'd lost too much already. Reagan. There was nothing that could bring him back. But Jack? Jack was here. He was hurt, but he was here. She told herself he would come back, over and over, every minute of the day, she told herself, but there was a small piece, a piece that she'd never admit to Jack, a tiny, dark, piece, that thought she'd lost him too.

Eloise fell into Jack's chest, and though he grunted in pain, he wrapped a bandaged arm around her as she cried into his wounded chest. "I'm sorry, Jack. I swore I wouldn't make you be the strong one, again. You're always a rock and I'm always this hot mess." She felt Jack's smile as he tried to tighten his grip on her, a soft grunt of pain followed his movements.

"Jack, what did I tell you about overdoing it?" A nurse walked in stayed by the door until Eloise stood.

"Sorry, Lydie. I promise it won't happen again." Jack's smile lit up the room, and Eloise could see the nurse watching him. Even injured, women found him attractive. That made Eloise smile. "Eloise, this is one of my nurses. Lydie, this is my Eloise."

Eloise wiped her face with one hand while sticking out the other. "It's nice to meet you." Lydie shook her hand, and then went to the opposite side of Jack's bed.

Eloise started to step back toward the door, but Jack gave her a look that clearly said *don't you dare*, so she remained on her side of the bed while Lydie and Jack talked about how he was feeling.

"Tomorrow, Jack." Lydie's eyes found the bandages. Eloise knew she was talking about changing his dressing, but wasn't sure why it was something that seemed like a secret.

"Whatever you say, Lydie." Jack rolled his eyes, which made Eloise smile.

"Eloise, it was nice to meet you. I'll give you both another hour or so and then he really does need to sleep." Lydie checked Jack's IV line, and then left.

"She likes you."

The way Jack smiled and his eyes lit, he already knew. "Why do you think we get another hour?" Jack scooted up in the bed a bit. "I told Chase and Stewart to stay with Allie and Emma, at the hotel, while you guys are in town. It'll be weird being in here alone."

"I wish I could stay with you."

"I don't think Lydie likes me *that* much."

"She might, but having me around won't help." They laughed, because they both knew Lydie didn't have a chance. Eloise trusted Jack, she loved Jack, and she knew he'd never hurt her that way. It was easy to giggle about women finding him cute, even flirting with him, and Eloise honestly didn't care if he flirted back, because she knew Jack's heart was hers.

"I wish you could stay too. But, tomorrow, you'll want to come later in the morning, after ten."

"Is this about changing the gauze?"

"You don't need to see it, Eloise."

"If you're not ready for that, I'll come after. But I'm ready for anything, Jack." Eloise set her hand on his arm lightly. "I'm here. I'm in this with you. All the way in."

Jack didn't answer, and Eloise didn't push. She would keep saying the words regardless if he answered or not. Eloise thought he looked like he was fighting tears, but didn't comment on that either. If Jack wanted to talk about what was on his mind, he would. Eloise didn't want him to feel forced, not anymore, not ever again.

Eloise hadn't taken much time to think about Jack's injuries. She knew that he was uncomfortable, that he was worried about his new appearance, but asking her to come later in the morning changed things. How would things be when they went home? Would he want her touching him the way she did before?

"Jack, I still want you. You know that, right?" Eloise asked, sick of trying to filter herself when she never did before.

"I don't see how."

"You can't tell me you didn't see it on my face the second I saw you." Eloise knew her eyes gave her attraction toward Jack away. They always had. It was another reason she stopped talking to him after Reagan. Reagan wasn't stupid. If he ever saw the way Eloise looked at Jack, he'd know how deeply she cared for him, craved him.

"I saw," Jack admitted. "One of my favorite things about you is that nine times out of ten, your desires are written across your face."

"They are not," Eloise almost yelled.

"Don't deny it. You're a terrible liar, your eyes always betray you. It's your longing that I loved seeing most. That look you have, the one that screams that you need my body on yours."

"And you believe the look?" Eloise set her hand on Jack's crotch, giggling.

"Every time, but, El, we can't, not here."

"Why not?" Her sheepish grin made him laugh, but her hand slipping under the sheet and between his thighs made him moan.

"Eloise," Jack bit out. "Stop."

"Or what?" Eloise slid her hand in Jack's sweats, under his underwear, and took him in her hand.

"You're going to be the reason I die." Jack's eyes shifted to the door, making Eloise laugh out loud. She knew he didn't want to get caught, but truth be told, she couldn't care less.

"Tell me you want me, Jack." Eloise continued to stroke him.

"I always want you, every second of every day." Jack's voice made her want to climb on top of him, ride him, and make all the distance and pain disappear. If she thought she could without hurting him, she would've already lifted herself up on the bed. Eloise took two steps closer to Jack so that she could push her mouth on to him. "El." Jack's entire body tensed, but Eloise had no intention of stopping.

CHAPTER 24

The next morning, Eloise woke up long before her alarm. She was surprised she'd slept at all. She still didn't know how to feel about Jack not wanting her to see his dressing being changed. They'd always been open, some would argue they were too open, and now he was shielding her from a piece of him. Was he worried she'd care about his looks? He had to know he meant more to her than that. It hadn't been about sex for a long time, well, not just about sex.

Eloise texted Allie and Emma before she left, but they both planned to stay exactly where they were with their husbands, and Eloise was thrilled that things were going so well for them. Eloise carefully curled her hair and took extra time on her makeup. It was barely after seven and she'd told Jack she wouldn't come before ten. She decided she'd do a little shopping before she went to see him.

Eloise parked her rental car in a plaza, then visited almost every shop she passed. She found some cookbooks she'd thought Jack would like, along with a black notebook and a set of pens in case he wanted to write out any recipes of his own. She knew he'd need someone to write for him, but she figured Lydie wouldn't mind, once Eloise went home. She got Jack some flowers, mostly because his room was so white, and a soft, fuzzy blanket that he could use instead of the hospital one. She bought him T-shirts two sizes too big so that Chase would have an easier time getting them on him, and multiple pairs of socks and silk shorts. She wasn't sure how long he'd have to stay, but she wanted him to be comfortable and knew he'd never ask her to get him anything. Eloise picked up the phone as she sat on a bench with all her bags.

"Hello." Nickie answered on the second ring.

"Nickie, I need some advice."

"Hey, stranger. How are you? How's Jack?"

"I'm good. He's good too. Mostly." Eloise had given Nickie a few text updates after she knew Jack was alive, but for the days she wasn't sure, it was silence. "I got him some stuff, to make him more comfortable. Shirts, cookbooks, socks, things like that. Can you think of anything else?"

"Buy him a Keurig. That hospital coffee is trash."

"I knew I called you for a good reason."

"A toothbrush would also be good. When my mom was in her car accident all she asked for was her own toothbrush."

"Got it. Good call. Anything else?"

"I think that about covers it, plus what you already bought. Are you sure he's doing okay?"

"He doesn't want me there this morning while they change his bandages."

"Oh," Nickie said.

"Exactly."

"El, it doesn't have to mean anything. Maybe he's self-conscious about it, maybe he's still just wrapping his head around the fact that he'll never look the same, but no matter what it is, it has nothing to do with you."

"I know that. I just wish he trusted me enough to be that vulnerable with me. The way I was after Reagan."

"You didn't do that all at once, El. Give him some time."

"He has all the time he wants. I'm not going anywhere."

"Keep telling him that. I love you, El, but Jack's always waiting for you to leave. Since he met you, he's said it was always you. You starting things, you ending things, he was always there. You need to make him believe that you're in this all the way."

"I told him I was."

"More than once, El. Every day you tell him, and you mean it."

"I do mean it, Nickie. I loved Reagan. You know I loved Reagan. Hell, I still love Reagan, and I know that love will always be there. But with Jack it's different and it always has been. I've never felt more like me, more open, more raw, more, just more, than I do with Jack. It's been that way since the day I laid eyes on him. Life just always got in the way. I got in my own way."

"You did get in your own way, El, but getting in your own way also led you to Reagan, and I think you were meant to love him too. Everything happens for a reason. But it's your time with Jack now, hold that close and remind him often that it's what you want."

"Thanks, Nickie. I love you."

"I love you, too, El, call me later."

"I will. Bye." Eloise hit end on her phone and then took a few deep breaths. She'd tell Jack every minute, if necessary, that she wasn't leaving. She just hoped he would believe her, and above that, she hoped he wouldn't be the one to leave her.

After buying a Keurig, and enough K-Cups for Jack to live at the rehab center for good, a new toothbrush, toothpaste, two coffee mugs, and getting all her bags into her rental's trunk, it was finally eleven. Before Eloise headed to the hospital, she stopped and got coffee, one for her, and one for Jack.

"Hey, handsome." Eloise pushed the door open, much more confident than the day before and set down the two coffees so she could remove bags from her arms.

"Wow, El, you ever planning on taking me home?"

"The second they let me, but until then, you may as well be comfortable here." Eloise picked up Jack's coffee and put it to his mouth.

"Thanks, beautiful." Jack sipped his coffee and Eloise tried not to stare at the newly placed bandages. Eloise set the coffee down and started to pull things out of bags. Jack smiled bigger with each new item. She covered him in the blanket, helped him brush his teeth, and set up the Keurig, giving him sips of coffee in between. Jack made a face after the sip he took once he brushed his teeth and Eloise tried to mimic his face, making them both laugh.

Eloise spent the whole afternoon with Jack and didn't leave until Lydie forced her out.

"I'll come back in the morning."

"You better." Jack tried to scoot up, but Eloise leaned down to kiss him instead, making it easier.

"He doesn't have to change his dressing tomorrow, so you can come as soon as visiting hours start at eight," Lydie said from the doorway.

"Thanks, Lydie," Eloise said. Lydie was actually very likeable and Eloise hoped they'd be able to stay friends. Eloise kissed Jack once more before turning to leave. She felt empty the second she couldn't see him anymore.

When Eloise got back to her hotel, she had a text from Allie asking her to go to dinner. Eloise replied that she'd be ready to meet them in an hour and then called Jesse to check on things at the house.

"Hello," Jesse answered.

"Hey, Jesse. I just wanted to see how things were going?"

"Excellent. Everything here is good. My boys have moved completely in, so hopefully you didn't change your mind on that, because we've taken over the cabin and the thing isn't finished all the way yet."

"I didn't change my mind. It'll be really great having people around. How are the animals?"

"They're all good. We adopted out two dogs yesterday to the same family. Roxy and Levi."

"That's great, Jesse." Eloise was a bit sad that she missed them going to their new home, but she knew Jesse would never let a dog go without vetting the family.

"I got their address for you. They said they'd love for you to visit Roxy and Levi in their new home when you get back."

"Thank you." Eloise swallowed so she didn't cry. She was more thankful for Jesse than she'd ever be able to say. He had become like a father to her, and his boys were such a great help, Eloise knew she'd love having them around too.

"Anytime, darlin'. We'll see you soon?"

"Yeah. I have a flight out the day after tomorrow. Jack has to stay for three to six months, depending on his progress, so I'll probably visit again before he comes home."

"That's great. I'm sure he's glad you're there with him."

"I'll call you tomorrow. I'm headed out to dinner. Thank you for taking care of everything."

"Be safe, hon. Everything will be fine until you get back. Have a good dinner."

"Thanks, Jesse. Have a good night," Eloise said before hanging up.

Eloise took a quick shower and texted Jack her plans with Allie before she started getting ready. Once she was dressed, she sent Jack a picture, a smiling one, and then five of her making ridiculous faces.

I wish you were coming.

Eloise sent him.

Me too. You look amazing, El.

Jack sent back with a picture of him making a sad face.

Thank you.

Eloise hit send as Allie knocked on her door. Eloise knew that someone, probably Nurse Lydie, was texting for Jack, but she tried not to think too much about someone else reading their messages.

The bar and grill that Chase chose had loud music playing, but it was folky and fun and Eloise found herself smiling. She clicked pictures of Chase and Stewart dancing with their wives for Jack, not sure if they'd make him sad or help him feel included.

The next morning, Eloise was at the hospital thirty minutes before visiting hours would start, two coffees in hand. She and Jack spent the day watching movies and talking. Eloise left twice, only to bring back food, and didn't leave until Lydie forced her to.

Eloise didn't want to think about tomorrow being her last day with Jack. On the one hand, there was no reason to rush back. Jesse reassured her every day that he had things under control. On the other hand, Eloise knew that she'd have a mountain of paperwork and grading to get to as soon as she got home. Her students never minded class being online, but she knew they got more out of face-to-face lectures and was excited about finishing the semester in a classroom.

Jack was asleep when she returned to the hospital the next morning, so she sat in a chair next to his bed and read while he slept.

"Hey, beautiful," Jack said, eyes still closed.

"How did you know it was me?"

"You smell better than the nurses." Jack opened his eyes.

"I guess that's a compliment." Eloise laughed and stood so that she could kiss him.

"It is." Jack sucked in a deep breath as she leaned down. "Things are going to be different now, El, and I won't lie to you, that scares me."

"We'll figure it out, Jack. Whatever it is, we'll get through it." Eloise wanted him to know she wasn't going anywhere and to believe that she was done running from her feelings for him.

"I can't hold shit on my own. I have no career anymore. I can't even cook now." Jack leaned his head back.

"I won't pretend to understand what you're going through. I can't imagine losing all the things that make me who I am. But you *will* keep getting better, Jack. I know you will. You'll cook again. And, as for the Army, I know that's going to hurt for a long time. I know you didn't want to be done." Eloise kissed his cheek. "I know it'll take time, but just remember you don't have to do anything alone. I'm here."

"I want to believe that. I want it to be true. That's what is keeping me breathing." Jack shut his eyes. Eloise understood that he didn't want to put so much pressure on her. He didn't want her staying because she felt like she couldn't leave.

"Jack," Eloise said. "I'm here because I want to be here, because I love you. You know me better than anyone. If I didn't want this anymore, I wouldn't have come here. This isn't about guilt or feeling bad for you, or feeling like I have to stay because you got hurt. I meant what I said when you left. We said no matter what." Eloise wiped a tear. She wasn't sad. She was relieved. She finally felt like she could tell Jack the things that crossed her mind, felt a little more like the girl she used to be and a lot less like the lost person she became after Reagan died.

"It's just hard, you know? You've never been good at staying when things got complicated. Whenever we got close, you always dated someone to stop us from getting any deeper."

"I was scared of how much I loved you. I know that doesn't really make sense. It was easier to pretend I didn't care than it was to risk being hurt by you. When you're young, you don't think about things working out, you only think about protecting yourself from potential pain, or at least that's what I thought." Eloise paused, but continued when Jack stayed quiet. "I wasn't ready for you, and I don't think you were ready, either, even though the feelings were there. We had a lot of growing up to do. I think I needed to love Reagan. I needed him to make me believe that something real was worth the risk."

"All of this will just take some time, El. This is so much change. Everything that's happened. I'm feeling pretty over-whelmed. I feel the guiltiest over you being the one who loses the most. You lost Reagan and now I feel lost too. It isn't the same as if I'd died, but the man I was before isn't coming back. You deserve the world, and I can't give you that. Not anymore, not when I can't even hold a pencil."

Eloise fixated her gaze on the door to keep herself from panicking. Why couldn't he just lie to her? Would they ever break this vicious cycle? In Jack's defense, he was always more willing in the past than she was to have something more serious. But now they both had their wishy-washy moments.

"Do you love me Jack? Do you still want to be together?" Eloise asked, refusing to just give in. "I know you're scared. Your whole world has been turned upside down, but you can't use that as an excuse."

"You know I do," Jack said without hesitating.

"Then be with me. Just be here, in this moment. I know it'll take time to convince you that I'm not going anywhere, and I'll put the time in, Jack, I will." Eloise wanted to tell Reagan all of this. She wanted him to know that she had to let him go. She wanted to be able to tell him that she'd always love him, always remember him, but that her heart had to heal in order for her to survive, and Jack healed her. Eloise made a mental note to visit Reagan once she returned home.

"I'm always with you, beautiful." Jack gave Eloise a sleepy smile, and she figured his IV was giving him his next dose of pain medication and he'd be out again soon.

E loise settled in on the plane the next morning, without attempting to stop her tears. She hated going home without Jack, hated the idea of walking into her house alone. Eloise felt the eyes of the other passengers on her. She despised people pitying her, feeling them wonder what had her looking like such a wreck. Eloise didn't like the uncertainty of when she'd see Jack again. The only positive was that because Jack was hospitalized, they could talk a lot without worrying about the Wi-Fi going out.

Eloise bought a notebook and a pen after she passed through security. She knew that Reagan may never actually know everything, but she had to try to tell him. She had to find a way to get closure, and make sure that if Reagan got the message, he knew that a part of her would always be with him.

Dear Reagan,

I should have written to you sooner, but I was so broken that the thought never crossed my mind. I want so desperately for you to know everything, for this letter to come as no surprise to you. I've never thought much about heaven, or what happens when we die. I feel like death is one of those things that you think will never happen to you, until it does. I never thought about losing you, Reagan. In my mind, you were always my future.

I need you to know that I never wanted anything else when I had you. I need you to believe that you were enough for me, because you were. I didn't settle, Reagan. I wanted you. I loved you. I chose you, every single day. I didn't expect Jack to show up the way he did, and maybe I should have told him to go, but I needed him, Reagan, I needed him so I remembered to breathe.

I didn't mean to love him. I feel beyond guilty about that every moment that I'm with him. If I'm being honest, though, I don't know how to stop loving him. I can't live the rest of my life feeling like I'm being suffocated. I hate asking you for forgiveness and understanding when I'm here and you're not. I hate being so selfish.

I miss you every time I take a breath. I used to wonder if loving Jack would make you think my love for you was less somehow, but I'd like to believe that you know that isn't true. A piece of me died the day you did. I've spent a lot of time trying to rediscover that part of myself, but now I know, that part of me is buried with you. Being with Jack doesn't mean I'm forgetting you. I will remember you and miss you for the rest of my life. I hope you understand, Reagan. I hope you aren't mad at me for being with Jack, for loving him.

I'll always love you. You will forever be connected to me, and I will live each day for us both. I know I have to let you go, let you rest. I know I have to move forward. I have to stop living halfway. I am sorry, Reagan. So sorry that I wasn't with you, that you aren't here, and that me being with someone else may leave you feeling betrayed. I know it's unfair for me to write this and use it as a way to make being with Jack seem okay. He'll take care of me, Reagan, and I know you'd want that. Want me to thrive, and to be safe. Your love for me will always be in my heart. You were always incredible to me, and loved me with your whole heart. I hope you felt me loving you with all of mine.

I hope that wherever you are, you're happy.

I love you. Forever.

-Eloise

Eloise read her letter, holding it away from her face so that her tears didn't ruin it. She folded it carefully in half and then in half again. She slipped it in the front pocket of her purse, and tried not to think about what Reagan's reaction would be, had he still been alive.

When Eloise landed in Grand Junction, she didn't go to her car. She booked a flight to Houston, then called Jesse so that he knew not to expect her for two more days. Eloise knew she had to give the letter to Reagan. She couldn't explain why, but she knew it would help her find closure. Eloise pulled out her phone once she was on the next plane to send a text to Jack.

I'm headed to Houston. I'll be back home in two days. I just thought you should know.

Houston?

I wrote Reagan a letter. I need to give it to him.

Please be careful, El. Let me know when you land.

I will.

Eloise sat down at Reagan's grave. She had rented a car in Houston and stopped to buy a small metal container for Reagan's letter.

"Hey, baby," Eloise said as she touched Reagan's headstone. "I'm sorry I didn't come see you before today." Eloise pulled the long-dead flowers out of the small holder and replaced them with the new ones she brought. She would have to ask one of her old coworkers to help check on Reagan. She could send them money and try to visit more, whatever she needed to make sure his resting place was better taken care of.

"I brought you something. A letter I wrote." Eloise opened the box and pulled out her letter, unfolding the two pages. She read the words to Reagan's grave, read them slowly, having to take breaks in between sobbing. When she finished, she folded the papers and put them back in their box. She used her hands to scoop out some dirt near the base of Reagan's headstone, digging a small hole to place his letter in. When Eloise covered the box with dirt, she felt like she could finally take a full breath. Relief washed over her, the letter serving the purpose of finding closure.

"I know you heard me, Reagan. I know you did." Eloise moved to her knees, leaning over to place a kiss on Reagan's engraved name. "Thank you for giving me this amazing life, for continuing to give me everything wonderful, even in death." Sitting with Reagan, a new thought found its way into her heart, something Eloise hadn't considered until now. Reagan sent her Jack. That thought filled her heart, and she had no doubt that it was the truth. Reagan did want her to be happy, because he loved her.

CHAPTER 25

S ix months of rehab felt worse to Jack than any deployment. He had undergone multiple procedures on his hands, arms, and chest to graft his new skin. Jack didn't have all his feeling back, and likely never would, but they made him work those muscles anyway.

Eloise had Jack set up at St. Mary's Hospital to continue working with an occupational therapist once he was back in Colorado. Jack was also encouraged, by his doctors, to join support groups and continue seeing a therapist, which he'd gladly agree to if they'd release him to go home.

Every couple of weeks Eloise offered to visit, but Jack usually told her that he'd be home soon and that she didn't need to make the trip. She always came anyway and stayed three of four days. He was grateful for her visits, but they were painful, too, because when she was gone all he did was ache for her. He honestly didn't imagine having to stay six months. He knew that all he'd have to do was ask, and she'd come, or stay longer, but he still felt guilty that she'd have to sacrifice so much to be with him.

Jack, Chase, Sam, Nolan, and a few other wounded vets had decided to continue their support group over video chat and met online every week. As much as he didn't want to admit it, it had helped Jack overcome a lot of his anxiety and feelings of being overwhelmed. The men and women in the group all worried about being a burden. Soldiers were used to being able to handle themselves and most everyone around them. Being wounded took that away. Jack had felt like he wasn't enough for Eloise since the beginning, but now he spent most days exhausted and he was still navigating those feelings.

The week Jack was set to go home, he felt excited and sad.

"We'll come visit," Nolan told him during their weekly support group. "Sam and I aren't far behind you in finally going home."

"You better visit. Eloise's place is great and she'd love to meet you guys," Jack told them.

"I'm already mentally packin', man," Sam said.

"Has it gotten any better? Your feelings about being with Eloise?" Nolan asked Jack. Jack had shared a lot about Eloise in his sessions.

"Yes and no," Jack answered. "I was always strong, solid. It sounds cocky, and I was that too." Jack laughed, repeating the words he'd said in sessions many times. "I don't know how to be there for her when I feel so, well, not strong."

"I felt the same," Sam said, another thing that had been said before. "But, the good ones, like my wife, like Eloise, they keep telling you you're enough and eventually you believe it too."

"That's true," Nolan said. "Relationships are about meeting the other person's needs. You can do that without being able to hold a fork."

"Hey," Jack said. "My fork holding time has been improving."

"You know what I mean."

"Yeah. I know. I just wish she didn't have to deal with it, you know, not after everything else she's lost."

"Do you still think she'll leave you again?" Sam asked.

"I worry less about that now. Eloise keeps talking about all the changes to the house, all the new animals, the new cabin, the five freakin' men she has living there, all her plans, all of which involve me. She seems more settled, more sure than she's ever seemed to me."

"The good news is if you can't give her what she needs…" Nolan raised his eyebrows. "Sounds like she has plenty of men who can."

"God, Nolan! Don't give him more to worry about," Sam said.

"You know what, jackass, my dick works fine." Jack had to laugh at Nolan's comment, because though Eloise could be a huge pain in the ass, she was the most loyal person he'd ever known. She'd never hide anything like that from him. The one thing he knew for sure, if Eloise wanted another man, she'd tell him first.

Jack got a lot of looks on his way home. People couldn't help but stare at his face and arms. He could have worn a long-sleeved shirt, but he wasn't going to hide from Eloise. If she accepted him, then he wouldn't hide from the world either. He was so nervous he thought he'd puke. He waited until everyone else got off the plane before he stood up. The flight attendant thanked him for his service and nodded as he stepped off the plane.

Jack stopped at the top of the escalator and looked down, finding Eloise. Shit, she looked incredible. Incredible and nervous. He hoped she was also excited. She wore jeans and a light-pink sweater that hung off her shoulder. Jack couldn't wait to touch that bare spot.

He placed his foot onto the step and started the descent. Two steps from the bottom he jumped off, his nervousness replaced with excitement. Eloise ran forward and jumped into his arms, kissing his cheeks and then his lips. He held her up under her bottom and leaned back just long enough to see her eyes before kissing her again. He never wanted to set her down.

Eloise shifted, breaking their kiss, tears streaming down her face. He set her back on her feet.

"Jack." Eloise ran her hands down his arms, examining his scars.

"It doesn't hurt." People walked by, staring as Eloise examined and touched his raw-looking skin. "I can cover them." Jack rubbed the back of his neck and awkwardly shifted his feet as he waited for her to say something.

"No." Eloise lifted Jack's chin with her fingers. "Look at me. You're as handsome as ever, and safe, and loved by me, and you never have to cover up anything about yourself."

Jack leaned down and kissed Eloise gently. They melted into each other, tears making their way silently down her cheeks as she smiled.

Jack wasn't sure why he was nervous about going back to Eloise's house, but figured it had a lot to do with all the new people who would also be there.

"I think you'll like Jesse." Eloise put her hand on Jack's as they drove to her house.

"And his sons?"

"Ethan and Kyson are both jokesters, sarcastic, and they party a lot. They are you about ten years ago, which is extra hilarious because they're close to our age. Markham is an extremely hard worker, but shy and quiet. The youngest, Bryke, is just nineteen. He competes in every extreme sport he can and drives anything with a motor like a pro."

"If you like them, I'll like them, El." Jack looked out the window. "They've been good to you and that's all that matters to me."

"Thank you, Jack. But I do hope you like them. Having a few friends around has been nice, hopefully they can be your friends too." Eloise paused. "We said we'd be honest, so I want you to know I'm not worried about you guys getting along, but I am worried about you sitting back and letting them take on the brunt of the work." Eloise sighed. "I know you'll have a hard time watching them do work that you can't anymore. I just hope that eventually you'll come to terms with it. I asked Jesse to warn his boys that you may be a bit standoffish, and to not expect much from you the first few days."

"Thank you. You didn't have to do that, but I appreciate it."

As Eloise pulled into the driveway, the whole gang stood out front. Jack waited as Eloise came around to open his door, something he still couldn't do alone. Eloise was there when his doctors told him he'd adapt, find new ways to do everyday things, and she knew Jack wanted to evolve as quickly as possible.

"Welcome home, Jack," Jesse said as Jack stepped out of the car. "Nice to finally meet you."

"Nice to meet you, too, Jesse. Thank you for taking such good care of my Eloise."

"Anytime, we've all come to love her." Jesse smiled at Eloise and she stepped forward to hug him.

"She makes it easy," Jack said as Eloise stepped out of Jesse's embrace.

"That she does," Jesse said. "This is Ethan, Kyson, Markham, and Bryke. My sons." Jesse pointed to each man as he said their name.

"Nice to meet you all." Out of habit, Jack started to hold out his hand, but stopped himself.

"Nice to meet you too." Ethan took the lead. "You need anything, just let us know."

"Eloise says you have it running like clockwork around here, so I'm sure I won't have much to need," Jack answered.

"I cooked, El," Ethan said. "Whenever you guys are ready."

"Thank you. Can you guys take Jack's stuff to my room? I want to show him the new additions."

"Of course." Ethan turned, along with his brothers, to grab Jack's bags.

Eloise walked Jack to the new cabin, and showed him the additional acres. A lot of the pets Jack remembered had been adopted and new ones had taken their place.

"I'll never cook again. Guess it's good we have Ethan," Jack said, feeling sadder than he thought he would be back home.

"You will, Jack. Everything will just take some time." Eloise stopped walking and pulled herself into Jack. When she kissed him, he immediately felt calmer, happier.

"I know you're right. It's just easy to get discouraged. I'll try to be more positive."

"You be whatever you need to, handsome." Eloise kissed Jack again before she kept walking, pointing out the changes and additions.

The next morning, Eloise had Jesse and his sons move all of Jack's things from his house to hers, but that wasn't what stood out the most to her. It was taking off her ring the first night they slept together in the master bedroom, surrounded by Jack's possessions.

"Eloise, you don't have to do this," Jack had told her.

"I know that, but it's time. I think Reagan would want me to be happy. He knew how much I loved him, but I think I'm finally to a point where I can love you and not feel guilty or like I'm betraying him." Eloise thought about the letter and visiting Reagan, and she knew what she said was the truth.

"Would you want him to be happy? If the shoe were on the other foot?"

"More than anything."

"Then I know he'd want the same." Jack held out his hand

and Eloise set her band in his palm. Jack wrapped his fingers around it, and she thought about everything they'd been through since the first day they met.

"It's always been you, El, since the day I met you. I never thought I deserved you. Hell, most days I still don't, but I love you and will spend the rest of my life making you happy." Jack set the ring on his nightstand. Her giving it to him was her way of saying she was letting Reagan rest, she was letting him go. It symbolized her giving herself to him and she hoped he knew that by looking at her. Jack had a lot of his own stuff to figure out now, stuff that wasn't there before, but Eloise was confident he'd do whatever he could to be the man he thought she deserved. He told her more than once he'd see a counselor and continue with his online support group or find a local in-person group. Jack vowed to Eloise that he'd stay mentally healthy for her.

The work with the animal sanctuary was always hard, but it was also fun and always something new and exciting. Jack was also working on getting another building built on the property to open a small restaurant, a dream he's always had and one that Eloise readily supported. She thought it would be a great way to help get more of the dogs adopted, if more people saw them.

"I love you, too, Jack. I always have. I love all that we are." Eloise rolled over on top of him, and he laughed under her weight as she leaned down to kiss him.

"I understand now what you meant when you told me you need something that was your own after losing Reagan. I feel like a big part of me is dead. Can a person mourn themselves?" Jack asked, still underneath Eloise.

"I think so. I did. It's okay to need something to help the remaining part of you heal, and that can be this restaurant." Eloise kissed Jack again.

"My dream will have to shift from chef to management, but I

think I come was come to terms with that." Jack said after Eloise broke their kiss.

Jack was supposed to meet with a contractor the next morning, and when he walked in the kitchen, Eloise was handing a man a plate of breakfast. He stood as Jack entered.

"Hello, Mr. Brennan. I arrived just a few minutes ago and your wife here said you were showering and insisted I eat breakfast. I hope that's okay." He nodded and then sat down.

"Of course it is," Jack said, not bothering to correct the "wife" part of his statement, instead he fed into it. "My *wife* is an incredible cook, and you deserve to eat before we get to work." He winked at Eloise and about melted at her smile. He walked toward her and wrapped her up in his arms, not caring one bit about the man eating at their dining room table.

"Wife, huh?" Eloise whispered in his ear.

"Will you?" Jack ran his lips along her cheekbone.

"Be your wife?" Eloise said a bit louder, noticeably shocked.

"Yes. I know this isn't the most romantic proposal, but I saw a window here and I'm taking it."

Eloise stepped out of Jack's embrace. Her startled face must have alerted the contractor because he told Jack he was going to take a look at what Jack planned to build and would meet him out there. Eloise barely registered what was said, but heard the sliding door close and knew he was gone.

"Eloise?" Jack shifted closer to her.

"Are you serious? Why?"

"Why did I ask or why do I want to get married?"

"Both."

"Because I love you. Because I've always loved you. Because we both deserve to be happy and you make me happier than I've ever been. I want to wake up to you every morning and fall asleep next to you every night. I used to believe I was your for-now guy, and maybe I used to be, but now I want to be your forever. I'm tired of one of us being ready and the other one being scared and then us switching roles. I want the permanence of you, beautiful, always."

"Yes."

"What?"

"Did you already change your mind?"

"No. I just can't believe it."

"I can't say no. I can't. My fear over losing you, over being disloyal to Reagan, all of it, is so outweighed by my fear of not being with you, of never running my hands over you again, of never being able to watch you smile again. I have no choice. No isn't an option."

Jack scooped Eloise up, and she wrapped her legs around his waist and her arms around his neck, covering him in kisses.

"I can't believe you said yes. We're going to spend the rest of our lives together." Jack set Eloise on the kitchen counter, and laughed as she pulled her shirt over her head.

"You have a house full of people here," Jack stated the obvious.

"They are doing chores. We have at least two hours." Eloise grabbed the bottom of Jack's shirt and pulled up.

"Don't gotta tell me twice." Jack's mouth met hers and Eloise reached down to undo both their pants.

When Jesse and his boys did return, Eloise and Jack were dressed and discussing everything that Jack had gone over with the contractor after their sex hiatus. Eloise knew that Jack would adapt, evolve into someone who had a life outside of the military, but it still scared her, and she assumed him too, to be essentially starting over.

"Good morning," Eloise and Jack said together as her kitchen filled.

"Good morning," all five men repeated back as they started to load plates full of lunch that Eloise had made. Jack usually stood behind her while she cooked, instructing her and Eloise loved it. It was his way of continuing to cook. With Eloise, he never felt embarrassed or shy. He was able to pretend for a bit that her hands were his as they cooked meals together.

Ethan made an extra plate and set it in front of Eloise, and Kyson did the same for Jack. The noise in the kitchen was Eloise's favorite part of her house, and Jack's too. It was a lot like back in college when his and Drake's house was a constant chaos of people and meals. Eloise looked around her table and squeezed Jack's thigh. She may never have children of her own, and though Ethan and Kyson were close to their ages, she felt older than them because of all she'd been through. Markham and Bryke were younger, adults, but young ones, and maybe Eloise could help them become the men they wanted to be. Jesse had been like a father to her over the last few months. Eloise also had Jack and would hold on to him like her life depended on it.

"Thank you for this life." Jack leaned over to whisper in Eloise's ear, making her think he could read her mind.

"Thank you, Jack. Had you not shown up, I never would have made it to this moment, and I love this moment," Eloise whispered back.

"I will always, always show up for you, beautiful."

"And I'll never, ever, run from you again, handsome," Eloise said before she pushed her lips to his.

E loise sat in her wedding dress, holding a picture of her and Reagan. It had been a year since Jack was medically discharged and though the year had brought challenges, it was also filled with more love and laughter than Eloise ever thought she'd have again.

Eloise kept one photo of her and Reagan out, but Jack never commented on it. When Jack had first come back, she wanted to hide her feelings for him from everyone, including Reagan and herself. Now, she wanted Reagan to know everything, and since writing him she'd often tell him about her life. That's why she kept the picture out. She needed to believe he was happy for her.

Chase and Allie, Nolan and Sam and their wives, Stewart and Emma, Jesse and his boys were there to celebrate Jack and Eloise. Nickie had been there for the last week to help get things ready, and Gage flew in two days ago. Jack didn't have any family to invite, but he'd told Eloise last night that everyone who mattered to him was there. Her mom got in late last night, and her uncle came too. Eloise knew that for a long time Jack felt like he was letting his own brother down, but over time, he realized Drake would be thrilled for him. Eloise had always loved Drake and knew, somewhere in the sky, he was proud of his brother.

"Knock, knock," Nickie said as she entered Eloise's room. "You okay?"

"Yes. I just was talking to Reagan. I hid Jack from him for so long. He has a right to about the wedding."

"I believe he knows." Nickie sat next to Eloise on the bed, her dress tight around her pregnant belly. "New memories, El. New life. It's okay to want those things."

"I do want them, and I want them with Jack." Eloise handed the photo to Nickie. "We were so happy when this was taken. It was the day we bought our house in Houston. We slept on the living room floor that night, in a sleeping bag. I feel like I was a different woman there."

"You're still you, El. Sometimes we have to change to survive. Isn't that how evolution works?"

"I think so." Eloise took the picture back, setting it on the nightstand, then gripped Nickie's hand. "Thank you, Nickie, for sticking with me these last two years. I know I didn't always make it easy."

"I'm just happy that you're here, El. That you're thriving and happy. You deserve this life you created and so does Jack. I know it came from a dark place, because it started with losing Reagan. But I know you finally believe he's happy for you, and we all believe that too."

"I used to want both. Right after Reagan died. I wanted him back, but I didn't want that to mean losing Jack. Isn't that insane?" Eloise let go of Nickie's hand and lightly clasped her own in her lap.

"It's not insane, El. It just means you weren't ready to let go of Reagan, and you weren't ready to love Jack."

"I wasn't ready. But sitting here now, I can't picture my life any other way. I feel horrible because this way can only happen with Reagan being dead."

"You can't blame yourself for what happened, El. If you knew, if you could've stopped it, he'd be here. But as shitty as it is, sometimes life just doesn't work the way we picture it."

"I know." Eloise placed her palm on her lips and concentrated on not crying and ruining her wedding makeup. "I loved him, Nickie, I adored Reagan. But I love Jack, too, and it's a different love. That's why I wrote to Reagan. I wanted him to know that I loved him, and that I never compared him to Jack."

"He does, sweetie." Nickie stood, held out her hand, and helped Eloise to her feet. "Let's get you married." Nickie pulled Eloise in, holding her close and kissing her cheek, then released her. Eloise took one deep breath before following Nickie out of the room.

"Don't let me trip," Eloise whispered to Jesse.

"I got you, darlin'. Don't you worry." Jesse tightened his arm around Eloise's, making her smile. Jack's eyes stayed locked on hers with each step. When Jesse handed her off to Jack, and the guests took their seats, Eloise finally looked at the decorations. Nickie, Jesse, and his sons had done an amazing job turning her property into the perfect setting. Eloise took in the details of the flowers, each tiny light, and read through the hand-painted signs as the officiant spoke, but when Jack said his vows, Eloise's attention was on him.

"Eloise." Jack gripped her hands. "I've been in love with you for over seventeen years. From the first moment I saw you, I knew I'd never meet anyone else like you. I know life has thrown things at you that most people wouldn't be able to handle, but you continued to fight, to be compassionate, and somehow your heart grew bigger when so many people's hearts would have shrunk and stayed dark. I promise you I will spend my life making sure you're happy, and that you always feel safe. You've driven me insane. Seriously, you are a pain in the ass." Jack paused when Eloise laughed. "But that's another reason I love you. You're challenging and fun, and unafraid of what the world thinks, which I know because I've carried you out of many a public place. Your spirit is truly free, and I promise that I'll never try and tame it. You've made me a better man from the first day we met, and I can't thank you enough for that. With you by my side, I know I can get through anything life has to offer. You've always been my light, beautiful, my best friend, and the only person I've never been able to live without. I love you." Jack finished and tears slowly fell down Eloise's face. He leaned forward and placed a quick kiss on her wet cheek.

"Jack," Eloise started. "Anytime I've found myself broken, you've been there. You have pulled me out of places so dark, and it's always been you. I believe that everything happens for a reason, and I believe that I met you all those years ago so that we could stand here today. I know we took the long way, but nothing has ever made me happier than knowing that in a few minutes I'll be your wife. I promise I will spend my life pushing your buttons and making you laugh. I will love you with my whole heart and I will never leave you alone." Eloise took a small step forward, her forehead almost touching Jack's. "I love the way you love me, Jack. The way you know me. The way you bring me comfort without trying. People search their entire lives to find what we've always had. You've always been the love of my life, and twice now, you've come without warning and captured my heart before I could say no. I love you. I will always love you." Eloise let go of one of Jack's hands to wipe her tears and then wiped Jack's as well, leaving her palm pressed against his cheek.

It took every ounce of restraint Eloise had to refrain from crashing into Jack before the officiant said the magic words. When "kiss the bride" finally left his lips, Jack kissed Eloise with a passion that had her believing they could kiss for hours, that it was everything, that if they both somehow disappeared, it wouldn't matter, because they would've experienced everything they'd dreamed of in that moment.

The clapping barely outlasted the kiss and when Eloise and Jack turned to walk back down the aisle, every person was smiling and on their feet. Jack kept walking, until he and Eloise were in their bedroom, behind a locked door. The intent was to change for their reception, but Eloise knew him well enough to know he'd have a few detours in mind.

"You look incredible, El." Jack kissed down her jawline.

"Back at you, handsome." Eloise pushed into Jack. Jack put his hands on her shoulders, turning her so that he could unzip her dress. She held her breath. Jack had actually practiced, *practiced*, unzipping things so that he could take her dress off, something she found incredibly sweet. When the fabric slipped off her shoulders, Jack followed the dress to the floor and Eloise stepped out of it.

Jack stood and Eloise watched his eyes scan her white lace lingerie as she unbuttoned and untucked until she could pull off his jacket and put her hands on his chest.

Eloise loved touching Jack, loved running her fingertips over his skin. The way his eyes danced as he watched her every move was enough to satisfy Eloise for a lifetime.

When Eloise was dressed and her makeup fixed, she walked out of the bathroom and found Jack sitting, also dressed, on their bed. The people at the reception were waiting on them, but Eloise doubted that they minded.

After a few moments of sitting on the bed together, Eloise finally told Jack they should get back. Everyone cheered as they entered their reception. When Nickie and Chase gave their toasts, Eloise and Jack were both in tears, from laughing at the memories they'd shared.

"Everything about yesterday was a dream," Eloise told Jack the next morning when he stirred in bed.

"I'm glad you enjoyed it, beautiful." Jack rolled over and kissed Eloise good morning. She still couldn't believe that he'd be kissing her every morning for the rest of their lives. Rossi climbed up on the bed, slowly, like maybe if she were quiet they wouldn't notice.

"Jack. I want you to know something." Eloise watched Jack's eyebrows rise. "I loved Reagan, I did, and I believe now that you can love a lot of people, but not like this. Love like what we have, I know people don't get it twice, hell, most people don't get it once."

"I know, El. I've always known that."

"Sorry it took me so long to catch up." Eloise climbed on top of Jack, pushing her mouth to his neck.

"You were worth the wait, beautiful." Jack arched his hips, his laughter at Eloise's groan filling the room.

Eloise thought about the day she met Jack and how far they had come. She thought about Reagan and how their love story would always be a part of her heart, but in a way that made her smile much more than it made her cry. She thought about the million other possibilities for her life had Jack not come to give her that tough love Nickie requested.

Jack and Eloise had decided against a honeymoon, so Jack could open his restaurant. It'd been four days since they married, and Jack still woke each morning thinking about it. If someone had told him two years ago he'd marry Eloise, he would've punched them in their lying mouth. Jack would be forever grateful that Eloise had Jesse to walk her down the aisle, something she hadn't had at her first wedding. Jack's breath still caught when he pictured Eloise the moment she stepped to the end of the aisle and met his eyes. He knew that memory would take his breath for the rest of his days.

Jack walked into the main room of his restaurant that evening and found Eloise's eyes first. She had pride written all over her face. The drive out to their place from town was a long one, but Eloise had told Jack not to worry about that, because she knew that once the word got out, people wouldn't mind making the distance for Jack's food. He spent the majority of his time planning the recipes and menus, but he cooked more than he thought he'd be able to, and his chefs were always willing to help him finish dishes if he ran into any issues. Eloise's property was never quiet anymore, and he knew she found as much solace in that as he did.

Opening night was everything Jack could have imagined, marrying Eloise was the only night that topped it. He'd named the place Fort Drake, after his brother, and hung a photo of the two of them above the bar.

"I'm so proud of you, handsome," Eloise whispered in Jack's ear, standing on her tiptoes to reach.

"I couldn't have done any of this without you, beautiful." Jack kissed her lips and looked at all the people. Every chair was filled. People were smiling, drinking, and eating, and Jack couldn't believe how great the night was going, considering most people had to drive an hour to get there. When Eloise agreed to the opening so close to the wedding, their friends were able to attend. Nickie singing and dancing in his place was a memory he'd always treasure.

"Congrats, man." Nolan slapped Jack's shoulder.

"Yes, congratulations," Sam followed.

"Thanks, you guys. And thanks for coming. Meeting you two knuckleheads was the best thing to come out of gettin' hurt," Jack said, pulling Eloise to his side.

"We also got to meet Eloise, and I think that's pretty great," Allie said as she and Chase joined the conversation. Allie hugged Eloise first and then Jack.

"She's all right," Jack said with a wink in Eloise's direction.

When Jack stood a couple hours later to thank everyone, he couldn't help but think how different his life would be had Drake lived. He wondered if Eloise still thought the same if Reagan had lived. People moving in and out of their lives, his brother, her husband, his mother, her dad, the soldiers Jack had lost, all the ones he'd saved who moved on with their lives, every person a puzzle piece in their story. Eloise said frequently that everything happened for a reason, but Jack sometimes struggled with the hard parts, the reason behind some of the agonizing, paralyzing pain that the two of them had endured over the years.

Jack found Eloise's eyes.

"Finally," Jack said to the crowd. "I'd like to thank my wife. A lot of you watched us get married a few days ago, and I'm so happy we're sharing another wonderful moment with the people we love. El, you are my saving grace. Thank you for always believing in me. Thank you for changing my life." Jack held up his glass and everyone followed. He walked toward Eloise and they clinked their glasses.

Jack took a step closer to his wife as she spoke. "Thank you, handsome." Eloise kissed him and then laid her head on his chest.

"For?" Jack kissed the top of her head.

"Changing my life," Eloise whispered into Jack's chest before tilting her head up to meet his kiss.

Thank you for reading!
If you enjoyed this book, I would greatly appreciate it if you

would take the time to leave a review. It would mean so much to me!

Catch up with Jack and Eloise
in The Grand Mesa Men series.
The first book of this spinoff
series is coming in 2021.

Stay updated by joining my newsletter.

CONNECT WITH ME ON SOCIAL MEDIA

I'd love to connect with you on social media.

You can find me on:
My Website | YouTube | Facebook
Twitter | Instagram | Patreon | My Blog

facebook.com/ShalanaBattles

twitter.com/shalanabattles

instagram.com/shalanabattles

youtube.com/authorshalanabattles